BRUCE'S STORY

Grandfather Patman smiled, first at one boy, then at the other. "I'd like to give each one of you boys two thousand dollars in cash. What you do with that money, as long as it's legal, is your business. The point is, four weeks from tomorrow night, when your parents get back from their trip, we'll see who's invested their money more wisely. Whoever has more money four weeks from now is the winner."

Mr. Patman looked stunned. "Father," he said, "are you saying—"

"I'm saying, the boys ought to fight it out, darn it!" Grandfather Patman cried.

"And whoever wins this contest gets the controlling shares of the company?" Bruce asked weakly.

"That's exactly right," Grandfather Patman said with a look of satisfaction.

Bruce felt sick to his stomach. He couldn't believe what he had just heard. He'd always known that he was going to inherit the Patman Corporation one day. Now his future had been yanked out from under him.

Well, he *was* going to fight it. He was going to fight it every step of the way. If Roger thought he was going to rob him of his inheritance, he was going to have to think again!

Bantam Books in the Sweet Valley High Series
Ask your bookseller for the books you have missed

SWEET VALLEY HIGH
Super Star

BRUCE'S STORY

Written by
Kate William

Created by
FRANCINE PASCAL

BANTAM BOOKS
NEW YORK · TORONTO · LONDON · SYDNEY · AUCKLAND

RL 6, age 12 and up

BRUCE'S STORY
A Bantam Book / June 1990

Sweet Valley High is a registered trademark of Francine Pascal

Conceived by Francine Pascal

Produced by Daniel Weiss Associates, Inc.
33 West 17th Street, New York, NY 10011

Cover art by James Mathewuse

ISBN 0-553-28464-9

Published simultaneously in the United States and Canada

Bantam Books are published by Bantam Books, a division of Bantam Doubleday Dell Publishing Group, Inc. Its trademark, consisting of the words "Bantam Books" and the portrayal of a rooster, is Registered in U.S. Patent and Trademark Office and in other countries. Marca Registrada. Bantam Books, 666 Fifth Avenue, New York, New York 10103.

PRINTED IN THE UNITED STATES OF AMERICA

O   0 9 8 7 6 5 4 3 2 1

One

"Hey, Rog!" Bruce Patman called to his cousin across the crowded lunchroom at Sweet Valley High. "Come over here. We need to talk strategy."

The cafeteria was buzzing with the usual lunchtime busyness: students eating lunch, talking to friends, and doing homework. Bruce had been looking for his cousin all morning. He was the only other person who could share his anxiety and his excitement about their grandfather Patman's arrival in Sweet Valley that very evening. "You've got to give me some moral support," Bruce said, an uncharacteristically pleading note in his voice.

Roger perched his tray on the edge of Bruce's

1

table. "I was supposed to have lunch with Ken and Lisa," he said, gesturing over to the nearby table where his friends were already sitting. Ken Matthews was an old friend of Roger's. Lisa DePaul was a pretty blond sophomore whom Roger had met in his Spanish class.

"Rog, don't abandon me!" Bruce cried, pretending to be terrified. "Not in my hour of need!"

Roger couldn't help laughing. Even though his cousin could be hard to live with, he could also be pretty funny when he tried. Roger was surprised to find himself thinking of Bruce in such a positive way. When he first came to live with the Patmans in their estate situated on a hill overlooking Sweet Valley, he might have described Bruce as spoiled, conceited, or stubborn—not funny. But over the past few months, Roger had come to care about Bruce. And *almost* to think of him as a brother.

Roger was as nervous about the arrival of Grandfather Patman as Bruce seemed to be. Maybe even more nervous. Bruce had at least *met* his grandfather, but Roger—the newest member of the family—never had. Roger pulled a chair up to Bruce's table and sat down. He looked at his roast beef sandwich. Suddenly he wasn't at all hungry. His stomach churned nervously.

"So, this is really it, huh?" Bruce said, sighing. He propped his head on his hands. "Can you believe it? It feels like just a couple of days ago that Mom dropped the bombshell. Six whole weeks of the old man. And I do mean *old*, Rog."

Roger laughed. "Come on, Bruce. He can't be all that bad. He *is* our grandfather."

It still gave Roger a shock to say "our" grandfather. A year ago, he would have thought that anyone who told him that he and Bruce Patman might share *anything*—let alone a grandfather—was crazy. Bruce was the richest boy in the whole school, and he always had been. He was the only child of Henry Patman, one of the wealthiest men in California. Bruce had always been given everything he wanted. He wore designer clothes, drove a fabulous black Porsche, and possessed the latest and biggest in every toy and gadget the day they hit the stores. On top of that, Bruce was drop-dead handsome. He had dark hair, broad shoulders, and a tennis player's slender build. He was the dream of most of the girls in town. The girls who didn't think he was perfect were the ones who had had run-ins with his king-size ego.

Not long ago, back when Roger Barrett Patman was still Roger Barrett, he would never have even talked to Bruce. Back then, Roger had tried his hardest to stay out of the way of the rich students at Sweet Valley High. That was because he had absolutely nothing in common with them. Roger's mother was very poor, and the Barretts had had only the barest necessities. Roger had always worked after school, not to earn money for himself, but to help his mother pay the rent. When he found out his mother had a heart ailment, Roger had felt as though his own life was ending as well. They couldn't even afford the money for the treatments his mother needed. But then, Bruce's father had mysteriously offered to pay for them.

But even the costly transplant operation that Mr. Patman helped arrange could not save her. Mrs. Barrett died. Overnight, Roger was left an orphan, with nothing to his name.

That was when something happened that

Roger couldn't have imagined in his wildest dreams. Henry Patman insisted that Roger come to live with his family, and he announced that Roger was the illegitimate son of his brother Paul, who had been dead for almost sixteen years. Overnight, Roger's life was changed. He had gone from rags to riches. But that didn't mean it had all been easy. Far from it.

"I guess being a Patman isn't all country clubs and credit cards," Bruce said, almost as if he were reading his cousin's mind. "Kind of scary meeting the man who made the family fortune, isn't it?"

"I don't know," Roger said slowly. "I have this image of us all kind of hanging out together. Grandfather Patman must know a million stories about my dad when he was little. I've kind of been looking forward to meeting him," he concluded.

Bruce rolled his eyes. "Roger, you can be unbelievably optimistic sometimes," he said. "Grandfather Patman isn't going to sit around and talk old times! He's a holy terror! He grills you about everything! Every grade on every test. How you spent every penny of your allowance." Bruce shuddered. "A two-day visit is bad enough! Six whole weeks of the dragon could be deadly!"

Roger gave Bruce a questioning look. He still couldn't believe his grandfather was that bad.

"Take it from me, Rog," Bruce insisted. "He didn't make the family fortune by sitting around talking about old times. He's a great business-man, but a real nightmare to live with. You should see what it's like trying to have a normal dinner conversation with him around. It's like eating with the New York Stock Exchange. But no point telling you all this stuff now. You'll see for yourself—tonight."

"I don't know," Roger said uncertainly. "I'm still looking forward to meeting him. He's fam-ily, after all."

"Another thing," Bruce continued. "Grandfa-ther's a real stickler for what he calls 'pride in your appearance.' Do yourself a favor and get a haircut before dinner tonight."

Roger frowned. Things were going well be-tween Bruce and him lately, but at times like this he couldn't help remembering those awful early weeks when he had first moved into the Patman mansion. Bruce had tortured him about everything: his clothes, his table manners, his lack of experience in formal social situations. Roger hoped their grandfather's arrival wasn't going to bring all that stuff up again.

"I'm sure Grandfather Patman will have more interesting things to think about than what I look like," Roger said lightly.

"Don't count on it," Bruce said. "I'm telling you, Roger. The guy could make the President of the United States feel insecure."

Roger felt his excitement over meeting his grandfather lessening. "Hey, we'll get through this, Bruce," he said. It felt funny to be reassuring Bruce, who was usually so confident. "And anyway," Roger added with a smile, "there're two of us and only one of him, remember?"

Bruce got up and gave his cousin a slap on the back. "You know something? You're all right, Roger. You're nowhere near as bad as I thought you were when Dad rescued you from the orphanage!"

"Thanks, Bruce," Roger said dryly. But he knew Bruce was only teasing him.

He and Bruce were beginning to treat each other like family. And it made Roger feel good to realize that for the first time, they were facing a problem together.

"What's up, Roger? You and Bruce looked pretty serious over there," Lisa asked. Roger had come over to join Ken and Lisa for the remaining minutes of the lunch period.

Roger smiled. "My grandfather is coming to visit for the next few weeks. His plane gets in this afternoon, so he'll be waiting for us at home when we get back. I'm a little worried about what kind of impression I'll make on him."

"Why? Has Bruce been telling you all kinds of horror stories?" Lisa asked.

The three of them chuckled together, and Roger thought again how glad he was to have Lisa DePaul for a friend. He'd never really known a girl quite like her before. She was bright, friendly, generous, and completely unselfconscious. Ever since the day when they had been assigned a project together in Spanish class, he'd enjoyed her company. She had blond, curly hair cropped short, and large eyes that lit up when she laughed. But even though Roger thought she was pretty, he was not interested in Lisa romantically. She was good company, and that was more than enough for him. He'd had enough of a romantic roller-coaster ride during his painful breakup with Olivia David-son.

"What's your grandfather like?" Ken asked.

"I'm not really sure. I know him mostly by his portrait in the living room at home." Roger frowned. "He's the one who started the Patman company." Roger shook his head. "It sounds to me like everyone's a little afraid of him."

"I bet you're not, Roger," Lisa said promptly.

Roger was quiet for a moment. Was he? The truth was, he didn't know what to expect. Bruce had told him some hair-raising stories about the last time Grandfather Patman came to visit five years ago. But Roger wasn't going to take Bruce at his word. He wanted to form his own opinion.

"Let's put it this way," he said lightly. "To-night I'll meet him. And he can't possibly be any scarier than I've imagined!"

It was hard for Roger not to feel insecure. As far as he knew, his grandfather hadn't known that his oldest son, Roger's father, had an ille-gitimate child until the rest of the world found out. In the letter announcing his arrival, Grand-father Patman had claimed he wanted to celebrate his seventieth birthday with family. "It is important to be with your family for such a momentous event," he had written. "This visit will also give me a chance to get to know Roger."

No wonder Roger had mixed feelings about his grandfather's visit! How on earth was he going to impress a big-deal business tycoon like Alexander Patman? Especially when Bruce was making it clear that his grandfather wasn't easy to please.

"Still getting dressed for dinner?" Bruce asked. He opened the door to Roger's spacious suite without bothering to knock. It was almost seven-thirty, and Miranda, the Patman's maid, had told the boys that dinner was about to be served.

"I'm dressed," Roger said. "How do I look?" He was wearing a pair of neatly pressed chino pants and a fresh white shirt. He hadn't had time to get his hair cut, but he hoped he looked presentable. He still hadn't met his grandfather, who had been resting in his room when Bruce and Roger got home from school.

Bruce was wearing a navy linen sports coat and an imported silk tie. The creases in his gray trousers looked as if they'd been cut with a knife. He had even slicked his hair back with a dab of gel. Bruce looked fantastic—his dark, chiseled good looks shown off to their best advantage. Roger had been struggling to decide whether or not to wear a tie. But once Bruce had burst in all dressed up, he felt a stubborn bit of pride creep in. He wasn't going to wear a tie just because Bruce was.

"Very daring, Roger. Very daring," Bruce teased him. Roger could tell from his cousin's voice that he was nervous. "Anyway, I wouldn't worry. Grandfather Patman will probably be so busy dragging you and me over the coals that he won't even notice what you're wearing."

"Look," Roger said uneasily, giving his hair a quick smoothing-over, "let's hope for the best, Bruce. It may not be all that bad."

Bruce paused to get one last glance at himself in the mirror. "Not bad," he praised himself, winking at his own reflection. "Good luck down there," he said. "If Grandfather kills me right

11

away, feel free to have my stereo. But if you touch my Porsche, I'll haunt you!" He chuckled. "Oh, well. What can we lose? The very worst he can do is write us out of his will and shortchange us a few billion dollars."

Roger sighed. "Come on, Bruce. Let's go down and face the music." At this rate, Bruce was going to make them both late—and that was hardly going to make a good impression!

Bruce stopped once on the landing between the second and first floors to recheck his hair in the mirror that hung there. "I like the way this gel makes my hair look," he said, turning his neck admiringly.

"Bruce, if you look at yourself in the mirror one more time, I'm going to kill you!" Roger exclaimed despairingly.

"I can't help it," Bruce said. "I get anxious about my appearance when I'm nervous."

Roger had to hide a smile at that one. *And all other times, too,* he thought.

"Darn," Roger said suddenly, stopping short on the third step. "Now you've got me really anxious. I guess I should put on a tie, after all. Will you tell them I'll be right down if I'm a minute or two late?"

Bruce nodded. "But don't take long. Remember Grandfather P. doesn't like people to be late."

Miranda was filling the Patmans' heavy crystal water goblets when Bruce entered the dining room. "Hello, Miranda," he said smoothly. "Are my parents downstairs yet? Or my grandfather?"

"They're just on their way. Your mother asked me to serve the first course promptly at seven-thirty," Miranda said.

Bruce nodded. *Good. I'm the first one.* He took his place, the chair right next to his father's, and while he waited he looked with pleasure around the massive room. Mrs. Patman had spared nothing decorating the mansion, but this room in particular struck Bruce as perfect. The table was long enough to seat twenty guests. Everything was costly and imposing—the Persian carpets, the candelabra, the draperies. Filled with contentment, Bruce settled back in his chair. For just a minute, he was reminded that there was nothing better in the whole world than being Bruce Patman. Here he was, still in high school, and he could have anything he wanted. When he had begged his father for a Porsche, his father gave it to him. He had unlimited use of credit cards, and looks and charm enough to have his pick of the girls at Sweet Valley High. *Or anywhere*, he reminded himself.

Bruce's thoughts were interrupted by the sound of footsteps approaching, then voices. His mother, his father, and Grandfather Patman. All of a sudden, it didn't feel so spectacular being Bruce Patman. Or any kind of Patman. Bruce felt his stomach tie into knots.

"Grandfather!" Bruce exclaimed, jumping to his feet.

Alexander Patman was a distinguished, awe-inspiring man. His hair was almost entirely silver, but he was as trim and muscular as he had been at forty. He was dressed formally, as always. He looked Bruce over without a smile.

"I see you look the same," he said finally, turning away as if he'd seen enough. "And where's the other boy? Where's Roger?"

Bruce was crushed. What kind of greeting was this? True, his grandfather wasn't usually very affectionate. But he seemed even sterner than Bruce remembered.

Roger opened the door and then slipped into the room. Bruce felt a stab of sympathy for him. Roger looked pale and nervous. And the tie he'd finally decided to wear wasn't worth being late for. His pants weren't dressy enough. And his shoes . . .

"Roger," Mrs. Patman said, regarding him coolly, "you're late."

Roger looked down. "Sorry," he mumbled.

"I'd like you to meet your grandfather," Mrs. Patman continued. "Alexander, this is Roger."

Upset over Mrs. Patman's icy comment, Roger put out his hand and said awkwardly, "I'm—uh, it's good to meet you. I'm Roger," he continued nervously as if Mrs. Patman hadn't introduced him. "Roger Barrett. Roger Barrett Patman, I mean." At that moment he wished there was a trap door that would open up in the dining room floor and that he would just disappear.

Alexander Patman's handshake was strong and firm. He raised his thick brows. "I see" was his only comment.

Mr. Patman cleared his throat. "Let's all sit down," he said, putting a hand on Roger's shoulder. Just then, Miranda appeared with the soup.

"Tell us *all* about Europe," Mrs. Patman said

to her father-in-law once they had all been seated and served.

Bruce tried to catch his cousin's eye. Even though Roger got along with his mother pretty well, he had to admit she could be pretty hard to live with. He didn't think she had ever been very fair to Roger.

"We want to hear everything," she continued.

To Bruce's surprise, his grandfather ignored his mother's question and turned to Roger. "Your father, Paul, was a great man," he said. "Both you boys could learn a lot from his example," he added, including Bruce in his gaze. Bruce shifted uncomfortably. He hated being lectured. Wasn't his grandfather here to relax? Bruce would much rather talk about the plans for his grandfather's birthday party. Besides, his grandfather almost always brought presents back for the family from Europe. Bruce had been hoping for some expensive clothing, at the very least. Maybe, he thought hopefully, the presents would come after dinner.

"Paul had the characteristics that make a truly great businessman," Grandfather Patman declared. Bruce knew what was coming next. "He

16

was industrious, persevering, and above all, hardworking," Grandfather Patman continued.

Roger was beaming. He obviously loved hearing about his father, who had died before he was born. Bruce decided to take matters into his own hands and try to change the subject.

"Grandfather, did I tell you about the tennis trophy I won?" he began.

Alexander Patman frowned at him. "Come now, Bruce. We're talking about something else."

Bruce could feel his appetite disappearing. Why did they have to talk about someone who'd been dead for sixteen years? Why couldn't they talk about something more interesting? *Like about me*, Bruce thought.

But when the conversation finally did turn to Bruce, he wasn't glad at all.

"I'd like to hear a little more about your grades, Bruce," Grandfather Patman said, taking a bite of the salad Miranda had served him.

Already? Bruce thought. Usually, his grandfather waited until he'd been back in Sweet Valley for at least a day before he brought up Bruce's report cards.

"I hope you're not going to tell me that you

haven't buckled down and shown an improvement," his grandfather added, folding his hands together the way he did when he particularly disapproved.

Bruce stared down at his plate. He didn't like the way this conversation was going.

"Now, look how young Roger here has taken after his father and developed industrious work habits," Grandfather Patman said, looking fondly at Roger.

Bruce felt himself growing angry. He couldn't believe this! Here Roger had slid into the dining room late, wearing a tie only because Bruce himself had pushed him into it. And who was getting picked on? This wasn't fair!

But during dessert, Grandfather Patman asked Roger if he had been following the debate within the Patman Corporation about whom to appoint as senior vice-president. Roger confessed he didn't know anything about it.

"That's a real shame," Grandfather Patman said disapprovingly. "You really ought to concern yourself more with the family company. I bet Bruce knows all about the issue, don't you?"

Bruce felt victorious. *As a matter of fact, I do,*

he thought happily. And he was only too glad to prove it by rattling off everything he had overheard his father saying about it on the phone just a few evenings ago.

Roger was the one who looked unhappy now. Bruce didn't blame him. He felt a twinge of sympathy for his cousin. But then he remembered his grandfather's praise for Roger's grades, and the twinge vanished. He hated his grandfather's hinting that Roger was a better grandson than he was. He would have to find a way to impress the senior Patman.

Two

The Patman house was completely changed by the arrival of Grandfather Patman. The family's normal routines were changed to accommodate him. Grandfather Patman liked breakfast served by seven. But he wanted only grapefruit and coffee to be served. He said people worked better when they had an edge of appetite. He jogged two miles after breakfast; then lifted weights before sitting down to study the stock market. "I have two mottos in life, boys," he announced to Roger and Bruce a few days after his arrival. "Get rich and work hard. I think you'll often find they amount to the same thing."

"Yes, sir," Bruce said. Roger looked uncomfortable. He had barely gotten used to having money. It was hard for him to throw himself behind the idea that wealth was everything.

"Just follow my example, boys, and when you're almost seventy, you'll be like me," Grandfather Patman went on. He slapped his stomach. "See? Not an ounce of fat. And incidentally, that's the way to run a company, too. No excess. No waste."

"No fun," Bruce muttered when his grandfather wasn't listening.

Roger grinned. "Hey, you weren't kidding about him," he said in a low voice. "Is he going to ease up, or does the torture continue?"

Bruce laughed. "It's barely beginning," he said. "Who knows what will be next? He may want to send us to boot camp before the week is out!"

Plans were already under way for Grandfather Patman's seventieth birthday party. It was going to be held a week from that Friday. Alexander Patman insisted he didn't want a fuss made, but Mrs. Patman had lined up a band and sent out formal, engraved invitations to all her friends. Bruce and Roger were allowed to invite as many classmates as they wanted, since the party would be held outdoors. "The more the merrier," Mrs. Patman said that morning, going over the guest list. One look at Roger changed her mood, however. "Roger, try not to invite too many of those ragamuffin friends of yours, won't you? Why don't you see if you can't meet some of Bruce's nice friends from the club?"

Roger had long since given up the hope of ever getting along with Mrs. Patman. At times like this, with someone like her father-in-law around to impress, she was all but unbearable.

"Maybe the night of the party is the time for me to announce my special surprise for you two boys," Grandfather Patman said, winking at them. "A party is a good time for a surprise, isn't it?"

Bruce was filled with excitement. At last, the present he'd been waiting for! He had begun to fear his grandfather wasn't going to give them anything. Secretly, he was hoping for cash so he could buy himself a new Windsurfer.

Just in case, Bruce decided to give his grandfather a couple of hints. Wednesday morning at breakfast, he described windsurfing to his grandfather, who listened attentively. "It sounds like a wonderful hobby," Grandfather Patman said at last. "I approve of sports that build up coordination and balance. Both are important qualities for an entrepreneur."

Bruce rolled his eyes. His grandfather clearly wasn't getting the hint. He decided to throw in some comments about how his own Windsurfer was scratched and how he'd like a shorter one, now that he was getting so good. His grandfather didn't look pleased.

"Don't be extravagant, Bruce. One Windsurfer sounds like more than enough to me."

Bruce frowned at his plate. At this rate, the next few weeks were going to be a real drag!

"I wonder what Grandfather's surprise is going to be," he said to Roger on the way to school. Bruce's mood had lightened as soon as he had slipped behind the wheel of his Porsche. "I really hope he can come up with a big fat check for us both. I'm down about a hundred bucks from poker, and I could use some extra."

Roger was surprised. "You play poker for that kind of money? Who do you play with?"

"Oh, just a few guys from the country club."
Bruce shrugged. "Do you think we'll make it
through Grandfather's birthday party? It's sound-
ing pretty deadly to me so far."

Roger shrugged and looked out the window.
"I feel a little sorry for him," he said softly. "I
get the feeling he'd rather have a small party
with just the family. But your mother's invited
the whole town."

Bruce raised an eyebrow. "Don't pick on my
mother. She can't help it if she thinks big. It
runs in the family."

Roger was about to reply when Bruce cut him
off. He had his eye on a group of girls walking
together toward school. "Hey, get a load of
Tracy Atkins," he said, letting out a low whis-
tle. "Did you see that new haircut? She looks
like a model!" Tracy was in the senior class
with Bruce, but he had barely ever noticed her
before. Bruce didn't understand what had come
over him, but he was transfixed. "She's gorgeous," he said.

"Hey, Bruce, watch out!" Roger cried suddenly. Bruce's steering had followed his gaze,
and he scraped the nose of his car against a
roadblock.

Bruce pulled the car to the side of the street, and he and Roger jumped out to inspect the damage. "Oh, it's nothing," Bruce said, still thinking about Tracy. "It's only a little scratch. I'll have Jim touch it up." Jim was a mechanic at Foreign Auto Body. Bruce always had him take care of his Porsche's little nicks or scratches.

"I've got to get to know Tracy Atkins," Bruce continued as he climbed back into the driver's seat. His face was set with a look of earnest concentration.

How had he overlooked a girl as beautiful as Tracy? *Patman, you must be slipping!* he told himself. He and Tracy had had a geometry class together their sophomore year. Once or twice he'd talked to her after class, but she hadn't seemed like his type at all.

But now Bruce was determined to make up for lost time.

Bruce had been hoping to reintroduce himself to Tracy that day at lunch, but by the time he got to the cafeteria, she was nowhere to be found.

Bruce didn't allow himself to get discouraged. He had decided to do as much research as possible that day. He was starting what he considered a mental "Tracy Atkins file." He wanted to know who her friends were, who she sat with during study hall, what she liked to do, and anything else he could find out. By the end of the day, he had learned that Tracy liked to do things with a few close friends. Lisa DePaul was one of her friends, and Bruce had already remembered that Lisa and Roger were good buddies.

So why not get Roger to get Lisa to bring Tracy to the party next week? Bruce thought. It seemed like a much better strategy than inviting her himself, since he remembered her as being shy. Bruce didn't want to come on too strong—not yet anyway. Besides, wasn't your family supposed to help you in times of dire need?

Bruce headed to his cousin's room that afternoon when he got home from school. "Hi," he said from Roger's doorway. He looked at him with his most affectionate smile. "What's up?"

Roger looked up from his homework. "Nothing, Bruce. What do you want?"

Bruce pretended to be hurt. "Is that any way to talk to your favorite cousin? I just want to talk, that's all." He sat down on Roger's bed without waiting to be invited. "What are you going to give Grandpa for his birthday?" he started.

Roger shrugged. "I haven't thought of anything yet. How about you?"

"I haven't thought of anything either," Bruce told him. "Maybe we can share a present. You know, go in on something together."

Roger looked suspicious. "Bruce, do you want something from me?" he said at last. "You're acting weird. Why are you being so nice?"

Bruce sighed. "You're wounding me, wounding me deeply. But if you have to put things in such crude terms, the truth is I wouldn't mind asking you for a tiny favor."

Roger closed his math book and rolled his eyes. "I knew it," he said. "OK, Bruce. What do you want?"

Bruce's eyes brightened. "Look, you and Lisa DePaul are good friends, right?"

Roger nodded.

"Have you asked her to come to Grandfather's party?" Bruce continued.

"Yes. She's coming," Roger said. "So?"

"Well, I found out today that Tracy and Lisa are close friends. Apparently, they went to camp together when they were kids, and even though Tracy's older, they've been like sisters ever since."

Roger groaned. "Bruce, forget it. If you think I'm going to be stupid enough to get involved in your love life . . ."

"You don't have to get involved. Just ask Lisa to bring Tracy with her. Please," Bruce begged. "Do me this one favor, and I'll owe you a big one."

Roger thought for a minute. "Well, OK. I'll ask Lisa," he said. "But promise you'll be nice to Tracy. You won't break her heart or anything, will you?"

"Who, me?" Bruce said, pretending to be shocked.

Bruce was delighted that Roger was going to help him out. It *almost* made up for the way Grandfather Patman was paying so much attention to Roger.

But Bruce's good feelings about Roger and the upcoming party were shattered at dinner that evening. They spent the whole first and second courses talking about the party. Bruce wasn't paying much attention to the conversation. He was too busy thinking about what he would wear, how he would introduce himself to Tracy, and how they would spend the whole night dancing together.

Then Mrs. Patman turned unexpectedly to Bruce. "And, Bruce, maybe you could help out by picking up some soft drinks at the store one day next week," she said.

Bruce nodded and opened his mouth to speak, but Roger cut him off.

"Isn't your car going to be in the shop?" he asked.

"Nah," Bruce said nonchalantly. "I'll take care of that some other time."

"In the shop? Why would your car be in the shop? I thought you told me it was serviced just last month," Grandfather Patman cut in, a look of disapproval on his face.

Bruce cleared his throat. "Well, I just nicked it a tiny little bit this morning, Grandfather. No big deal. It'll be good as new in five minutes flat." He tried to tell his grandfather all about Jim and how great an artist he was when it came to touch-up jobs, but his grandfather clearly wasn't interested.

"Useless extravagance!" he retorted, wadding up his napkin and hurling it down on the table. "Bruce, you are going to have to learn that money does not grow on trees! That car you drive cost more than my first house. Don't you think you'd better learn to drive it a little more carefully?"

Bruce was stung. He'd never heard an outburst like this before. He looked in his parents' direction for help, but they were both embarrassed and uncomfortable, uncertain about how to respond.

"I'll try to be more careful from now on, Grandfather," Bruce mumbled, his face turning red.

"I should hope so," his grandfather said angrily.

Bruce glared at Roger, whose expression was completely blank. Why would Roger bring up his accident unless he wanted to make Bruce look bad in front of his grandfather? *Well*, Bruce thought, furious, *two can play at that game!*

*   *   *

On Friday, a special assembly was called at Sweet Valley High. Bruce had hung around outside the door of the auditorium for as long as he could, hoping to catch a glimpse of Tracy. Once he was inside, he saw she was sitting in one of the front rows, next to Lisa. Bruce hoped Roger had already asked Lisa to invite Tracy to the Patmans' party, since there was no way he'd ask Roger again. Not after the way Roger had treated him the night before.

Mr. Cooper, the principal, called the students to order and made a few announcements. Then he said, "The main reason for holding this assembly is to introduce a very special community program that will be going on for the next several months. I'm going to hand the mike over to Mr. Collins, who's closely involved with the program and who can tell you all a little more about it."

Everyone cheered. Roger Collins was a handsome young English teacher who looked a bit like Robert Redford. He was one of the most popular teachers in the school.

Mr. Collins put up his hand to stop the applause. "Thanks, guys. Let me make this as

31

brief as I can, because I know you all want to get back to class."

This brought more cheers and laughter from the students.

"This is a very special program I'm about to describe to you," Mr. Collins said seriously. "It's called SAVE. It was started by a group of community leaders who want to help save the Nicholson School. Nicholson is a school for special-needs children from the ages of five to twelve. Due to fiscal problems, the Nicholson School will have to close its doors at the end of this year unless ten thousand dollars is raised. And raised *quickly*. The whole community is doing what it can to help."

Bruce had his eye on Tracy, who was hanging onto Mr. Collins's every word.

"The PTA has asked us to elect student representatives to help out with SAVE. We have to move on this right away. There'll be a meeting next week with the PTA and with other community organizers to plan local events to raise money. In your homerooms, you will be asked to write down the name of the person from your class who you think would do the best job. Then we'll tally up the votes and announce whom you have chosen as reps on Monday."

The mood in the auditorium grew solemn as everyone tried to think who would be the best for this sort of job. Bruce himself didn't find it a very absorbing issue, but he couldn't help noticing that Tracy Atkins appeared very concerned.

He didn't particularly care about good causes himself. But if Tracy did, then so did he.

Three

Bruce wasn't sure at first what woke him Sunday morning. He never set an alarm on weekends. Then he realized someone was knocking on his door.

Grandfather Patman opened the door and barged in without waiting to be asked. "Wake up, Bruce. Sleeping all day isn't going to get you anywhere. When I was your age, I'd already run three miles by this time on a Sunday morning. Your cousin Roger's already awake," he added.

Bruce hid a groan. He was sick and tired of

hearing about how hard his grandfather had worked all of his life. The only thing that was worse was hearing how great Roger was.

At brunch, Bruce accidentally dropped a glass, and it shattered.

"Never mind, sweetheart," Mrs. Patman said, patting Bruce on the arm and calling to Miranda to clean up the mess.

Grandfather Patman was horrified. "You can't mean to tell me that you're not even going to ask Bruce to clean up his own mess!" he exclaimed.

Everyone looked around in embarrassment.

"What are you doing?" Bruce growled when his cousin leaned over to wipe up a few splashes of orange juice near his chair.

Roger felt mortified. And, of course, Grandfather Patman saw the whole exchange.

"You see, Roger knows what it means to work," Grandfather Patman said. "Not like you, Bruce. You're used to being taken care of. You're used to having everything given to you on a silver platter. That's why you're so careless with your possessions."

Bruce was so angry that he felt as if he were

35

being suffocated. He suffered in agonizing silence all through the rest of the meal. There wasn't any escape—they all had to stay in the dining room, even when brunch ended. That was when Alexander Patman decided to distribute sections of the newspaper. "Roger, may I pass you the business section?" he inquired.

Roger shook his head. "No, thanks," he said, reaching for the Sunday magazine.

Bruce felt his spirits lift. This was almost good enough to make up for his own humiliation. And the best part was, Roger had no idea how much he had upset his grandfather!

Alexander Patman waited a minute, then cleared his throat. "I must have heard you wrong. Did you just say 'No, thanks'?"

Roger nodded. "I never read that section. It's a little dry," he said, unaware of his grandfather's rising temper.

Grandfather Patman smacked the paper on the side of the table, his face beet red. "Dry? Dry? Is that how you refer to the information we all need to make our company grow? Why, do you realize that unless you stay on top of the most important day-to-day events in the business world, you can't possibly be any good to yours or any other company!"

"*I'd* like the business section, Grandfather," Bruce said pointedly, stretching out an eager hand. "I always read it," he added, giving his cousin a meaningful look.

"Oh, *really*," Roger said. More than a little sarcasm was evident in his voice.

"Yes," Bruce said, irritated. "*Really*, Roger. Just because *some* people around here couldn't care less what happens in business doesn't mean—"

"Boys!" Mr. Patman exclaimed, cutting them both off. "Let's stop this bickering and go outside and enjoy the day!"

Bruce frowned. He didn't feel like enjoying anything, least of all the company of his rotten cousin Roger.

"Hey," Jessica Wakefield said Monday at lunchtime, gesturing with a french fry to the spot nearby where Bruce and Roger were arguing noisily. "What's going on with those two?

I thought they were getting along so much better these days."

"Don't talk to me about Bruce Patman," Amy Sutton said. "That boy is nothing but trouble."

Jessica took a bite of her sandwich. "Yeah, but you're not completely objective, Ame," she pointed out. "I seem to remember a time when you were plenty interested in everything Bruce did."

Amy made a face. "It's a time I like to forget, if you don't mind," she said lightly. "Anyway, he and Roger are probably arguing about something earth-shattering, like who has to get gas for the Porsche." She giggled.

Jessica didn't look satisfied with her friend's remarks. "I've had a funny feeling lately about Bruce. You know that really nice senior, Tracy Atkins? I saw Bruce following her down the hall today. He looked so pathetic, just like a lovesick puppy."

Amy flipped back her hair. "I don't know who she is, and I'm not really interested," she said coldly.

Jessica knew Bruce was still a touchy subject for Amy. After all, Amy was part of the reason

38

Bruce had broken up with Regina Morrow. The breakup had been so traumatic for Regina that she had let herself be taken in by the wrong crowd. She had experimented once with cocaine and had had a severe reaction and died. It was a painful thing for all of them to remember—especially for Amy.

"I'll point her out to you the next time I see her," Jessica said. "Anyway, it looks to me like Bruce has got a bad case of infatuation." She giggled. "Either that, or he's attached to Tracy Atkins with Velcro!"

Amy just rolled her eyes. "Poor girl," she said dryly.

The following Tuesday morning, the decisions on student representatives for the SAVE Fund Drive were announced in homeroom. Elizabeth Wakefield couldn't believe it when she heard she had been picked as the representative for the junior class. Her homeroom teacher announced her name first and then read the rest of the nominees. "Dirk Pierce will be representing the freshmen; Lisa DePaul, the sophomores; and Tracy Atkins, the seniors."

"Hey, well done," Jessica whispered to her twin sister. "I mean, if you like that sort of thing," she added immediately.

Elizabeth laughed. It was a long-standing joke in the Wakefield family that Jessica wouldn't volunteer for a good cause unless every mall in California was closed and every boy banished from the state.

Elizabeth was a little worried by the way her classmates were treating the SAVE project. Most of them seemed completely unconcerned. Drumming up interest in a school nobody knew anything about wasn't going to be easy. *Well,* Elizabeth told herself, *we'll just have to do something to change that!*

Bruce was doing everything he could to keep Tracy in his line of vision in the crowded high school hallway. This took real effort, since he had an armful of books and was trying to smooth his hair back with one hand. He'd just come out of homeroom, where the SAVE representatives had been announced. Ordinarily, Bruce didn't pay much attention in homeroom. But

when he heard Tracy's name, he sat bolt up-
right. Tracy! She had won the seniors' rep
position!

Which was a perfect chance to talk to her.

The only problem was that Tracy seemed to
be in a hurry to get to class.

"Hey, Tracy!" he called. He was a little out of
breath when he finally caught up to her.

She looked fantastic. She was wearing a slim
dark skirt and a soft-blue denim shirt and cowboy boots.

"Tracy, I just wanted to tell you I'm glad
you're going to be our rep," Bruce said. He
knew that sounded a little bit inane, but he
figured he had to start somewhere.

Tracy stared at him. Up close, her eyes were
a lovely shade of light green, with flecks of
warm amber in them. She smiled, her eyes fixed
firmly on his. "Thanks," she said softly. "I'm
embarrassed to admit this, but I'm not sure I
remember. . . . Have we met?"

Bruce cleared his throat. "Yes, but I can see I
didn't make much of an impression," he said,
trying to keep his tone light. Tracy raised her
eyebrows but didn't smile.

Boy, he thought. *This is one serious girl!*

"I'm Bruce," he said quickly. "Bruce Patman."

"Oh, yes," she said. "I know who you are. Your family runs the Patman Corporation, right?"

"Right!" Bruce said, relieved. He leaned back against the locker behind him, ready to start *really* talking now that the introductions were over. Now that she knew who he was.

"Listen, I'm sorry, but I've got a test this period. I've really got to run," she said earnestly. And before he could say another word, she was gone, slipping off down the hallway as if it didn't make one single bit of difference to her that she had just blown a chance to talk to him!

Bruce felt miserable as he watched her disappear.

Roger was in a rotten mood on Tuesday. He still hadn't recovered from spending the weekend with Grandfather Patman. Every time he had turned around, his grandfather seemed to be criticizing him—or even worse, comparing him with Bruce. Why couldn't he be interested in the family business, as Bruce was? Why didn't he want to read the business section of the newspaper, the way Bruce and his father both did? It was infuriating. Roger felt as if he could never measure up to Bruce, and it made him hurt and angry.

He had tossed and turned all night long. Now he couldn't even concentrate in class. The only good news he could remember hearing since his grandfather had arrived over a week before was that Lisa had won the student-representative position for the Nicholson School Fund Drive. It cheered him up a little bit to think what a great job she would do.

"You four are going to be fantastic!" Roger told Lisa during lunch. "I can't imagine a better group of reps. I bet the Nicholson School gets saved in no time!"

"Thanks," Lisa said. "The four of us are going to meet this afternoon to talk about some ideas we have. We have to get organized, since later on in the week we meet with the PTA and the other committee leaders." She grinned. "Any input you've got would be great."

"At this point, I don't feel like I have much to

contribute—to you guys or to anyone else," Roger told her.

"Why?" Lisa asked him with genuine concern.

Roger filled her in on his weekend with his grandfather.

"Poor Roger." She patted him on the arm. "Let's do something fun together this afternoon. Why don't you come with me to the SAVE meeting, and then we can go to the beach when it's over?"

Roger shrugged again. Maybe going to the meeting wasn't such a bad idea. At least it would take his mind off Grandfather Patman.

That afternoon the SAVE reps had their first meeting. The other three reps chose Elizabeth Wakefield to be in charge of running their meetings and to deal with administrative details.

"OK, guys, let's get started," Elizabeth said. Lisa had already explained to her that Roger would be sitting in on the meeting.

"The PTA has asked us for suggestions on an event we could hold to raise money. They'd like us to bring some ideas to the meeting this week. Why don't we brainstorm for a little while and see what we can come up with. . . ."

For a few minutes, the five of them threw ideas around. But none of the events they came up with seemed big enough.

"You know, something like a community market might be a good idea," Tracy suggested. "We could set up stalls down by the harbor."

"That's a great idea!" Elizabeth exclaimed. "What sort of things do you think we could sell?"

Tracy was about to answer when the door to the classroom opened and Bruce burst in. Smiling, he looked from one to the other. Finally, his gaze rested on Tracy.

"Bruce," Elizabeth said, clearly annoyed, "what are you doing here?"

Bruce cleared his throat. "Uh, I was looking for Roger," he said.

Roger felt himself growing angry. He was sure that Bruce wasn't there to see him. He wanted to talk to Tracy, no doubt. Or at least make sure she noticed him.

"Maybe you two could talk about whatever

you need to talk about in the hallway. We have business to take care of in here," Elizabeth said quietly. She wasn't usually so cold. In fact, Elizabeth was one of the most friendly girls in the school. Roger could tell she was just trying to be firm to make sure the meeting ran smoothly.

But getting Bruce out of the classroom now that he and Tracy were in the same place was easier said than done. "Hi, Tracy," Bruce said, sitting down on the chair next to her and giving her his most engaging smile. "I don't know if you remember this, but you and I were in a math class together once. Remember, Mr. Jordan's geometry class sophomore year? Which reminds me, how was your test today?"

Tracy smiled, although she seemed a little puzzled. "It was fine," she said slowly. "But what—"

Elizabeth cleared her throat. "Roger, Bruce—if you could just talk about whatever you need to talk about in the hallway and let us finish our meeting . . ."

"Bruce, what is it?" Roger demanded when the two of them were out in the hall.

"Boy, she's cute," Bruce said, grinning. "Think she likes me? Tell me the truth."

Roger rolled his eyes. "Bruce, I really don't know. Look—"

"Oh, there really was something I wanted to ask you," Bruce continued. "I don't want you to think I just burst in there to see Tracy."

Roger waited silently for what was coming next.

"I need to borrow your car. I've got a couple of errands to run on my way home." Bruce had finally put his car in the shop, and he had ridden to school that morning with Roger.

Roger could feel himself getting angrier and angrier. "Sorry, Bruce, but I happen to need my car. Lisa and I are going to the beach after this meeting."

"What am I supposed to do about my errands?" Bruce demanded.

"How should I know? Find somebody else. Take the bus," Roger retorted. He could tell from the angry look in Bruce's eyes that Bruce would eventually make him pay for that comment; but he didn't care. He was fed up with being nice to his cousin.

Alexander Patman was in unusually high spirits on Tuesday night. He spent most of dinner reminiscing about how he had built up the Patman Corporation with only a few thousand dollars to his name. "And look what an empire it's become!" he exclaimed.

Mr. and Mrs. Patman couldn't get a word in until they were having dessert and coffee. "Everyone," Mrs. Patman announced, "Henry has something he'd like to tell you."

"As you all know," Mr. Patman said, "our company has been doing more and more business recently with a Japanese firm named Mitsu. Some of our top clients there need to discuss some delicate matters with me. So I've decided to take a trip to Tokyo."

Mrs. Patman was beaming. "But that's not all," she went on. "I've managed to convince your father that he and I need a vacation. So instead of letting him fly off by himself for a few frantic days, he and I are going to combine business with pleasure and take a trip to the Far East."

At first, their announcement didn't really sink in. "That sounds great," Bruce said, concentrating on his chocolate mousse. "When do you guys take off?"

"Saturday." Mrs. Patman said. "I can't believe how much there is to get accomplished
before we go, Henry," she added. "I have to
buy a completely new wardrobe." She glanced
at her father-in-law. "I mean, I'll have to pack a
few things," she corrected herself quickly. "And
we'll need to call our contacts in Japan. We'll
need to make all kinds of arrangements! Besides, there's Grandfather's party to think
about," she finished. "There are a lot of things
to do."

Bruce suddenly realized what his mother was
saying. "Saturday? You're leaving *this* Saturday? The day after the party? But—" He paused.
"How long will you be gone?"

"A month," Mr. Patman said, taking his wife's
hand in his. "A much-deserved month. Fortunately, your grandfather is here to look after
you boys, or we wouldn't be able to stay away
so long."

Bruce felt as if he was going to choke on the
chocolate mousse. His parents were going away
for an entire month and leaving him alone with
Grandfather Patman and Roger? He couldn't
believe it. It was worse than being abandoned.

"I think it's wonderful," Alexander Patman

said. "It'll give me a real opportunity to get to know the boys." He smiled from one to the other. "So often, these visits can be forced or too formal. But this way, we won't be able to pretend. It'll be a real learning experience—for us all."

Bruce stared at his parents with growing horror. This was going to be a total disaster.

Four

Tracy had given a great deal of thought to the question Elizabeth had brought up at the SAVE meeting. What was the best way to get other students interested in the project? She was spending her study hall trying to work out some ideas before the representative's meeting that afternoon. In fact, she was so deeply absorbed in what she was doing that she hardly noticed when Bruce Patman came over to her table. He set his books down, sighed loudly, and when she looked up, he smiled at her.

"Tracy!" he exclaimed. "What are you doing here!"

Tracy laughed. Was it her imagination, or had there been an awful lot of coincidental "collisions" between Bruce and her lately?

"Tracy," Bruce said, his brown eyes fixed sincerely on hers, "I really want to help you guys with the fund-raising drive. Will you let me know if there's anything I can do to help?"

"That's really nice of you, Bruce," Tracy said slowly, looking shyly at him. She didn't know what else to say. But it was nice having him pay her so much attention!

Tracy barely knew Bruce. She had heard a few of the rumors after Regina's tragic accident. She knew that Bruce was from one of the wealthiest families in the entire valley—and that was about it. Why Bruce would want to have anything to do with her was beyond her comprehension. After all, he could go out with any of the girls at school—or in the whole town, for that matter.

Tracy didn't take Elizabeth and Lisa seriously when they teased her about Bruce at the meeting later that afternoon.

"Seems like you've won us a major supporter,

Tracy," Elizabeth said, smiling. "Bruce has been by three or four times today—just to let me know how much he wants to help us."

The student representatives for the SAVE Fund Drive had gotten permission to use the classroom next to the *Oracle* office as their headquarters. Elizabeth had already made a sign for the door, and her twin sister Jessica had contributed a suggestion box just outside. "In case any of the rest of us come up with brilliant schemes," Jessica had remarked, her blue-green eyes sparkling.

Tracy had always admired the Wakefield twins. They were a legend at Sweet Valley High because of the contrast between their identical appearance and their vastly different personalities. Elizabeth was the more serious twin. She wanted to be a professional writer, and she was getting experience by working on the staff of *The Oracle*, Sweet Valley High's student paper. Jessica loved change and adventure. She preferred the kind of school activities that put her in the limelight. she was co-captain of the cheerleading squad and an active member of Pi Beta Alpha, an exclusive sorority.

Tracy had always wanted to get to know the twins better. She hoped that being a rep for the SAVE fund would make that possible.

One thing Tracy could tell—Elizabeth wasn't exactly a Bruce Patman fan. Elizabeth wasn't the sort of person to make unkind comments about anyone, but Tracy could pick up a negative reaction from Elizabeth whenever she mentioned Bruce.

"Of course, Bruce has the money to be a big help," Elizabeth mused, twirling her pencil around. "He could probably help us a great deal—if he really wants to."

Tracy felt her cheeks color slightly. Despite herself, she was flattered to think Bruce might be interested in her. *What's wrong with me?* she asked herself sternly. *Bruce Patman is from a world as different from my own as I can imagine! Thinking about him is probably the stupidest thing I could possibly do.*

Tracy had never had a boyfriend. She was the oldest in a family of six. Since both her parents worked, Tracy had to help a lot around the house, especially with her youngest brother, Jeremy, who had been born with a rare muscular disease that impaired his growth. Jeremy was in the second grade at the Nicholson School. He was the reason Tracy cared so much about the SAVE project. She couldn't bear the thought of the Nicholson School's closing. If it did, her parents would have to send Jeremy to a school in Los Angeles. That would mean he couldn't live at home, and *that* was too awful a thought to consider.

Tracy loved her family with all her heart. She never minded how much time she spent with them or how little time was left over for her to be with people from school. Of course, sometimes she wished she could be a little bit more like the other students she knew. Like Elizabeth, for instance. Elizabeth had a wonderful boyfriend, Todd Wilkins, and the two of them seemed to have so much fun together. Tracy had never met a boy she liked as more than a friend, and she had told herself that sort of thing would wait until she was a little bit older. But something in the way Bruce had smiled at her this afternoon in the lunchroom . . .

I'm just nuts, she told herself. *Bruce Patman would never be interested in me.*

Still, after the SAVE meeting that afternoon, Tracy did something she hadn't done in a long, long time. She stopped in the girls' bathroom on the first floor and stared long and hard in the mirror.

There she was—Tracy Atkins. Her long, silky black hair had recently been cut in a sophisticated new style, which Tracy's mother had chosen for her. And she had to admit that the way her hair framed her face suited her. Her almond-shaped green eyes shone in a new way, and the elegant lines of her cheekbones and her neck were revealed for the first time. Tracy didn't have a lot of money to spend on clothes, but she loved to sew, and she was able to design and make dresses unlike anything her classmates wore. She loved fashion and dreamed of becoming a designer. "You don't look half bad, Tracy Atkins," she told herself.

And who should she bump into on her way out of the bathroom but Bruce!

"Hi," Bruce said, his face lighting up. "Tracy, I was hoping to run into you again today. Did Roger or Lisa tell you that we're having a big party for my grandfather tomorrow night?"

Tomorrow night? That's Friday! Tracy thought. She shook her head slowly. "No, they didn't," she managed to get out.

Bruce's expression darkened. "My cousin hasn't been very cooperative lately," he muttered. Then he smiled. "Well, anyway, we are— and I'd like you to come. My grandfather's turning seventy, so we're having a big bash— Patman-style," he added, looking pleased with himself.

Tracy took a deep breath. What did "Patman-style" mean? Hundreds of people milling around in fancy clothes? She would have been much more inclined to say yes if Bruce had said it was something small and informal.

Still, Bruce was looking at her with such a hopeful expression. He seemed to really want her to be there.

"I don't know. Sometimes I have to help out at home on weekends," Tracy said slowly.

"Well, if you could come, I'd be one happy guy. I mean that," Bruce said. He didn't sound cocky, the way he had earlier. He sounded sincere. Tracy lowered her gaze shyly.

"I'll try," she said softly.

*　　*　　*

Bruce walked around the Patman estate on Friday evening with a feeling of pride. The house, surrounded by well-maintained grounds, always looked beautiful, but it was especially magical that night. From the grounds in front you could see the lights of the valley twinkling below, and from another direction you could see the gentle crests of whitecaps in the ocean. *This is the life*, Bruce thought, smiling. He felt on top of the world. He thought of Tracy seeing all this for the first time. He knew the minute she saw the way he lived, she would be won over. That was the way it always was. Girls might be a little resistant at first, but the Patman wealth was always too much for them. *Tracy would fall in love with all this*, he thought.

The only thing troubling Bruce was the knowledge that his parents would be leaving the next morning for the Far East. Already, their bedroom looked more like the inside of a suitcase than anything else.

Bruce saw a shape out in the twilight. It was Roger, standing under the trees, his hands in his pockets. "Hey, Roger!" Bruce called out.

Roger looked startled. "Bruce! I thought you'd be inside, spending time with your parents before they go," he said.

Bruce shrugged. "Why should I? They have Miranda to help if they need it." Bruce could feel his good mood ebbing away. Seeing his cousin reminded him of how strained relations with his grandfather were. Everything Roger did lately rubbed Bruce the wrong way.

"What did you decide to give Grandfather Patman for his birthday?" Roger asked.

Bruce shrugged. "I haven't found anything yet. But I will. Why? Have you found him something?"

Roger didn't answer, and Bruce felt waves of fury wash over him. Of course Roger had a present. He was probably just waiting for the perfect moment to give it to their grandfather so that Bruce would look bad in comparison. He was fed up with his cousin.

"By the way," Bruce said acidly, "thanks for taking all the trouble to ask Tracy to come tonight."

"I tried, but—"

"Sure, Rog," Bruce said. And before Roger

could say another word, Bruce spun on his heel and left.

Bruce thought his grandfather's birthday party was a smashing success. The food was delicious, and the Latin-American band his mother had hired was wonderful. Bruce danced every dance he could with Tracy. She looked stunning in an off-white, one-shoulder dress.

"You look wonderful," he told her right away, giving her a big smile.

When she smiled back at him, he knew she was glad to be there. His confidence lifted enormously.

Almost a hundred guests had been invited to the party, and the mood was festive and warm. Dinner was served buffet-style on the terraces. Bruce made sure to bring a plate heaping with food for Tracy and him to share. Like the music, the food had a south-of-the-border theme. It was spicy and delicious, and there were lots of iced drinks to wash it down with.

"So, what do you think of all this?" Bruce asked Tracy, looking happily out over the terraces.

"It's an impressive house," Tracy answered, but she didn't look impressed. In fact, Bruce thought she looked a little bit put off.

This was obviously going to be harder than he thought it would be. Bruce decided to redouble his efforts. He told Tracy about the new Windsurfer he wanted to buy. "You should see it, Trace. It's incredible, entirely state of the art. . . ."

Tracy still didn't look impressed. In fact, she seemed a little uncomfortable.

"Is something wrong?" Bruce asked.

"Maybe I should go and find Lisa," Tracy said in a distracted voice.

Bruce moved a little closer to Tracy so he could smell the soft scent of perfume on her hair. "You know," he said, "I'd love to take you to a club in L.A. sometime. I know a really wild place that you can only get into if you know the right people. We could even go tomorrow night. . . ."

Tracy pulled back. "That doesn't really sound like my kind of thing," she said politely.

Bruce couldn't believe his ears. What girl in her right mind wouldn't jump at that kind of invitation?

"Thanks anyway," she said.

"You're a funny girl, Tracy Atkins," Bruce said softly, letting his hand brush hers. Her cheeks colored, and she looked shyly down at her lap. Bruce felt an overwhelming desire to kiss her. But he held back.

Talk about mixed messages, Bruce thought. Tracy truly seemed to like him. She had definitely been happy to see him when she first arrived that evening. And she wouldn't have agreed to come to the party if she didn't like him. But Bruce couldn't figure out why she didn't seem more excited by the estate and even worse, why wasn't she interested in going to L.A. with him.

It didn't make sense. But Bruce wasn't prepared to give up yet. Not after the beautiful blush his touch had evoked.

"You know something, Trace?" Bruce said, leaning closer to her, "I think there's something happening between us. Something that just needs a little bit more time to develop."

Tracy looked embarrassed. "You're pretty sure of yourself, aren't you?" she said with amazement.

"Yeah," Bruce said, still staring into her eyes. "I am."

Tracy didn't respond, but Bruce's confidence didn't waver. He knew something magical was going to happen between them. It was only a question of *when*.

"This has been a terrific party," Alexander Patman said at midnight. Most of the guests had gone, and the last few were saying their goodbyes. Mr. and Mrs. Patman both looked tired, and they still had some packing to do before they were ready to leave the next morning. But Grandfather Patman clearly wasn't ready for the evening to end yet.

"When you get a chance," he said, his eyes twinkling, "I'd like to take you and the boys aside and tell you about the surprise I have planned for them."

"How about right now? I won't stay awake that much longer," Mrs. Patman said. "We have a long flight ahead of us tomorrow."

"Fine," Grandfather Patman said.

The Patmans sat down around a patio table and waited for Alexander Patman to speak.

"I want you to know, first and foremost, how much I appreciated this party," he began. "I suppose a moment like this presents itself as an opportunity to look backward as well as forward. I've been very lucky in my life. I've had both a wonderful family and a wonderful career. And I hope very much that the Patman Corporation will live on long after me as a testimony to what I dreamed of accomplishing when I was young—about the same age as you boys are now," he added.

Bruce was anxious to hear about the surprise. His grandfather could be so long-winded sometimes.

"Now, being here with you boys for the past week has made me do a lot of hard thinking. I always assumed that the company would pass down from me to Henry and then to Bruce."

Bruce sat up straighter.

"But now that I see there's another young Patman around, it doesn't seem that simple to me. Why shouldn't Roger have a hand in the company in the future as well as Bruce?"

Dead silence greeted this question. Bruce couldn't believe his ears. His grandfather had to be kidding!

"Now, I spoke on the phone today with my attorney, and I've told him that I think my will ought to be altered." Grandfather Patman smiled. "The thing is, I'm not sure *how* to alter it yet. And that's where the surprise comes in."

Bruce was sure everyone else could hear his heart pounding. This was his entire future his grandfather was so casually talking about altering! And all because of his rotten cousin. Bruce couldn't look Roger in the eye. He felt dizzy.

"My feeling is that you boys ought to have to work to earn your chance to control the Patman Corporation. Why should it just be handed to either of you when Henry retires? If you're the right man for the job, then you're the right man to fight for the job. I wanted to give you boys a chance to show you're made of the stuff that company presidents are made of." Grandfather Patman smiled, first at one boy, then at the other. "So here's what I propose. I'd like to give each one of you boys two thousand dollars in cash. What you do with that money, as long as it's legal, is your business. The point is, four weeks from tomorrow night, when your parents get back from their trip, we'll see who's invested his money more wisely and who's made it grow. Whoever has more money four weeks from now is the winner."

Mr. Patman looked stunned. "Father," he said, "are you saying—"

"I'm saying the boys ought to fight it out, darn it!" Alexander Patman declared. "No foul play, either," he warned them. "As of today, that two thousand has to cover everything. I want you two to give me your credit cards, your checkbooks, every bit of money you have. I'll keep them in custody for the month. May the best man win!"

"And whoever wins this contest gets the controlling share of the company?" Bruce asked weakly.

"That's exactly right," Grandfather Patman said with a look of satisfaction. "Now, doesn't that seem like a good way to elect a company president? Just like in the old days, when gumption and hard work got you somewhere!"

Bruce felt sick to his stomach. He couldn't believe what he had just heard. For his entire life, he'd known that one day he was going to inherit the Patman Corporation. Now his future had been yanked out from under him.

Well, he *was* going to fight it. He was going to fight it every step of the way. If Roger thought he was going to rob him of his inheritance, he was going to have to think again!

Five

Bruce sat on the edge of his parents' bed, watching them finish packing. It was Saturday morning, and they were leaving in less than an hour for the airport. "It just isn't fair," Bruce said for at least the dozenth time since his grandfather's astonishing announcement the night before. "Dad," he pleaded, "can't you talk to him? This seems insane to me!"

Mr. Patman shook his head. "Bruce, if there's one thing I know about your grandfather, it's that he can be extremely stubborn. I think the best thing I can do is stay out of this for now."

Bruce was miserable. "And he really has the right to change his will, just like this!"

Mr. Patman shrugged. "Of course he does. It's his will, Bruce. You know as well as I do that the control of Patman Corporation still lies with him. I may be president, but he's chairman of the board. He has the right to do whatever he wishes."

Mrs. Patman came over, and gave Bruce a soothing hug. "Don't worry," she whispered when Mr. Patman was busy on the other side of the room. "You'll win the contest. You've always had an excellent head for business."

Bruce was secretly pleased. His mother was right. It was silly to let his grandfather's challenge get to him. He was bound to make more money in four weeks than Roger was. "Roger'll probably keep the money in his piggy bank," he said with a mean snicker.

"Now, listen to me, Bruce," Mr. Patman said firmly. "I know your grandfather hasn't exactly made this easy, but I'd really like to ask you to cooperate with your cousin. We're going to be far away, and we don't want to have to worry about you two boys."

"Oh, there won't be any reason to worry, Dad," Bruce said seriously. But he didn't intend to cooperate with his cousin. He intended to *win*.

"OK, boys, let's have it all. Your checkbooks, your credit cards, the whole works." Alexander Patman crossed his arms and looked expectantly at the table. Roger emptied out his pockets.

Bruce sighed. "Here," he said finally, tossing everything onto the table with an attempt at nonchalance.

"Is that everything?" Grandfather Patman's eyes looked like ice, and Bruce felt his stomach churn. "I guess I've still got a credit card or two upstairs," he muttered. Just then, he hated his grandfather.

"Go get them. We'll wait," his grandfather said firmly.

Five minutes later, Bruce had given his grandfather every last penny he had—and every credit card. In exchange, Grandfather Patman counted out twenty crisp one-hundred-dollar bills for each boy. "There you go," he said with a satisfied smile. "Two thousand dollars each. It will be four weeks until your parents come back from the Orient. Let's see what you two can do with your money between now and then."

Bruce casually crumpled the bills into his pocket. It made him want to laugh, watching Roger fold them carefully. "Watch it, Rog. Looks like you may have creased that one."

"Now," Grandfather Patman said, "I'm off for my jog. With all this celebrating and leave-taking, I haven't had time to work out for the past two days." He glanced at his stopwatch. "Either of you want to join me?"

"No, thanks," Bruce and Roger said in unison. They glanced uneasily at each other, then away.

A week ago, Bruce and Roger would have shared a laugh about their grandfather's enthusiasm for running. It was strange how impossible that seemed now. Bruce could hardly wait to get Roger out of his sight.

It was Saturday, and for Bruce, that meant it was time to do something really self-indulgent. The question was, what? It was strange to see his wallet empty. *Oh, well*, Bruce thought, *I have two thousand dollars.* He could see no reason not to dip into it every now and then if he really needed to. *I can always earn it back*, he told himself.

The first thing Bruce wanted to do was think of somewhere wonderful to take Tracy. Maybe a special concert?

Less than an hour after his parents had left for the airport, Bruce jumped into his car and headed toward downtown Sweet Valley to a ticket office where he could find out what was happening in the area.

Bruce thought about Tracy all the way to town. He couldn't get her image out of his mind. Her soft dark hair, her huge, sexy eyes. She was beautiful. And there was so much more to her than most of the girls he'd dated. She didn't seem the slightest bit vain. He longed to get beyond that cool, reserved manner of hers. Maybe if he could find some great little place to take her to that night . . .

Bruce was so absorbed in his thoughts that he didn't even see the stop sign at the next intersection he came to. He slammed on his brakes to keep from running into the Camaro that zipped through the intersection in front of him. He did hit the car, but not very hard.

The woman driving the Camaro jumped out of her car. "You idiot!" she hollered at him.

She calmed dow when she realized the Camaro wasn't even nicked. She took Bruce's phone number and insurance information, even though there wasn't a single scratch on her car. Bruce's was another story. One front fender was badly dented.

"I can't believe it," he moaned. "Of all the rotten luck!" Bruce knew his grandfather had been annoyed with him for scratching his car last week. He was really going to love *this*!

"I won't tell him," Bruce decided then and there. He would take the car back to the auto-body shop and pay cash to have the fender bumped out.

Bruce called Jim, the mechanic, who assured him that he could take care of it. "But it's going to cost you, Bruce. If you've really crushed the fender, it'll be four or five hundred dollars," Jim said.

Bruce didn't like the sound of that, but what choice did he have? At least getting the car fixed would save him hours of sermons from his grandfather on how careless he was, how he didn't know the value of money, and how his grandfather didn't have a car until he earned the money to buy one himself.

Bruce dropped the Porsche off at Foreign Auto Body. Jim promised him he would take care of it as soon as possible. Even so, Bruce would have to leave the car there for a few days. The repairs would cost four hundred and fifty dollars.

Oh, well, Bruce told himself in the taxi from the auto-body shop to the Ticketron office. He would figure out a way to earn the money back. Right now he had more important things to think about. Like what kind of concert would impress Tracy the most.

There was only one that looked at all interesting to Bruce—a reunion concert of a band that had been very popular ten years ago. They were expected to perform to sellout crowds that night outside Los Angeles. The only problem was that the tickets were fifty dollars each. "But well worth it," the guy at the ticket office had assured him. "This is the concert of a lifetime. They're never going to perform together again."

"Oh, all right," Bruce said, peeling a one-hundred-dollar bill out of his wallet. He was having a very expensive morning!

Roger was sitting by the Patmans' pool reading a novel, when Bruce sauntered over.

"Trying to catch a few rays, Rog?" Bruce's voice sounded even less pleasant than usual. "I'm surprised to see you out here relaxing. I would've thought you'd be ironing your money or something."

Roger took off his sunglasses. "To tell you the truth—"

But Bruce didn't give him a chance to finish. "You'd just better watch out, Roger. Because I'm going to make ten times the money you do," he said. An instant later, he dived into the pool, making sure to splash Roger and his book.

Roger was annoyed. He had wanted to tell Bruce that he thought their grandfather's contest was a rotten idea and that they should try to convince him to change his mind. Roger thought relations had been strained enough lately between him and Bruce without involving them in a contest guaranteed to turn best friends into enemies.

But the more obnoxious Bruce was, the less Roger felt like trying to make up with him. Maybe he ought to go ahead and work on the contest as hard as he could. For once, Roger wanted to show Bruce that he was his equal—or better.

Forget being a peacemaker, Roger told himself. *If Bruce wants a fight, I'll give him a fight to remember.*

"Listen, Rog, I was wondering," Bruce said, drying himself off after his swim. "Are you using your car tonight?"

"Why?" Roger asked suspiciously.

"Well," Bruce began carefully. "Actually, I'm taking Tracy to a concert and my car has been making this funny little knocking sound. I don't want to take it on the freeway."

Roger raised his eyebrows. "Actually, I need my car tonight," he said. "A group of us are going to the Beach Disco, and I promised Lisa I'd drive."

Bruce looked at him sullenly. "So, what am I supposed to do?" he grumbled.

Roger shrugged. "Hire a limo," he said in a mockingly sweet tone of voice. It was just the tone Bruce sometimes used with him. "You've got two grand. You can afford it. Or ask Grandfather if you can borrow one of your parents' cars."

Bruce gave him a dirty look, and Roger felt triumphant. The truth was, Lisa was driving that night. But he didn't want to use his car; he wanted to save every penny to invest, and that meant not buying gas. He certainly didn't want *Bruce* using up his gas. And he knew Bruce would never dare ask his grandfather to use one of the other cars—then Grandfather would ask too many questions.

If this was going to be all-out war, Roger certainly wasn't going to give the enemy any ammunition!

Bruce hid his bicycle behind the bushes and rang the Atkinses' doorbell. After several minutes, Tracy opened the door.

"Bruce!" she exclaimed. Her eyes brightened at once, and Bruce hid a smile. She was glad to see him, all right. *I probably brightened up her whole Saturday just by dropping by*, Bruce thought proudly. He felt a little awkward about not hav-

ing a car. But he was fairly sure he could borrow one from one of his friends.

"How're you doing? I wanted to make sure
you got home safely last night," Bruce said,
giving her an affectionate smile.

Tracy smiled back. "I did. And it was a really
fun party, Bruce. Thanks again for inviting me."
She cleared her throat. "Is that—uh, is that
why you came by?"

"Well, that and the fact that I happen to
have come by two tickets to the Starfest concert
in L.A. tonight. I was hoping you would want
to go with me." *Boy*, Bruce thought, *Tracy must
be feeling very lucky, having all this attention lav-
ished on her!* How often did girls get asked
out to a once-in-a-lifetime concert such as the
Starfest?

But Tracy didn't look impressed. "Well, Bruce,
ordinarily I would have liked to go, but—"

"But what?" Bruce cut in. He couldn't believe
his ears. Didn't Tracy realize that this was a
dream of an invitation? From the modest look
of the Atkinses' home, she couldn't be used to
being offered fifty-dollar concert tickets.

"I have to baby-sit tonight, Bruce," she explained. "My parents hardly ever get out, and I

promised I'd stay home and take care of my younger brothers."

"Get another baby-sitter," Bruce suggested. "Can't your sister sit?" Tracy had a fourteen-year-old sister.

Tracy shook her head. "No, she can't. Anyway, to tell you the truth, I'm a little tired. I'm not really up for a big drive tonight. But thanks for thinking of me." She gave him a nice, sincere smile, but he couldn't help but notice that she didn't seem particularly upset about turning him down.

Bruce was shocked. Was Tracy nuts? "Listen—" he began, sure he just hadn't emphasized how special the concert was.

But Tracy seemed to hear something inside that caught her attention. "Oh, dear," she said. "That's my little brother now. I'd better go, Bruce. But thanks again for last night—and for the invitation to the concert."

And before Bruce could say another word, she had closed the door.

"Unbelievable," Bruce muttered. Had he completely misread Tracy the night before? He could've sworn she was interested in him.

Now he was stuck with a hundred dollars'

worth of tickets for a concert that evening. And he didn't even have his car.

Bruce sighed deeply. Obviously, it wasn't his day.

Twenty minutes later, Bruce was strolling through the front entrance of the Sweet Valley Country Club, enjoying the familiar atmosphere of luxury and privilege. The club seemed like a good place to try to sell his tickets. Bruce was proud of himself for having made the effort to stop off at the club—especially since he had to ride his bike. He was trying to make money. If he could get his hundred dollars back—or even sell the tickets for a little more—so much the better.

It was a gorgeous afternoon, and most of the people at the club were lounging by the pool. Bruce strolled around, looking for familiar faces, but most of the club members there were closer to his parents' age than his own. Not exactly the right crowd for the Starfest Concert.

Just when he was about to give up, Bruce ran into Judd Phipps, a tall, lanky guy whom Bruce knew well. Judd was the organizer of the poker game Bruce frequented.

"Judd!" Bruce called to him.

Judd came over, tennis racket in hand. "Bruce! How are you, buddy?" he asked, slapping Bruce on the back.

"Fine, fine. Judd, it's your lucky day! I've got two tickets to the Starfest Concert tonight I'm selling," Bruce said. "Interested?"

"No, thanks. I've got a hot date tonight," Judd said.

"So take her to the concert," Bruce said. "Come on, Judd. It's a chance of a lifetime."

"Nah," Judd said lazily. "I don't think so, Bruce. But listen, I've been meaning to call you. Are you up for some poker Thursday night?"

Bruce was about to say no, since he had to be careful with his money, when it occurred to him that this might be his golden opportunity. He'd always been a good poker player. With his skill, why couldn't he win big on Thursday night? In fact, a few Thursdays in a row and he could easily turn his two grand into at least twice that much.

"Absolutely," Bruce said warmly.

He felt so good about his prospects for making big money at poker that it didn't even bother him that he hadn't sold the tickets. In fact, Bruce was in the mood to be generous. Maybe he would take one of his friends to the concert —as long as he could find someone whose car wasn't in the shop!

By the time he left the club, Bruce was as cheerful as if he'd already won ten times the amount his grandfather had given him. *This is exactly the way the rich get richer*, he thought. They relaxed, had fun, and did what came naturally to them. What could possibly be easier?

Six

Roger got to school early on Monday morning. He wanted to go to the library and look up a few books about self-made men. Maybe they would give him ideas on how to turn his two thousand dollars into more.

Lisa was in the library, checking out some books. "Roger! What are you doing here?" she asked as soon as he walked in the door.

Roger sighed. His grandfather had sworn them to absolute secrecy about the competition. Much as he would have loved to, he couldn't tell Lisa what was going on. He felt as if he would have benefited from confiding in her. She was so calm and reasonable, and he really trusted her opinion.

"You know, being part of the Patman family, I feel like I need to learn a little bit about the business world," Roger told Lisa. "How people like Alexander Patman do what they do."

Lisa nodded. "My dad's always going on and on about his clients," she said. "Now that he's a senior partner in this investment company, he sees lots of people like your grandfather. And it sounds to me like none of them are very easy to give advice to!"

Roger stared at Lisa. He had completely forgotten that her father was an investment counselor. This was a dream come true! "Lisa," he said, trying to conceal his excitement, "does your father buy and sell stock for people, or just tell them what to do?"

"Both," Lisa said. "Why? Are you considering a career as an investment counselor?"

Roger laughed. "Not at all. But would you mind if I gave your father a call? There's something I have to ask his advice about."

"What's that?" Lisa asked.

Roger shook his head. "I can't tell you yet," he said. He knew Lisa probably thought he was acting strangely, but he couldn't help it. He'd just had a wonderful idea. Why not invest his two thousand dollars in the stock market? Wasn't that how most big business moguls made their fortunes?

Monday afternoon, Roger dropped by Mr. DePaul's office. Mr. DePaul was one of the senior partners at the largest investment company in downtown Sweet Valley. Roger doubted he would have even gotten five minutes with Mr. DePaul if he weren't a friend of Lisa's. He owed her a big favor.

"Now, Roger, what can I do for you?" Mr. DePaul asked after offering Roger a seat in his plush office.

"I'm interested in investing some money in the market, sir," Roger told him. "But I really don't know how to start."

Mr. DePaul smiled at him. "Now, why would you want to invest in the market? The stock market can be very risky. I lost my shirt when I was your age."

"My grandfather thinks it's one of the best ways to learn investing," Roger said boldly.

That wasn't true, but Mr. DePaul seemed to believe it.

"Yes, I suppose that could be true—as long as you're extremely cautious," Mr. DePaul replied. "You have to understand, Roger, that even for people like me, who have spent their whole lives studying the market, the process can be more than a little like gambling. What you want to do is balance risk with security. Put some of your money somewhere safe, and just use part of it in the market. Does that make sense?"

Roger nodded. But he was convinced that he *needed* to take a risk. Otherwise, he would never make his money grow. *This isn't the time to be cautious*, he thought. *If there ever was a time for big risks, this is it!*

"So, how do I buy some stock?" he asked eagerly.

Mr. DePaul put up one hand. "Take it easy," he said. "First, you need to decide how much money you want to spend. Then, choose a stock or a number of stocks to purchase." He cleared his throat. "You'll have to ask your father to buy the stock for you, since you're not eighteen. And then all you do is follow it and see how you're progressing."

Roger hadn't realized he wasn't old enough to buy stock. However, he was determined not to allow that rule to ruin his chances. "Mr. DePaul, my uncle, who's my legal guardian, is in the Far East for a month. I wanted this to be a surprise for my grandfather. Could you buy the stock for me if I gave you the money?"

Mr. DePaul frowned. "Ordinarily, I'd say no. But I've known your uncle for a long time. If you can assure me that this is your own money and that he wouldn't mind, I suppose I could buy the shares for you."

Roger's face lit up. It was as if he had already tripled his two thousand dollars.

Mr. DePaul's intercom buzzed. "Sorry to interrupt," came his secretary's voice, "but it's the call you've been waiting for from New York."

"I'd better take this," Mr. DePaul said, giving Roger an apologetic smile. "Why don't you come back tomorrow, and we'll choose a stock or stocks you think you might like to buy."

Roger thanked him. He was already excited about what he was about to do. He got even more excited when, on his way out, he heard two of the company's employees deep in conversation. They were talking about a stock called Robotech. Roger couldn't quite make out what they were saying, but he could see how animated they were. Stocks were so exciting! Roger could hardly wait to play the market himself.

Bruce didn't reach Judd Phipps until Tuesday. He had been leaving messages for him since Sunday, and as the date of the poker game got closer, Bruce grew more and more anxious to reach him. He had spent half an hour with his calculator and realized that, at the rates they usually played for, he wasn't going to be able to win back even enough money to cover his car repairs, let alone to win the contest. But then Bruce had come up with a terrific idea. He wanted to raise the ante from a dollar to ten dollars. That way, he could make some big cash fast and spend the rest of the month dating Tracy Atkins, while Roger suffered! It cracked Bruce up, watching his cousin trying to save money. Roger wasn't even using his car these days, probably so he could save the gas money!

"Judd, it's Bruce," he said when Judd came to the phone. He knew Judd didn't like to waste time, so he immediately explained his proposal.

"You want to raise the stakes to ten dollars?" Judd repeated incredulously. "Bruce, we aren't all made of money the way you are. That's pretty high-stake poker."

Bruce was annoyed. He hadn't expected Judd to give him a hard time. "Come on, Judd. We aren't babies anymore. The reason the game isn't more exciting is that nobody cares much about losing or winning fifty dollars. Let's make this the real thing."

Judd was quiet for a minute. "Well, I'll have to check it out with the other guys." He still sounded uneasy. "You really think this is a good idea, Bruce? We want to have fun, remember. We're not in this to wipe out each other's bank accounts."

Bruce knew that the best way to get Judd to agree was to let just the right amount of contempt creep into his voice. "It's up to you, Judd. It's your poker game. I just thought now that we're all a little older we should make it a little more real. A little more challenging."

"OK, Bruce. If no one else objects, we'll raise the stakes," Judd said abruptly.

Bruce was elated. "Great! See you on Thursday night, Judd!"

Judd sounded a big angry. "Right. See you Thursday." And before Bruce could say another word, Judd had hung up the phone.

Whistling cheerfully, Bruce strolled down the long hallway toward his bedroom.

"Hi, Rog! What're you doing?" he demanded, opening the door to Roger's bedroom without knocking.

Roger was deep in the business section of the *Los Angeles Times*. He snapped it shut the minute he saw Bruce.

"What do you think you're doing, Bruce? Haven't you heard of knocking?" Roger said angrily.

"Just wanted to hear if you'd come up with any brilliant moneymaking schemes, coz," Bruce said sweetly.

"As a matter of fact, I have. But they happen to be none of your business," Roger said coldly.

"Oh, is that so? And I suppose you think you've really found a way to wriggle your way into controlling the family fortunes?" Bruce's voice was heavy with sarcasm. He shook his head with mock pity. "Poor Roger. Poor, poor Roger."

"Bruce, get out of here and leave me alone," Roger said furiously.

"Does that mean you don't want to hear about my brilliant plans to double my money in less than one evening?" Bruce asked blithely. He leaned against the doorjamb and folded his arms. "I don't intend to work for my money, Rog. I don't think that's very appealing. No, my idea is to earn while I play." He grinned. "Poker, that is. High-stake poker. And I intend to win every last hand! Just wait and ask me on Friday how big my earnings were. The whole contest will already be over!"

On Wednesday morning, Roger had the first appointment of the day with Mr. DePaul. He could feel his heart pound with excitement as the secretary showed him into the office and closed the door.

"Well?" Mr. DePaul said inquisitively, taking off his glasses. "Any ideas, Roger? Did you look over the business section as I suggested?"

"Yes," Roger said, "and I know which stock I want to buy."

Mr. DePaul looked surprised. "Really? Which stock is that, Roger?"

"Robotech," Roger said.

Mr. DePaul stared at him. After a minute, he put his glasses back on. "Robotech? Who have you been talking to?"

Roger decided not to mention the men he had heard talking outside Mr. DePaul's office. "I read all about it in the business section. The article said the company is going to be bought out by a big company that specializes in software and that Robotech is the best growth stock around." Roger could barely contain his excitement.

Mr. DePaul frowned. "Well, there've been a number of speculators cashing in on what seems to me to be nothing more than rumor. Roger, I'm not sure a safer, more stable stock wouldn't be better for you."

"I'd . . . well, I'd really like to give Robotech a try, sir," Roger said quietly.

Mr. DePaul shrugged. "Fine. It's up to you. Let's see," he said, tapping some keys on his computer. "Robotech is selling at fifteen dollars a share today. Up five dollars a share from last week." He narrowed his eyes. "Looks like a lot of people are interested in this stock, Roger. Does that worry you?"

"No, sir," Roger said. He didn't want to admit to Mr. DePaul that he wasn't sure whether that meant he ought to be worried or not. All he wanted was to make money—fast. And he was convinced that investing in Robotech was the way to do it.

"Fine," Mr. DePaul said. "How many shares would you like to buy?"

"A hundred," Roger said promptly.

"A hundred? You want to invest fifteen hundred dollars?" Mr. DePaul stared at him.

Before Mr. DePaul could object, Roger pulled an envelope out of his pocket and started counting out bills. "Please," he said, his fingers trembling slightly. "Will you buy the shares right away?"

Mr. DePaul sighed as he took the money. "Well, Roger, I'll be crossing my fingers for you." He didn't look very happy.

The SAVE representatives were excited Wednesday afternoon. They had just come back from their first meeting with the PTA and local community leaders, and their idea to organize a Harbor Days festival had been approved with overwhelming support by all present.

"Let's hear it for Tracy and Harbor Days!" Elizabeth Wakefield sang out, and the other members applauded loudly.

Tracy smiled. She was as pleased as everyone else that the project had been approved and that so much had been accomplished during the meeting. Harbor Days would be held on two consecutive Saturdays. Local shopkeepers would be invited to set up stands, and restaurants would be invited to sell food and ice cream. It would be open to the whole community. The PTA planned to ask a local band to play, so there would be entertainment as well. The first Harbor Day would be a week from the coming Saturday, and the second would be the following week.

Tracy and Elizabeth's most important contribution had been the suggestion that students could set up booths to sell things as well. Like the local shopkeepers, they could keep half the proceeds they earned, and the other half would go to the Nicholson School Fund.

"I can tell, it's going to be a fantastic success," Elizabeth said, her eyes shining.

"We still need to publicize Harbor Days and get as many students as possible involved," Tracy added. "And we don't have much time." The rest of the students still didn't seem very interested in the SAVE Fund Drive. That bothered Tracy a great deal. The Nicholson School meant everything to her. The school had given her brother Jeremy so much confidence, and he had made many friends. He adored going there, and she knew he would be heartbroken if it was forced to close.

"Are you worried that more students haven't volunteered to help out?" Elizabeth asked her.

Tracy nodded. "We need to think of some way to bring the Nicholson School's crisis home to them," she mused.

"Well," Elizabeth said, smiling, "at least you've managed to get one student interested. What's going on with Bruce Patman, Tracy?"

Tracy shrugged. She felt a little shy talking about Bruce. "I guess . . . well, he seems interested," she said softly.

"In the project or in you?"

Tracy laughed. "Look, I can be honest with you, Liz, can't I?"

"Of course you can," Elizabeth said.

"I just don't know what to do about Bruce," Tracy said anxiously. "I think he's a nice guy. And the truth is, I'm kind of—well, I can see liking him as more than just a friend. I guess I'm more than a little bit interested myself."

Elizabeth hesitated. "It doesn't sound to me like there's much of a problem," she said slowly.

"Well, there is. I don't quite trust him. I think he's funny, and smart, and—" Tracy took a deep breath. "Well, I'm pretty attracted to him. But I'm not sure how responsible a person he is deep down. I'm not sure what kind of a boy-friend he'd be."

"Have you two gone out much?" Elizabeth asked.

Tracy shook her head. "No. He's asked me, but I keep finding excuses not to go. Maybe I'm just a little afraid," she said suddenly. "I don't have much dating experience. Liz, were you afraid before you and Todd started going out together?"

"Not really," Elizabeth said. "But I'd say if

you like Bruce, why not go out with him? That's the best way to find out what you two are really like together."

Tracy nodded slowly. "Maybe you're right," she said, fiddling with her bracelet. Her heart beat a little bit faster when she thought about accepting a date with Bruce. *Why not?* she asked herself suddenly. Bruce was lots of fun, and he really seemed to like her. *Why not just give him a chance?*

Seven

Bruce could hardly wait for the poker game to get started.

They were playing at Judd's house. The game started at eight o'clock sharp, and the rule was that whoever wasn't there by eight couldn't play. Bruce made sure he was there in plenty of time. He had brought ten crisp one-hundred-dollar bills, a thousand dollars. He figured he would intimidate Judd and some of the others by flashing the money around.

Six boys showed up to play. Usually Bruce knew several people in the group, but that night he didn't know any of them except Judd. They were all from Judd's high school, the next town over. But they looked like an innocent group to Bruce. He didn't think he had anything to worry about. In fact, he was certain that within hours his troubles would be over. *If it's not too late, maybe I'll stop off at Tracy's house on the way home and see if she has any plans for the weekend.* Once he had pocketed his earnings, he could take her wherever she wanted to go. The sky would be the limit!

Judd announced the rules. "The ante is ten dollars," he said with a quick sidelong glance at Bruce. "We've got three colors of chips: red, green, and blue. Red is worth a dollar, green is worth five dollars, and blue is worth ten dollars."

The group around the table fell silent.

"You *sure* we want to go that high?" a guy named Marshall asked.

Judd nodded. "I'm sure," he said. "Remember, if you're in, you're in. Anyone who wants out, let me know now."

All six boys agreed to stay in. Bruce sat at the head of the table, with Marshall on one side of him and someone named Rod on the other side. At the other end of the table was Judd, with Arthur Marks on one side and Tony Dent on the other.

Judd dealt for five-card stud, which had always been Bruce's favorite game. He was sure it was a sign of good luck that Judd chose it first.

Bruce was dealt a jack, a ten, a four—then another jack! He felt his heartbeat speed up. A pair of jacks! His last card was a two. Bruce expertly maneuvered his cards around to line up the pair. This was the beginning of a long winning streak, Bruce was certain.

"Let's put in ten," Judd said lazily, rolling in a chip. Bruce looked at him carefully. Judd was raising the ante by ten dollars. What did that mean? It wasn't that high a bet. Maybe he had a pair, but it was probably a low pair. There was no way Judd could beat a pair of jacks.

"Forget it," Arthur said, throwing down his cards. "I'm out."

Tony and Rod dropped out, too. That left Marshall, Judd, and Bruce.

"I'll see your ten," Marshall said. He looked a bit nervous.

Good, Bruce thought. *If he looks nervous, that means he doesn't have anything.*

"See you ten," Bruce said, "and raise you twenty."

100

Marshall drew a deep breath. Bruce almost laughed out loud. Marshall obviously didn't know the first thing about playing poker. You *never* showed any emotion about what was in your hand. If you did, your opponents knew how to bet. "I'm history," Marshall said, throwing in his hand.

"I'll match you," Judd said quietly, pushing two chips over toward Bruce.

"Show me what you've got, Judd," Bruce said confidently.

Judd turned his cards over and slid them across the table.

Bruce felt his mouth go dry.

Three eights. Judd had three of a kind. He had won the hand.

"What have you got, Patman?" Judd asked.

Slowly, agonizingly, Bruce turned his hand over. It wasn't just losing the money that bothered him, though that was bad enough. Losing the hand had hurt his pride. But he was determined not to lose confidence. He was going to play much harder and keep this from happening again.

By ten o'clock, Bruce was in total despair. They had played every card game they knew—

five-card stud, five-card draw, blackjack, high-low—and Bruce had lost at them all.

At first, the losses weren't that big: a thirty-dollar hand, a fifty-dollar hand. By nine o'clock, Bruce was down three hundred dollars, and he started betting more aggressively. He figured his only chance to win back what he'd lost and start to make some money was to change his strategy. But the plan backfired. Instead of losing thirty or fifty dollars a hand, he started losing a hundred dollars a hand.

By ten-thirty, Bruce was down seven hundred dollars. It was a disaster! Bruce tried to hide his anxiety, but he was stunned. Whoever heard of losing that kind of money playing poker?

Judd was the big winner. He was six hundred dollars ahead. Most of the other players were either up or down by about fifty dollars. It was humiliating to Bruce to be losing so badly. Not only that, it was horrifying. Bruce couldn't even let himself think about the consequences. Not yet.

"Listen, I think we'd better stop," Judd said after Bruce lost a hand of five-card draw. His losses now totaled almost eight hundred dollars. "This is ridiculous, Bruce."

Bruce didn't know how to react. On the one hand, he knew he should stop playing, but on the other hand, it made him furious to have to take their pity.

Slowly he got to his feet. He was too upset to even respond. He knew he had to get out of Judd's house as quickly as he could.

The poker game had been one of the biggest mistakes of Bruce's life.

"I may have just thrown away my share of the Patman Company," he whispered to himself as he stepped outside into the clear evening air.

Friday, during lunch, Roger was engrossed in a book called *How to Invest Your Money*.

"Roger," Lisa called to him as she hurried up to his table, "I just got a message in the office. It was from my father. He says he's been trying to get in touch with you all day. He wants you to call him right away."

Roger almost dropped his book, he was so excited. He hadn't expected results so quickly! Maybe he was already a millionaire!

Roger called Mr. DePaul from the pay phone across from the principal's office. Mr. DePaul was in a meeting, but his secretary said she would get him. "He told me to interrupt him if you called," she said.

Roger's hopes soared. This was good news for sure!

Mr. DePaul came on the phone an instant later. "Roger, listen. I don't usually advise clients in this way, but seeing as you're underage and new to this racket . . . I wanted you to know that Robotech shot up from fifteen dollars a share to twenty this morning. That means it's doubled this week alone."

"That's wonderful!" Roger cried.

"Well, it is and it isn't. No one knows for sure what's going on, but there's a rumor around my office that the takeover may not go through after all. If that's true, the stock could collapse on Monday. My advice to you is to sell today. You'll have a nice profit, and you can reinvest in a safer stock," he added.

Roger could barely suppress his delight. It was working! What incredible luck. He'd invested fifteen hundred dollars—and made five hundred in just one day! But he couldn't understand why Mr. DePaul wanted him to sell the stock. That didn't seem like a very good idea to him. "Mr. DePaul, thanks for your advice, but I really think I want to hang on to it," he said quickly.

"Well, it's up to you. I just wanted to warn you," Mr. Depaul said. "You're sure?"

"Absolutely!"

Roger could already see the look on Bruce's face when Roger was declared the winner of the contest.

Bruce was in a rotten mood Friday. Every time he thought of what had happened during the poker game the night before, he felt sick to his stomach. He still didn't know how he could have lost that much money.

But Bruce felt a tiny bit better when he noticed Tracy in the hall in front of him. She was just about to disappear inside the SAVE office when Bruce caught her by the arm.

"Tracy Atkins," he said, "just the person I've been looking for."

Tracy's eyes brightened. "Uh, hi, Bruce," she said.

Bruce's gaze dropped briefly, and he caught sight of a poster Tracy was holding in one hand. "What's that?" he asked, leaning closer to get a better look.

Tracy glanced up at him shyly. She seemed extremely aware of just how close he was standing.

"It's our poster for Harbor Days. We're trying to get as many students interested in participating as possible," Tracy said.

"What are you asking students to do?" Bruce asked, trying to sound interested.

Tracy explained how Harbor Days was going to work. "The shopkeepers and the students who set up booths get to keep fifty percent of what they earn, although they can contribute more to the fund if they want to," Tracy concluded.

"That sounds great," Bruce said. And it really did.

Bruce realized that if he could come up with a really clever product to sell at Harbor Days, he could earn back some of the money he'd lost, *and* get to spend time with Tracy! The minute he thought of it, Bruce realized how ingenious it was. Besides, he would be raising money and helping the community at the same time. His grandfather was sure to approve. Bruce felt his bad mood disappear instantly. He couldn't believe how he'd let himself get so down about that stupid little poker game. It was only money he'd lost, and the great thing about money was that there was always more of it!

"Tracy," he said, "do you think you could help me figure out something I could sell at Harbor Days?"

Tracy looked surprised. "You? I mean, uh; sure, Bruce." She cleared her throat. "I didn't mean to sound like that. It's just, well, I can't imagine why—"

Bruce cut her off before she could go any further. "I definitely want to be part of Harbor Days," he said firmly. "I care a lot about the cause." *Especially*, he thought, *since I get to pocket fifty percent of my earnings!*

"Well, great," Tracy said, smiling. "Welcome aboard, Bruce."

Tracy went into the office and set the poster down. She looked around her, a distracted expression on her face. "I know there are about ten things I wanted to take care of, but I can't seem to remember them," she murmured.

Bruce followed her into the office and leaned against the door frame. "So listen, I'm not very good at this kind of thing. I'm definitely going to need lots of help coming up with an idea." *Especially in the evenings,* he added to himself.

"Well, I'll do what I can," Tracy said. "But I don't know how much help I'll be, thinking of innovative things to sell. Do you have any ideas?"

Bruce's eye fell on a black notebook lying on the office desk. "I've got it!" he cried, snapping his fingers. "You know, I have a notebook almost exactly like that one. But mine is filled with names and addresses." He winked at her. "Names and addresses of the greatest girls in town. I bet I could run off copies of that book and make a fortune!"

Tracy's eyes widened. "You mean sell the names and addresses of girls you've gone out with? Are you serious?"

"I know it's a pretty generous idea," Bruce said modestly. "But it's worth it for a cause like this—"

"Bruce," Tracy cut in firmly. "I don't think that sounds particularly tasteful. Or even particularly legal. Maybe you'd better come up with something that won't be so offensive to your old girlfriends." She sounded angry, and Bruce looked at her with concern.

What had he said wrong? He thought it was a great idea! *Maybe Tracy was jealous*, he thought.

"But you know," Tracy said, "you have quite a reputation around school. You might be able to capitalize on that. How about something like 'The Bruce Patman Guide to Dating'? You could put it in general terms so you wouldn't offend any girl in particular. And I bet a lot of people would want to buy it. At least, just to see what you have to say."

Bruce was delighted. "I like that," he said. " 'The Bruce Patman Guide to Dating.' I can see it now." Then Bruce remembered he wanted Tracy's help on this, and he forced a panicky look to cross his face. "But I have no idea how to start something like that! Will you help me, Trace?"

He crossed the room and took her hand in both of his. He looked at her imploringly. She stared down at his hand. "I guess so," she whispered.

Bruce tightened his hold on her hand. "Thanks," he whispered.

She smiled at him warmly. *Try to put that technique in a dating guide*, Bruce thought. It would never work in a million years. Either you had the Patman touch or you didn't!

Eight

Roger couldn't wait for the weekend to be over. He wanted the stock market to open so he could see whether or not his Robotech stock continued to climb in value. *It will*, he thought eagerly. *I have to show Bruce that I can do this stuff as well as he can.*

"Good morning, Roger," Grandfather Patman boomed, sitting down at the table across from his grandson. "Reading the stock page, I see. Well, it's always good to keep yourself informed, though I hope you yourself stay away from risky ventures like stock. The way I see it, the only shares to worry about are those you own in your own company." He chuckled dryly. "Although I have to admit I've seen others make a pretty good profit in the market. I guess I was just always a little too afraid of the risks involved myself."

Great, Roger thought. At least he knew now that it was a good thing he had kept his experiment a secret from his grandfather. Better not share it with him until he'd made his fortune!

Just then, the kitchen door flew open, and Bruce came in, carrying some paperback books.

"Good morning, Bruce! Come to join us for breakfast?" Grandfather Patman said cheerfully.

Bruce shook his head. "I've got to get going. I'm meeting Tracy Atkins before my first class starts." He gave Roger one of his smuggest grins. "I happen to have a little business venture I'm getting started for Harbor Days." He turned to his grandfather. "Nothing like a venture that helps the poor *and* makes money. Right, Grandfather?"

"Why, that's right, Bruce," Grandfather Patman said.

Roger couldn't believe his ears. "You're selling something at Harbor Days? You? I can't believe you'd do something that wasn't for profit!"

Bruce shrugged. "Well, as a matter of fact, it *is* for profit. The reps from the SAVE project have been trying to come up with some scheme to get more students from school involved. They decided that anyone who sets up a booth at the harbor can keep half the profits they make. The rest goes to the fund. They're advertising it in school today. I just happened to have gotten the inside scoop."

Roger couldn't stand how smug his cousin looked. "What are you planning on selling, Bruce? Old paperbacks?" he demanded, raising his eyebrows at the books.

"These are just for reference. The book I'm selling is one of my own," Bruce said. Then, clearly for his grandfather's sake, he added, "I may be home a little late after school today. The project I'm working on is going to eat into my spare time."

"That's all right, Bruce," Grandfather Patman said. "Hard work is its own reward."

Roger said goodbye to his grandfather and followed Bruce outside.

"What's the matter, Bruce?" he said, once their grandfather was out of earshot. "Didn't your little disaster at the poker table teach you anything?"

"Who told you about that?" Bruce asked angrily. "I told Judd to keep his mouth shut!"

Roger laughed. "Yeah," he said, "and a lot of good that did, too. Judd's told everyone at the club that you lost a fortune, Bruce." He grinned. "Come to think of it, I'm surprised Grandfather Patman hasn't heard yet."

Bruce looked as if he was ready to take a swing at his cousin. "If you say one word to him, Roger, I'll . . ."

But Roger just laughed. He wanted to win. And whatever it took, he was prepared to do it.

"What do you mean, the stock is dropping?" Roger asked. He had called Mr. DePaul from a pay phone at school.

"Just what I said, Roger. I warned you about this. The takeover deal fell through. Investors are pulling out of the company faster than you can say 'Robotech.' The stock is down ten points since the market opened this morning." Mr. DePaul cleared his throat. "If I were you, I'd pull out—fast."

"OK," Roger whispered. "What do I do?"

"Call me back in five minutes. I'll call my trader and try to sell your stock right now."

Those five minutes felt like an eternity to Roger. He was furious with himself. If only he had taken Mr. DePaul's advice and sold his shares on Friday! Finally, it was time for him to call Mr. DePaul back.

"I'm sorry, Roger. I sold your stock for eight dollars a share—that was the best I could do. I'm afraid you lost quite a bit of money."

Roger tried to steady himself. He had lost seven hundred dollars.

He thanked Mr. DePaul and slowly hung up the phone. When he stepped out of the phone booth, he caught sight of Lisa. She was hanging up a big poster outside the main office.

The poster read: "Save the Nicholson School— and make money for yourself—at Harbor Days!"

Roger looked at the poster for a long minute. It explained all about the fair, and promised that half the profits from booths could be kept by participants.

It might not be as fast a way to make money as the stock market, but it would be safer. And Roger was convinced that if Bruce could think of something to sell at Harbor Days, then so could he. In fact, he would think of something better—something that would make more money.

Roger might have lost money with Robotech, but Bruce had lost money playing poker. And that meant Roger was still in the running. He still had a chance to blow his cousin out of the competition completely.

"You have some really good ideas here," Tracy said, turning to Bruce. "You have a sense of humor about yourself. That's important." Her eyes were shining.

Bruce dropped his hand onto hers and gave her fingers a squeeze. "Thanks, Tracy. That means a lot to me, coming from you."

Tracy cleared her throat and turned back to the notebook Bruce had brought to the office with him. They were looking over Bruce's ideas for his book during their study hall on Wednesday. Tracy had made Bruce feel great about the project. She praised his writing and laughed at his jokes. Tracy actually seemed to get a kick out of Bruce's "dating tips."

Bruce had organized his book into a series of chapters. The first chapter was called "How to Let the Girl of Your Dreams Know You're Alive"; the second, "The Phone Call"; the third, "What to Drive, What to Wear, and What *Not* to Say: A Beginner's Guide to the First Date." Bruce had already written a few funny stories to be included in each chapter.

"This is fantastic!" Tracy exclaimed. "You've got a talent for this kind of thing! Did you ever think about writing comedy or working for television when you graduate?"

Bruce couldn't remember the last time he'd heard a genuine compliment like that. But he couldn't figure out why Tracy wouldn't agree to go out with him. For the first time ever, his dating tips weren't working!

"There's still a lot you have to do before Saturday," Tracy reminded him. "You need to have the book printed, bound, and figure out how much you're going to charge for them." She grinned. "From what I've seen so far, I think you'd better print a lot. I'm sure these are going to go like crazy.''

Bruce leaned closer to her and let his fingers brush against hers. Her blush boosted his confidence. "How about coming out to dinner with me tonight?" he whispered. "Let's combine business with pleasure." His eyes fixed on hers. "It would mean a lot to me if you'd let me take you out, Tracy."

"I'd like that," Tracy whispered softly.

Bruce could feel his heartbeat speed up. Finally! This was the moment he'd been waiting for. *Patman*, he congratulated himself, *you're a genius. No wonder people are going to be lining up to buy your dating guide.*

"Great," he said, giving her a big smile. "How 'bout I pick you up at seven o'clock?" Bruce had had to use part of his grandfather's two thousand dollars to get his car out of the shop.

"That sounds—" Tracy began. But before she could finish, Bruce leaned over and gave her a quick kiss on the cheek. Tracy looked stunned, and Bruce could barely contain his delight.

Chapter Six, he thought as he scooped up his jacket, *"Keep Your Date Surprised."*

"See you," Bruce called behind him as he sauntered out of the office. He hadn't felt this good in a long, long time. He really liked Tracy and he had a feeling that the evening was going to be magical.

Bruce looked around him with pleasure. His favorite Italian restaurant was even more charming than he had remembered.

Tracy looked beautiful, too. Her hair was swept back behind her ears, which showed off her high cheekbones. She was wearing tiny stud earrings and a simple dress. She looked elegant and sophisticated. Bruce definitely approved.

"Let me," Bruce said, pulling out her chair for her after the hostess had shown them to the table.

Tracy shook her head. "You're too much, Bruce. Is all of this going into your dating guide?"

Bruce grinned. That was something else he liked about Tracy: she didn't let him get away with much. She was too smart for that.

"I think I'll keep this private," he said, giving her hand a squeeze. "Just between you and me."

She squeezed his hand back, and a current passed between them.

Dinner was wonderful. The food was delicious. Bruce found that talking to Tracy was easier than he ever could have imagined. They talked about a million different things, and he felt as though they had known each other forever.

"Did you hear about Roger's great idea for Harbor Days?" Tracy asked him.

"Great idea?" Bruce said, alert at once. If Roger had any sort of idea, great or otherwise, he certainly wanted to know about it!

"Lisa called right before you picked me up," Tracy told him, "and she said Roger had decided to sell something at Harbor Days. I'm surprised he didn't mention it to you," she added, clearly puzzled. "Anyway, he's going to buy a bunch of canvas caps with visors and paint them with whatever slogans or designs people want." She giggled. "Whoever would've guessed both of you Patmans had so much creative talent?"

Bruce gave her a weak smile.

So Roger was going to sell something at Harbor Days, too. That worried Bruce. He had seen a brochure from an investment firm on Roger's desk. He had a feeling his cousin had bought some stock. By now he'd probably doubled the money they had been given. And by the time Bruce had paid for dinner that night, he was going to be well on his way toward being broke.

Bruce decided he was going to have to do something about his cousin's plan to sell painted caps. Even if it meant he had to play dirty.

Nine

Bruce woke up early Saturday morning and bounded out of bed. He was certain that the weekend would be terrific, and he could hardly wait for it to begin.

It was the first day of Harbor Days. Bruce admired the neatly packed boxes of the "Bruce Patman Guide to Dating." They were laser printed and spiral bound, just as Tracy had suggested.

Business sense and beauty, Bruce thought with satisfaction. *What a dynamite combination!* It had been Tracy's idea to make the dating guide look like a book, instead of just pages stapled together. It had also been her idea to charge more for each book to help pay for the cost of having them bound. Bruce still wasn't convinced people would want to spend five dollars to read his words of wisdom on the opposite sex. But Tracy had assured him his books would sell well.

Bruce could hardly wait to thank Tracy in the way he thought she truly deserved. *Maybe tonight*, he thought. Tracy had invited him over to her house for dinner that evening. Bruce didn't need a dating guide to tell him what *that* meant. He whistled happily as he rummaged through his drawers for the perfect shirt to wear.

One quick check in the mirror and Bruce was ready. He ran downstairs, making sure as he passed Roger's door that it was still closed.

Bruce headed back to the garden shed near the Patmans' pool. If he hadn't seen his cousin sneaking back there the afternoon before, he might never have discovered where Roger stored all the materials for his Harbor Days project. But following Roger for the past few afternoons had been enormously instructive. Bruce had learned that Roger intended to hand-make each cap in front of his customers. He'd had a long discussion with the man at the paint store and had finally selected spray paint that was guaranteed to be a hundred percent waterproof.

Bruce surveyed Roger's materials. There were stacks of white painter's caps packed in neat plastic bags and stored in the corner of the shed. And there was a box of spray paint.

It took Bruce only a couple of minutes to drag the box of paint out of the shed and shove it deep into the bushes surrounding the pool. He grinned as he brushed off his hands. "Now," he said to himself, "the replacement!"

Bruce crawled under the next bush and pulled out an identical box, filled with identical cans of spray paint. Identical in almost every respect, that is.

The only difference between the cans was that the ones Bruce dragged into the shed bore the tiny words "water soluble." Bruce knew Roger would never take the time to recheck his paint before using it. He had no reason to suspect that the paint wasn't the paint he had bought.

Deep down, Bruce was sure his grandfather would approve of what he was doing. This was the kind of behavior that built business empires! You had to know what you wanted and be prepared to do anything to get it. That was the whole meaning of competition.

Bruce hurried back inside for breakfast. Harbor Days started at ten o'clock, and he wanted to be on time.

Roger was downstairs, eating a bowl of cereal and reading the paper.

"Looking forward to Harbor Days?" Bruce asked Roger innocently.

"Yeah, I am," Roger replied. "I think it's going to be fun. Besides, it's for a good cause."

Bruce had almost forgotten that he would have to give half of his earnings to the SAVE fund. *Darn*, he thought. *That means I have to sell twice as many dating guides*. He grabbed a sweet roll and ate it in two big bites.

"What are you selling, Bruce?" Roger asked him. "You never told me."

"Never mind, Roger," Bruce said. "You'll find out soon enough." *And you can be sure it's going to be a much greater success than your painted caps*, he added silently.

Poor Roger, he thought as he hopped into his Porsche a few minutes later. The poor guy really didn't know the first thing about competition. Roger didn't have the faintest idea what foul play was and how much it could come in handy. And Bruce certainly didn't have any plans to teach him!

Tracy surveyed the harbor and grinned. "Liz, you were absolutely right about this. It's fantastic!"

Tracy, Elizabeth, and Jessica were putting the last-minute touches on the Information Booth the representatives had set up near the entrance to the harbor. It was nine-thirty, and Harbor Days was just about to get started.

Local shopkeepers, restaurant owners, and Sweet Valley High students had set up booths on all four boundaries of the park, leaving the central green clear for people to walk around and admire what was for sale. Some of the booths were filled with food, some with games, others with clothing. People were already walking around and enjoying the beautiful weather before the fair actually started.

"You think we'll raise a lot of money for the Nicholson School?" Elizabeth asked.

"I hope so," Tracy said, surveying the crowds.

It surprised Tracy how much she was looking forward to seeing Bruce. Thinking about him coming over to her house for dinner that night made her heart beat more quickly.

Elizabeth seemed to read her mind. "Looking for someone?" she asked lightly.

"Uh, no, not really," Tracy stammered. "I was just—"

"You must be looking for Bruce," Jessica interrupted her.

Tracy gave her a tiny smile. "I admit it. I told him I'd help him with his booth."

"Be careful, Tracy," Jessica said. "I've seen Bruce break more hearts than I can count. And even if he doesn't break your heart . . ." She shrugged. "Well, he just doesn't seem your type. You deserve a nice boy to go out with, not a creep like Bruce Patman."

"Jessica!" Elizabeth cried. "That isn't a very nice thing to say. How do you know Tracy doesn't really like Bruce?"

Jessica gave her sister and Tracy a nonchalant shrug. "Just watch out, Tracy. You're far too good for Bruce," she warned.

"Sorry about my sister. She can be a little blunt," Elizabeth said when Jessica had hurried off to sample the doughnuts being sold at one of the booths.

Tracy considered asking Elizabeth for advice. Elizabeth and her boyfriend, Todd Wilkins, were considered the perfect couple at Sweet Valley High. They were both good-looking, smart, and well-liked by everyone. Tracy was sure Elizabeth must have a secret opinion about Bruce. Was he really a creep, as Jessica said? Tracy wished she trusted her own opinion more, but she just didn't know that much about boys. Still, she had a hard time believing Bruce was as bad as Jessica made out. He struck Tracy as friendly, thoughtful, and kind, and he wasn't at all stuck up, the way Tracy had feared he might be.

On the other hand, she hadn't introduced him to her family yet. Tonight was going to matter a lot to her; it would give her a chance to see what Bruce was like deep down.

Bruce was making his way toward the Information Booth, carrying a box full of dating guides. He was searching the crowd for Brian Webster, a young boy he knew from the club.

Good, Bruce thought. *There he is!*

Brian was a mischievous ten-year-old with

lots of freckles and a mean smile. He already had the reputation of being a troublemaker. *My kind of kid*, Bruce thought, grinning. Just then, Brian spotted him and came running over.

"Hi, Brian," Bruce said. "Do you remember what you're supposed to do, or should I tell you again?"

"I remember," Brian said. "I'm supposed to start a big water balloon fight right in front of your cousin's booth. And make sure I get water all over his caps. Right?"

"Right," Bruce said, patting him on the head. "Well done."

"Can I have my money now?" Brian demanded, sticking out his hand.

"Brian, let me give you a business tip. Never pay anyone until the job is done," Bruce said sternly. "If you do a great job and really make a mess, I'll give you an extra five dollars. Until then, nothing."

Brian stuck his lip out. "OK," he muttered.

Just then, Tracy wandered over to them. "Hi, Bruce! Let's get you set up!"

"Go on. Get out of here," Bruce grumbled to Brian. Then he turned to Tracy and gave her a big smile. "Hi, Trace!" he said brightly. "Ready to do business?"

"You bet I am," she told him.

"You're the greatest to help me set up my booth," Bruce said warmly.

"I sure am," she agreed cheerfully, following him over to the spot where his booth was going to be.

"You were absolutely right about having these bound," Bruce said, opening a box of books and holding one up. "Don't they look great?"

"Hey, Bruce, what are you selling?" Winston Egbert demanded. Winston, a junior at Sweet Valley High, was widely acknowledged as the school clown. Winston had been strolling around the park with his girlfriend, Maria Santelli. Maria was also a junior at Sweet Valley High.

Tracy and Bruce started unpacking the books while Winston read some of the choicer passages out loud.

"Hey, get a load of this," he cried, waving a group of his friends over. "Want to hear Bruce's tips on dating?"

"Wait a minute," Bruce said, snatching the book out of Winston's hand. "You want to read that, you've got to pay for it. Five bucks."

Winston's face fell. "Oh, all right," he said, pulling a five-dollar bill out of his pocket.

Bruce grinned from ear to ear. His first sale! He felt as if Winston was giving him a five-hundred-dollar bill.

"Listen to this," Winston said. " 'What do you say to a girl you've just met who you want to go out with? A, You're gorgeous. B, I drive a Porsche, want a ride? C, You're in for the best time of your life now that you've met me. D, All of the above.' " He shook his head. "Can you tell that Bruce wrote that, or what?"

"Let me see it, Winston," Aaron Dallas, another Sweet Valley High student, demanded.

Winston pulled back. "No way. You heard what Bruce said. If you want it, you have to pay for it."

Bruce couldn't believe his ears. Winston couldn't have done a better job advertising his books if Bruce had paid him.

People started crowding up to the booth to buy their own guides. Bruce looked over the crowd and smiled triumphantly. The stack of bills in his pocket was growing thicker and thicker. As far as he was concerned, Harbor Days was a smashing success!

"Hey," Tracy said suddenly, putting her hand on Bruce's arm. "What's going on over at Roger's booth?"

131

Bruce looked up, surprised himself. He had forgotten all about Brian Webster. He was supposed to wait for the fair to get going—until enough people had bought painted caps from Roger—and then open fire.

As Bruce and Tracy watched, Brian grabbed a water balloon from the booth Amy Sutton and Cara Walker had set up. At their booth, you could buy a chance to throw a balloon at Steven Wakefield, the twins' older brother. But Brian didn't throw his balloon at Steven. He threw it at another sixth-grade boy, who ducked as if he had been expecting to be a target. The balloon hit Ronnie Edwards right in the head and exploded against his brand-new painted cap.

"Hey!" Ronnie cried. He wiped off his face, then started chasing Brian.

But, by then, several other little boys had joined in the water-balloon war, and there was no stopping them. Ronnie gave up trying to catch Brian when he discovered a more serious problem. His cap! Instead of the beautiful red, white, and blue design he'd paid three dollars for, his cap was a blurry mess. And he had paint all over his face and T-shirt.

"Roger, what's the deal?" Ronnie demanded,

marching up to Roger's booth, an indignant look on his face. "I paid for a painted cap, not a painted face."

Roger stared at the cap in alarm. "That shouldn't have happened," he muttered. "I made sure I had waterproof paint."

Ronnie picked up one of Roger's cans of paint. "Yeah, right," he said. "Is that why it says 'water soluble' on the can?"

Roger grabbed the can from him, a look of confusion on his face. "But . . ." he began.

The three girls who were about to buy caps from Roger put their money back in their pockets. "I don't want my hair turning green," one of them said.

"Hey, wait a minute," Roger said.

"I'd like my money back, Roger," Ronnie said calmly, wiping off his face with his shirt. "I really don't think a face full of paint ought to cost me three bucks."

Bruce had overheard most of Roger's conversation with Ronnie. As soon as Ronnie had disappeared into the crowd, Bruce stepped up to Roger's booth. "Well, well, well, Rog," he said, giving his cousin a mocking grin. "Run into a little trouble with your paint, or did you plan this effect?"

Roger's face was red with fury. "I don't suppose you had anything to do with this," he hissed.

Bruce's eyebrows shot up. "Me?" He pretended to be shocked. "How could I possibly have anything to do with it?"

Bruce stood to one side of Roger's booth and watched as one person after another came back with their caps and demanded refunds. The word about what had happened to Ronnie had spread quickly.

"Looks like this just isn't your day, Roger. But don't worry. I'd be glad to pay you to help me sell my books. I'm doing such a booming business that I can't handle it all myself."

"Then you'd better hurry back," Roger said angrily.

Bruce could barely hide his joy. He couldn't possibly have hoped for a more triumphant start to Harbor Days!

"Your books were a huge success today," Tracy said happily. "You must've made a fortune!" They were driving to Tracy's house for dinner after putting in a long day together at the harbor. She wasn't nervous about introducing Bruce to her family anymore. The more time she spent with him, the more she felt that Bruce was a terrific guy.

"I did make a fair amount of money. And I'm going to give *all* of it—not just half—to the SAVE project," Bruce said.

Tracy was overjoyed. "Bruce, you're incredible," she said softly. "I knew you weren't the way . . . well, the way some people said. I could tell how considerate you are." She knew then and there it would be all right to tell Bruce about her brother. If anyone would understand about Jeremy, Bruce would. "Can I tell you something before we get to my house?"

Bruce nodded. "I hope you're beginning to feel that you can tell me anything—anytime," he said.

"My younger brother *goes* to the Nicholson School. His name is Jeremy. He's not seriously disabled, but he does need special attention." Tracy fiddled with her seat belt. "I adore Jeremy. I'd do anything in the world for him. The money you earned today may keep Jeremy in a school that is extremely important to him."

"You're kidding," Bruce said. He seemed

slightly uncomfortable, but Tracy wasn't surprised. He was probably just embarrassed that she was making such a big deal out of his generosity.

"I don't usually tell people much about my family unless I know them really well. I'm kind of shy, I guess," Tracy went on a little uncertainly. "But I'm really glad I'm getting to know you, Bruce. You're different."

Bruce pulled the car up in front of the Atkinses' split-level house.

"Tracy," he said, turning to her with an earnest expression in his eyes, "may I kiss you?"

Tracy felt her heart speed up. Besides the quick brush on the cheek Bruce had given her earlier, he hadn't really kissed her yet. Not a *real* kiss. Silently, she nodded.

Bruce leaned close and cupped her chin in his hand. Everything flew out of Tracy's mind. All she could think of was the softness of Bruce's lips against her own and the pounding of her heart.

This is it, she thought giddily. *This is love!*

Ten

On Sunday morning, Bruce sat at the Patmans'
dining room table studying a tally sheet of his
total expenses from the "Bruce Patman Guide
to Dating" and his list of profits from the first
day of sales at Harbor Days. He had done very
well. Even after the money he'd put into laser
printing and binding, he'd come out five hundred dollars ahead. If he could just think of a
good idea for next Saturday's Harbor Day and
do as well then as he had the day before . . .

Only one thing worried him. He was afraid
that Roger might come up with a great new
idea himself. Bruce was pretty sure Roger had
suffered a big loss on his painted caps. But then

there was the investment folder of Roger's he had seen. What if Roger was making a fortune in the market? Bruce might still be behind.

Just then, Roger came into the dining room. He looked furious.

"I don't suppose you know anything about the box of paint I found hidden in the bushes out by the pool, do you?" he demanded.

"What paint? What bushes?" Bruce said innocently.

"Don't start with me," Roger practically yelled. "I know what you did! I'm not stupid! You switched paints on me—and then you got that little Webster kid to start the water-balloon fight and ruin my project! You really are a major jerk!"

"Whoa!" Bruce said, putting up both hands. "I can't believe this, Roger. We're almost brothers. How can you accuse me of doing such a terrible thing?"

Roger glared at him. "I know you're not going to admit it. But I also know you did it! And I'm telling you right now, Bruce, that if I get half a chance to get you back, you can count on the fact that I'm going to do it!"

Silently, Bruce watched Roger storm out of the room. *This isn't good*, he thought.

Bruce was going to have to keep a close eye on Roger, that much was clear. He had to make sure Roger didn't do anything to keep him from making money *and* that Roger didn't come up with a successful moneymaking scheme of his own. But how could he do that? Especially now that Roger was onto him? It was impossible. That is, it was impossible—unless he could get someone else to do it for him! Someone who knew Roger really well, someone Roger trusted. . . . And then it hit him. The perfect plan!

Tracy was good friends with Lisa DePaul, and Lisa was one of Roger's best friends. Why not get Tracy to find out—through Lisa—if Roger had anything planned for next Saturday? If he did, Bruce could try his hardest to wreck it again!

The only problem was finding a way to get Tracy to spy for him without her suspecting what he was up to.

That afternoon, Bruce dropped by Tracy's house uninvited. Luckily for him, Tracy answered the door. She seemed surprised to see him, but happy he was there, too. "Just coming by to say hi?" Tracy asked after she had invited him in and he had greeted her mother.

"To say hi, thank you for a terrific dinner last night," he said, "and to ask for your advice. I'm worried about Roger."

"Why?" Tracy asked.

"Well, because of what happened to his caps yesterday. He's taking it very hard. I want to help him out, but I know how proud he is."

"Well," Tracy said, "it isn't like he needs the money. The fact that he tried to help the SAVE project is what really counts."

Bruce thought for a minute. "Well, Roger's going through a very competitive time right now, Trace. You can imagine how hard it is adjusting to life in a new family. And with my parents gone and my grandfather here, things have gotten even more difficult for him. I'm only telling you this because I trust you so much," he added quickly. Tracy gave him an encouraging smile. "The truth is, it's just going to kill him if he can't make a successful product, I know it. Especially since our dating guides were such a hit," he added.

Bruce noticed that Tracy looked very concerned. He was impressed by how well he understood Tracy after knowing her for such a short time. She had fallen into his trap, just as he had thought she would.

She looked thoughtfully at him. "So, you want to help him come up with an idea for next week?" she asked slowly.

"Well, I'd love to, but Roger's too proud to let me help him. I think I'd better just figure out some way of finding out what he's thinking of selling and then help him—without his knowing," Bruce concluded.

"That is really a generous thing to do," Tracy said. "But I don't know how . . ." Her eyes brightened suddenly. "Hey, I have an idea! Maybe I can ask Lisa if she knows if he has anything planned yet. They tell each other everything!"

Bruce had to work hard not to smile. *Good thinking, Tracy!* he thought. "That's a fantastic idea, Trace," he said out loud. "Could you really do that?"

Tracy nodded. "Sure—and I will. For you," she added.

Bruce was just about to thank her with a kiss

when Mrs. Atkins came back into the living room, carrying two bowls filled with ice cream. "Bruce, you made a big hit with Jeremy last night. I told him you were here, and he asked me to bring you some of his favorite ice cream."

"Oh, that *is* high praise!" Tracy said, her eyes lighting up. "Bruce, wait till you taste this. It's the best ice cream in the whole world, my grandma's special recipe." She passed Bruce one bowl and took the other. "Grandma really ought to sell this stuff," she added, taking a bite. "I bet she'd make a fortune."

Bruce took a bite. "Wow," he said, surprised. "I've got to tell you, I didn't think this could be as good as the ice cream at Casey's. But it's better. It really is." The ice cream had a smooth texture and a rich taste. "What flavor is this?"

"Peach raspberry. Isn't it yummy?"

Bruce took another spoonful. "You know," he said, inspired, "you're right about selling this. Why don't we sell it next week at Harbor Days?"

Tracy's face brightened with excitement. "And give all of the proceeds to the Nicholson School?"

"Uh, sure, of course," Bruce said weakly.

Tracy set her ice cream down and gave him a

hug. "If Grandma says it's OK, we've got ourselves a wonderful product. And Grandma will
definitely say yes, too. Especially if she knows
it's all for Jeremy."

"Well, kids," Grandfather Patman said, "how's
the contest going? Will you tell me how your
investments are paying off, or would you prefer
to keep me in suspense?"

Sunday dinner was the least formal meal of
the week at the Patman house. That night, the
three of them were having soup and salad. But
Roger felt as if the dinner was dragging on and
on. He couldn't stand being in the same room
with his cousin, the traitor.

"Oh, it's going great, Grandfather. At least, it
is for me," Bruce said, turning to his cousin with
a pitying smile. "How's it going for you, Roger?"

"You'll find out soon enough," Roger said as
calmly as he could.

Roger had never been as angry with anyone
as he was with Bruce that weekend. Every time
he thought back on the humiliating experience
of having to refund money for his caps, he
wanted to scream.

He wasn't going to let Bruce get away with it. He was determined to get even.

Roger had already come up with something to sell at next Saturday's fair. He had called up Jim Roberts, a classmate who was a talented photographer, and asked him if he could enlarge some of his photographs and sell them as portraits. Jim had made a name for himself around school when his photo of Shelley Novak, one of the stars on the girls' basketball team, had won first prize in the *Sweet Valley News* photography contest. Roger was positive he would be able to sell a lot of Jim's photos. Many of them were candids of students at school or people in the community. This time, Roger was going to make absolutely certain Bruce didn't find out what he was doing. Only one person in the whole school knew, and that was Lisa. He had called her that afternoon to discuss the idea with her because he knew he could trust her.

"We'd better not talk about results yet, Grandfather," Bruce said. "We wouldn't want to jinx each other or anything. Would we, Rog?"

Grandfather Patman smiled from one boy to the other. "Well, I hope you two are learning a lesson about competition. Because once you're out in the business world, competition is the name of the game. You'll have to fight for *everything*. As I always say . . .''

Roger felt like groaning. The truth was, he *was* learning a lesson about competition. But he didn't think it was the lesson his grandfather was hoping he'd learn.

He was learning that he liked Bruce a lot less than he had before the contest started. And he liked himself less, too.

"It's so good to be alone with you," Bruce said tenderly as he gently kissed Tracy's neck. It was Monday evening, and they were parked at Miller's Point, overlooking the valley.

Tracy shivered and moved a little bit closer to him. Bruce had to hide a smile.

He felt that he had never been more charming or romantic. He seemed to know just what to say at the right minute. He complimented Tracy on her hair, her outfit, and her perfume. Finally, she begged him to stop. But that was only because she wanted him to kiss her! Soon they were curled up in each other's arms.

"You're amazing, Tracy," Bruce told her, pulling back to look admiringly into her eyes.

"I've—I've never felt anything like this before. It's kind of scary," she whispered back.

"Hey," Bruce said tenderly, stroking her hair. "There's no hurry, Trace. We'll just take things one step at a time and see what happens."

"I should be getting home," Tracy said softly. "Even though it's been a wonderful evening, Bruce."

Reluctantly, Bruce turned on the engine of the Porsche. "Do you want to have lunch together tomorrow at school?" he asked.

"Sure," Tracy said warmly. "Hey, I almost forgot to tell you. My grandmother's given us the go-ahead to use her ice-cream recipe for Harbor Days!"

"Fantastic!" Bruce said, his eyes lighting up.

"Which reminds me. I talked to Lisa this afternoon, and I asked her what Roger was planning to sell next week. She didn't want to tell me because Roger swore her to secrecy. *You* never would have been able to drag it out of her, but I managed! Do you promise not to tell Roger you know?"

"Oh," Bruce said as sincerely as he could. "I won't tell him. I promise."

"OK, then," Tracy said. "He's going to enlarge some of the photographs Jim Roberts has taken this year and sell them as portraits. It sounds like a great idea, especially since so many Sweet Valley students will be at the harbor and will want to buy photos of their friends. Jim's also done a lot of photos of local celebrities, which people will probably snap up. So don't worry, Bruce. It sounds like Roger's come up with a good idea all on his own."

It is a good idea, Bruce thought. *But luckily, it's also an idea that can easily be destroyed.*

"Thanks, Trace," he whispered.

"Anything to help you help Roger," Tracy said sweetly. So sweetly that Bruce *almost* felt a twinge of guilt.

Eleven

Tracy woke up early Tuesday morning and immediately thought back to the evening before. It had been perfect. Was this what it felt like to fall in love? she wondered happily.

She got out of bed and walked slowly over to her dresser. It took a superhuman effort for her to get dressed and go downstairs to help with breakfast. All she could think about was Bruce. She could hardly wait to meet him at lunchtime. Would they do something special together next weekend? Were they starting to act like boyfriend and girlfriend?

"Did you get the message from Lisa last

night?'' her mother asked her at the breakfast table.

"No, Mom. What did she say?"

"You and the other reps are supposed to meet before your first class to go over some figures from Saturday's fair. Apparently, you reps are going to meet with the PTA and community leaders this week. She said you all need to figure out how much money the Sweet Valley students have raised for the SAVE fund so far."

Tracy glanced at her watch. She was going to have to hurry. Breakfast was just going to have to wait!

Twenty minutes later, Tracy walked into the SAVE office. Lisa was the first one there. She was fiddling with a pencil and flipping through the sales records from Saturday. "Hey, Trace," she said. "We made out great on Saturday. We raised fifteen hundred dollars for the project!"

"That's really wonderful!" Tracy said. She looked at the figures over Lisa's shoulder.

"Bruce sure seemed to be a success with those dating guides of his," Lisa said. "When we get his fifty percent, we'll know for sure, but it looked like he was doing well."

Tracy frowned. "You haven't gotten his money? And it isn't fifty percent, either. Bruce is giving the fund everything he made."

Lisa looked astonished. "Bruce? No way!" she said. "You've got to be kidding me!"

Tracy had a nervous feeling in the pit of her stomach. She felt as if Lisa wasn't being fair to Bruce. Just because he was from a wealthy family didn't mean he couldn't work hard for a good cause. Tracy tried her hardest to hide her anger.

"Well, anyway, we haven't gotten anything from him yet," Lisa said calmly.

Tracy took a deep breath. She felt as though she ought to say something in Bruce's defense. After all, they were dating now. Bruce mattered a lot to Tracy, and she wasn't going to just sit there and let him be criticized. "Lisa, I don't think you're being very fair about Bruce. First of all, he worked really hard on those dating guides, and he isn't going to keep one single dime for himself. I'm sure he'll hand it in this morning. Not only that, but he's going to work at Harbor Days again this coming week."

Lisa looked at Tracy skeptically. She didn't say anything in response.

Tracy felt her anger rising. "Come on, Lisa! Be fair! Wait! Here's another thing—he's going to all kinds of trouble to help Roger this week, since Roger's caps turned out to be such a disaster last week. I think that's amazingly nice of him."

Lisa looked at her in disbelief. "Tracy, you must be out of your mind! Can't you see what kind of person Bruce really is? He wouldn't help Roger unless there was something in it for him. And for your information, Roger's caps didn't run because Roger was too stupid to know to use waterproof paint. Somebody deliberately switched Roger's paint cans so he ended up using water-soluble paint instead of the paint he bought!"

Tracy stared at her. "You're kidding," she said. "But—"

"I didn't want to tell you this because I wasn't sure how you'd take it," Lisa continued, "but Roger thinks that Bruce is the one who did it. In fact, he has pretty good evidence."

"Bruce?" Tracy repeated incredulously.

"That's what Roger told me yesterday. He called me, and he was in a really rotten mood. And when I asked him why, he just started going on and on about Bruce." Lisa bit her lip. "He made me swear not to tell one single soul about his photography project, and I lied and said I hadn't and I wouldn't. So don't you tell *anyone*, Tracy Atkins, and that includes Bruce!"

Tracy suddenly felt sick to her stomach.

Hadn't she been the one to tell Bruce about Roger's painted caps? The conversation she had had with Bruce came flooding back to her, and she could hear Bruce asking if there was any way that she could find out what Roger was going to sell next. . . .

But it didn't make sense. Why would Bruce want to hurt Roger? "Look," Tracy said uncomfortably, "these guys have more money between them than the rest of us have put together. Why would they care about making a couple hundred dollars at a charity fair?"

Lisa shrugged. "Beats me. All I know is that Roger's been acting like a completely different person for the past few weeks. He talks about money *all* the time. First it was the stock market, and now it's Harbor Days. I don't know what's behind it, but if I were you, I'd be careful around Bruce. I just don't trust that guy, Tracy. And I don't think you should, either."

Tracy didn't answer. She was feeling increasingly uncomfortable and confused. She wished she could stay angry with Lisa, but suddenly she remembered that Lisa was her best friend in the world. Was it possible she had misjudged Bruce so completely?

It just didn't make sense that the son and nephew of one of the richest men in all of California would be fighting over proceeds from a charity fair. But why hadn't Bruce given any of his earnings from Saturday's fair to the SAVE fund yet? And why was he so eager to "help" Roger with his photography project? Had Bruce really been the one who destroyed Roger's caps?

All these questions led to the most painful question of all. Why was Bruce suddenly so interested in *her*? Tracy wondered. Unless it was because she was on the SAVE project with Lisa, and she was the perfect person to use to find out what Roger was doing and when he was doing it.

It made Tracy heartsick to be so suspicious, but she didn't intend to let Bruce Patman use her. She was going to find out what was going on once and for all!

Tracy met Bruce outside the Sweet Valley High cafeteria at lunchtime.

"Hi, Tracy. How's it going?" Bruce said. He leaned toward her to give her a kiss, but she turned her head away. "Hey, what's the matter?"

Tracy crossed her arms and looked up at him. "You tell *me*. You said you were going to give everything you earned to the SAVE fund. How come you haven't handed it over yet? It was supposed to be in by yesterday afternoon."

Bruce squirmed. "I was going to. It's just—"

Tracy didn't even let him finish his sentence. She turned and stomped off.

Bruce stood there, stunned. He didn't believe Tracy could be that mad just because he hadn't come through with a few hundred dollars for the SAVE fund. But that left him without an explanation as to what he could have done wrong. Bruce planned to work his way back into Tracy's affections by buying her something really stunning after he won the contest. But that meant he had to win, and that meant he had to turn a basement full of cream into ice cream!

By Wednesday afternoon, Bruce had assembled all the equipment and ingredients he needed and was ready to start making the ice cream. He was in the middle of reviewing his notes on how to run the ice-cream makers he had rented when the door to the basement opened and he heard footsteps on the stairs.

It was Roger. He was holding a big box in his arms.

"Roger, what are you doing here?" Bruce demanded. The last thing he needed was his cousin getting in his way.

Silently Roger surveyed the equipment and the ingredients Bruce had assembled. "Making some ice cream, Bruce?" Roger asked in a nasty voice.

"As a matter of fact, I am. So do me a favor and get lost," Bruce snapped.

"Why should I, Bruce? Maybe I can help you. Considering all the help you gave me with my caps last weekend, it's the least I can do."

Bruce swallowed. He had never heard Roger sound like this before. "I didn't touch your stupid caps," he lied. "And I think you should stop blaming your mess on me."

"Fine," Roger said shortly. "I'll get lost, Bruce. But don't forget: I owe you one." And before Bruce could say another word, Roger spun around, and still carrying the box, disappeared upstairs.

Great! Bruce thought. *Now Roger knows where my project is!* What was going to keep him from doing something awful to it? Unless he sat guard for the next three days, Bruce didn't see any way to protect his ice cream. Something told him that the next three days weren't going to be easy ones.

If Tracy's mood had been bad on Tuesday, by Wednesday it was rotten. She wasn't any closer to knowing what was going on with Bruce. When she had asked him about the money, he hadn't given her a real answer. She was afraid to ask him about Roger's caps. What if she was wrong? The uncertainty was driving her nuts. Was she crazy, or did she have reason to suspect him?

Wednesday night, Tracy almost convinced herself she was jumping to conclusions. She stared sadly at the telephone in the kitchen. Where was Bruce now? What was he doing? Why didn't he call? Her hand inched toward the receiver, but she stopped herself before she picked it up.

I am not calling him! she told herself. *Not until I know for sure what kind of guy Bruce really is.*

That evening, she went over and over the events of the past few days in her mind. Finally, she came up with what seemed to her like a good plan. She would follow Bruce the next day after school and see what he was doing. At the very least, she would learn more about him. And at best, she'd get some kind of answer about his relationship to Roger—and to her.

Bruce rubbed his eyes. He was exhausted. It was almost midnight on Wednesday, and all he

157

wanted to do was to go upstairs and crawl into bed. But he couldn't. What if Roger crept down and unplugged the freezer and turned his wonderful ice cream into peach-raspberry soup?

Bruce sighed and shifted uncomfortably. He had decided the best thing was to hide out of sight in a dark corner of the basement. That way he would be ready to spring out if Roger came downstairs. Too bad he hadn't thought a little more about comfort when he had decided to spend the night in the basement. His back ached, his legs ached, and there was so much dust down here that he was beginning to sniffle. Bruce stretched his neck from side to side, thinking how dumb he would look to someone who didn't know what was going on.

It is dumb, he thought suddenly. *Why are Roger and I going through this?*

Just then, he heard a stair creak. This was it! Roger was sneaking downstairs with a flashlight!

Bruce watched the circle of light bounce across the floor. Then he saw his cousin. Roger was in his pajamas, and he looked worried. He glanced around several times, as if to make sure nobody was watching.

Nice try, you little rat, Bruce said to himself as he watched Roger tiptoe toward the freezer. He couldn't believe Roger really thought he was stupid enough to leave his treasure unguarded. *I guess that's just the difference between us*, he thought smugly. *Roger let his caps get ruined. I'm not that dumb!*

Bruce was about to jump out of the shadows and confront his cousin, when something told him to wait just a minute or two longer. Something strange was going on. Roger wasn't doing anything to the freezer at all!

In fact, he crept right up to it, looked at it, paused, and walked away. He didn't even bother opening the door and looking inside.

Bruce was completely confused. It wasn't as if Roger knew he was lurking in the shadows, ready to pounce on him.

He had the perfect opportunity, Bruce thought in disbelief, *and he didn't use it. He left my ice cream alone.*

Bruce waited until Roger had gone back upstairs before inching out of the shadows, stretching his legs, and hurrying over to double-check the freezer. Everything was intact. The freezer was still plugged in, and the ice cream was fine.

Roger must be even stupider than I imagined, Bruce thought. He didn't see any reason to sit guard any more. If Roger was too much of a sissy to fight back, why should Bruce lose sleep over it?

"Are you OK, Tracy? You seem a little down," Elizabeth said.

It was Thursday after school, and Tracy was sitting out on the lawn with Lisa and Elizabeth. She was trying to make conversation about the SAVE Fund Drive and the upcoming fair on Saturday, but her mind was somewhere else. She was waiting for Bruce to come out of the building.

Tracy shrugged. "I'm fine. Just a little distracted," she said. "I guess I've been thinking about the Nicholson School and whether or not we'll raise enough money to save it."

Lisa cleared her throat. "It must be really hard for you," she said softly, "especially because of Jeremy."

"Who's Jeremy?" Elizabeth wanted to know.

"My younger brother," Tracy said. "He's been a student at the Nicholson School for two years.

160

He's a wonderful kid, but he has a genetic muscular disease and needs special help. He's in the second grade now, and all his friends are there. Which makes me all the more . . ." Her voice trailed off. *All the more furious at Bruce Patman*, she was thinking, *for promising to give money to the school and then keeping it for himself.* What she said was, ". . . all the more determined to help them in any way I can."

Elizabeth patted her on the arm. "From the way the drive is going so far, it looks like the school *will* be able to stay open. I know we can't get our hopes up too early, but things look promising."

Tracy didn't answer. She had just seen Bruce come out of the building and stroll across the parking lot to his Porsche.

"Listen, guys, I've got to run," Tracy said as casually as possible. She got smoothly to her feet, slinging her bookbag over her shoulder. "See you tomorrow."

"OK, Tracy, see you," Lisa said.

"Bye," Elizabeth added.

Tracy headed toward her parents' car, keeping an eye on Bruce. She was only a few cars behind him as he pulled out of the parking lot. She would be able to trail him with no trouble!

Bruce made one stop on his way home—at Corner Camera. Tracy couldn't believe she was actually following him. She felt like a detective! But she was determined to find out the truth about Bruce, whatever it took.

Corner Camera was large enough that Tracy could slip through the front door without Bruce's noticing her. He was deep in conversation with a man behind the counter. Tracy crouched down in the second aisle and pretended to examine a stack of frames. She was invisible to Bruce, but she could hear every word of his conversation with the salesman.

"Let me see if I understand you," Bruce was saying. "Photographic paper cannot be exposed to any light at all, is that right?"

"That's right. If it is, and you try to print on it, the images will barely come out," the man behind the counter said pleasantly. "Just make sure to keep the paper sealed up in a dark place until you use it. Otherwise, all that expensive paper will go to waste. For your information, we don't guarantee the photographic paper we sell. If you expose it, the loss is yours."

Bruce nodded. "Thanks for your help," he said.

Tracy waited until Bruce was outside again before she stood up. The sinking feeling in her stomach was even stronger now.

She knew exactly what Bruce was going to do. He was going to ruin the paper Roger was planning to use to print his photographs for Saturday's fair.

Twelve

It took Tracy a lot of nerve to do what she did next.

But she knew she wasn't going to have a moment's peace unless she knew what Bruce was up to.

Bruce parked his Porsche at the top of the Patmans' driveway and headed around the side of the house. Tracy parked her car on the street and ran on tiptoe through the open gate and up the side hill, stopping to duck behind a tree whenever she thought Bruce might be looking in her direction. But he was so absorbed in whatever he was doing, he didn't notice her. He headed straight for a shed near the pool.

"Darn it," Tracy whispered as he opened the door to the shed and slipped inside. If Bruce did something to Roger's photography materials while he was in the shed, how was she going to know?

Then she noticed a window on the side of the shed. It was higher than eye level, but if she pulled one of the pool chairs over, she would just be able to see inside.

Tracy had to know what was going on. She tugged a chair over and climbed up, then peered into the dark interior. She didn't even care anymore if she got caught.

It was the gardener's shed. She could see hoses coiled up, watering cans, rakes, and a lawn mower. Bruce had his back to her; he was bending over a table that was shoved up against one wall. As her eyes adjusted to the dim light inside the shed, Tracy saw what Bruce was doing. He was stacking up boxes of photographic paper, and he had a pair of scissors in one hand. Obviously, he was just about to slit open the boxes and carry the paper out into the sunlight. The paper would be destroyed, and when Roger tried to print his photographs, they wouldn't come out.

Tears of pain and anger flooded Tracy's eyes as she jumped off the chair and ran with all her might across the green lawn and down the steep hill toward her parents' car. She couldn't bear to confront Bruce right then. She needed to be alone with her disappointment and anger.

But she intended to talk to Bruce as soon as she pulled herself together. She wasn't going to let him get away with this. Whatever it took, she was going to expose Bruce for what he really was!

The minute Tracy got home, she went right into the kitchen. She was relieved to see nobody was in there. Without pausing to think, she crossed the room, picked up the phone, and dialed the Patmans' number.

Roger answered.

"Roger, it's Tracy Atkins. Don't ask me how I know, but trust me on this one. Bruce just ruined your photographic paper. He exposed it to the light—or if he hasn't yet, he's about to."

For a few seconds, there was dead silence on the other end of the line.

Then Roger said, "Tracy?" He sounded shocked and confused.

Tracy hung up the phone. She didn't have anything else to say to Roger. She had done what needed to be done, and that was that.

Seconds later, the phone rang. Tracy knew it was Roger calling back. She wanted to let it ring, but if she did, her mother would answer it. On the third ring, Tracy scooped up the phone.

"I can't tell you how I know, Roger," she said breathlessly.

There was a pause. And then a voice said, "Know what?" It was Bruce.

Tracy was shocked. Just the sound of Bruce's voice was enough to bring all her rage flooding back. "I don't want to talk to you, Bruce," she said coldly.

"Tracy, I deserve an explanation. Up till four days ago, you and I were really starting to get something off the ground! Then you just suddenly cut me off. If I did something offensive or acted like a jerk or something, I think I deserve to know."

Tracy couldn't believe her ears. How dare Bruce act so innocent? She had almost been taken in. But now she knew the truth. This nice-guy stuff was just an act. *There ought to be a label on every one of his dating guides,* she thought angrily. *Warning: This Guy Is Not What He Pretends To Be.*

"Let's just leave it at this: I misunderstood a few fundamental things about you," Tracy said.

"Like what?" Bruce demanded. "And why have you been talking to Roger about me behind my back?"

"I haven't—" Tears of confusion sprang to Tracy's eyes.

"I need to see you, Trace. Please. At least tell me in person what's going on," Bruce begged.

"I'll talk to you in school tomorrow. But that's it," Tracy said. And for the second time in ten minutes, she hung up on a Patman.

Only this time, she burst into tears as soon as she had slammed down the receiver.

Bruce paced back and forth in his bedroom.

168

Had Tracy somehow found out his plan to ruin Roger's photographic paper? It seemed impossible. After all, Tracy had more or less dropped out of sight this past week. How could she have found out? And it was obvious she had told Roger something. But what?

All in all, it had been an unsettling couple of days. Ever since he had seen Roger walk away from a perfect opportunity to destroy his Harbor Days project . . .

Maybe that was why Bruce hadn't been able to go through with his plan this afternoon. It wasn't as though he hadn't tried. The scene was vividly implanted in his mind: He was standing in the shed, ready to drag the boxes of photographic paper into the sunlight and open them. Roger would never have the time or the money to replace all that paper. So his photos would be ruined—just as his caps had been.

Why had Roger let him get away with ruining his caps? Was it because Roger was just too scared to fight back, or was it maybe because he was capable of staying above that kind of dirty fighting?

Bruce didn't know. All he knew was that he

couldn't make himself ruin the paper. He wanted to, but he just couldn't do it.

The next day at school, Bruce was eating lunch with a few of his friends when Tracy came up to their table.

"I'm ready to talk to you now," she said. "Alone."

Bruce had hoped Tracy would cool down overnight, but she seemed even angrier than she had been the day before.

"I want to know something, Bruce Patman," she told him as soon as they had gotten outside. "Just exactly who do you think you are, using me and lying to me and pretending as if you really care about the SAVE project, when the truth is you don't care at all?"

Bruce couldn't believe his ears. "What the heck are you talking about?" he said. "What do you mean that I 'used' you? What for?"

"For getting information about Roger from Lisa DePaul," Tracy said angrily.

Bruce was taken aback. It was true that he had found Tracy's friendship with Lisa to be convenient lately, but he had hardly *used* her!

"Why would I want to do something like that?" he asked incredulously.

"Don't ask me. Maybe you can tell *me* that. All I know is that you've lied to me." Tracy's eyes shone with angry tears. "You pretended to be one thing, and it turns out you're just a great big fake."

Bruce shook his head. "Just tell me," he pleaded, "exactly what I did wrong."

"Fine!" Tracy said. "First, you never turned in the money you promised the fund. Second, you ruined Roger's caps. Third, you wrecked his photographic paper yesterday afternoon. Don't deny it," she added quickly, seeing the look on his face. "I was there, and I watched the whole thing."

"You were . . . where?"

"I followed you," Tracy said, holding her head high. "I watched you stop in at the photography store, I heard your conversation with the salesman, and I followed you all the way home."

Bruce was starting to get mad, too. "Well, you should've stuck around awhile. You would have seen that I didn't do it. I planned to, but I didn't."

Tracy stared at him for a minute. "You admit

171

it? You admit you intended to ruin your own cousin's project—for a charity fair?"

"Sure," Bruce said. "But the point is, I didn't do it! Just quit yelling for a minute, Tracy, and give me a chance to explain myself."

"I am *not* yelling," Tracy said coldly. "And I can't imagine any explanation that would justify your behavior. To hurt your own cousin is bad enough, but to deliberately steal money from the kids at the Nicholson School—that's really scummy, Bruce."

Bruce shifted uncomfortably. "Listen, Tracy, I swear to you that I didn't destroy Roger's paper. I was going to, but I didn't. Now, will you just give me one second so I can try to explain myself?"

"Go ahead," Tracy said. But from the look on her face, Bruce had the impression she wasn't going to be very forgiving.

"It's going to take a couple of minutes," he said, letting out a deep sigh.

Tracy just looked at him. "I'm waiting," she said.

Bruce wasn't used to being in this position. Usually when someone got mad at him, he didn't bother to stick around and defend him-

172

self. "Never apologize, never explain" was what he always told himself. But he really wanted Tracy to understand—even if it meant breaking the promise to his grandfather to keep the contest a secret.

"It all started when my grandfather came to stay with us," Bruce began. "See, my grandfather came up with this idea to have a contest between Roger and me to see which one of us is the better businessman," Bruce went on. A note of bitterness crept into his voice as he thought about how unfair his grandfather had been. "The object was to take a certain amount of money and invest it. Whoever has more at the end of next week is the winner. And the prize is pretty big. See, this contest determines which of the two of us is going to run the Patman Corporation after my father retires."

Tracy looked at Bruce in disbelief. "So that's why you've been involved in Harbor Days? To see if you could edge out Roger and win this ridiculous contest? I thought you were different, Bruce. Everyone told me not to trust you, but I did. *I* thought you were capable of caring about people."

"But the contest . . ." Bruce began weakly.

Tracy's eyes were cold. "Forget the contest, Bruce. I really don't care about it. It sounds sad to me that your grandfather would set up something like that, and even sadder that you and Roger were both willing to play the game. But right now, I'm thinking about kids like my brother, who need people like you to raise money on their behalf. If everyone acted the way you and Roger have, the school would close down in a second!" Her eyes flashed. "I thought you were somebody I could care about, Bruce. Well, I guess I just ought to be thankful I found out what you're really all about before I let you get to me!"

And with that, Tracy turned on her heel and strode off, leaving Bruce staring after her in anguish.

"Boy, Patman, way to go," he said sadly.

The thing that really made him sad was that Tracy was right about the contest with Roger. Bruce should have trusted his instincts right from the start and stood up to his grandfather and told him it was a bad idea. Instead, he had thrown himself wholeheartedly into the competition.

She was also right about the Nicholson School.

Trying to win money at poker was one thing, but using a charity drive to win the contest wasn't exactly fair.

Worst of all, he had ruined his relationship with his cousin forever. And that was something Bruce knew he would regret for the rest of his life.

Thirteen

Roger frowned as he looked down at the piece of photographic paper he was testing. The paper seemed perfectly fine. None of the seals on the boxes had been tampered with. And when he opened a box and tried a piece of the paper to see if it was all right, he couldn't see any evidence that it had been exposed.

"Weird," Roger mumbled. Then a scowl crossed his face. Maybe Bruce just hadn't gotten around to destroying the paper *yet*. Maybe he'd told Tracy that he intended to, and since she was such a nice person she had called and warned him. She had said something over the phone like "If he hasn't done it yet, he's about to. . . ."

That made sense. Terrible sense.

For a minute, Roger almost wished he *had* gone ahead and melted his cousin's ice cream. If Bruce was going to play dirty, why not sink to his level?

Because it takes a true man to fight fair—that's what his mother had always told him. A lump formed in Roger's throat at the thought of his mother. Now that the Patmans were gone and he and Bruce were alone with Grandfather Patman, Roger missed his mother more than ever. He knew that if she were still alive, she would be proud of him for fighting fair. And he was determined to try his hardest to behave in a way that would have made her proud.

Roger looked with pleasure at the negatives Jim Roberts had given him. If everything went the way he planned, the portraits he was going to make would be a huge success. He had to do everything possible to keep Bruce from ruining them. He'd already bought a heavy-duty lock from the hardware store. He planned to lock the shed every time he came in or out.

*   *   *

"Tonight is Friday," Grandfather Patman said cheerfully at dinner that night. "Your parents get back a week from tonight. I think we ought to plan a surprise welcome-home party for them. What do you think?"

Bruce poked at his food. He appeared miserable, and he made no attempt to answer his grandfather.

Roger cleared his throat. "That sounds nice, Grandfather." He couldn't wait until they got back and this ridiculous contest was over.

"Let me just remind you both," Grandfather Patman continued, "that Friday marks the last day of your competition. How are you two doing, by the way? Any news for me on your investment strategies?"

Bruce sighed so heavily that both Roger and Alexander Patman looked at him in surprise. "Can I be excused, please?" he said moodily. "I'm not feeling very well."

"What's the matter, Bruce?" his grandfather asked quickly.

"Nothing. I just need to lie down for a little while," Bruce said.

Grandfather Patman watched him leave the

room in silence. "I don't think Bruce is looking well. Do you?" he asked Roger.

Roger didn't answer. But once he thought about it, he realized that Bruce *did* look kind of different. He was pale, and he seemed too quiet, not at all his usual arrogant self.

"I'm sure he's fine," Roger said shortly. *Maybe he's worn out by trying to destroy all my projects,* he thought.

Over dessert, Grandfather Patman told Roger that he wanted Bruce and Roger to invite all of their friends to the welcome-home party. "I'll invite a few people myself. And after the party, we'll have our announcement," the elderly man concluded. "We can tell your aunt and uncle which one of you two has won the competition."

"Sure, Grandfather," Roger said. He couldn't imagine anything worse.

Bruce woke up very early Saturday morning. He immediately jumped out of bed and ran downstairs to the basement and checked on his ice cream. There it was, neatly packaged and ready to be taken to the harbor.

All the joy had gone out of this project for

Bruce since his fight with Tracy. But he was determined to sell as much ice cream as possible that day. She might not believe he was going to give a penny to the Nicholson School, but she was wrong. And Bruce intended to show her just how wrong.

Bruce was one of the first people to arrive at the harbor. Elizabeth Wakefield was the only one of the SAVE representatives to have arrived. She gave Bruce a strained smile when she saw him setting up his booth.

"Giving it another shot this week, Bruce? We never got your contribution from last week."

"You'll get your money," he told her. "I needed to buy supplies for this week. But today I plan to make you guys a bundle."

Elizabeth raised her eyebrows. "Or somebody, at any rate," she said smoothly.

Bruce shrugged. Let her think what she wanted to. He wasn't going to let it bother him!

That day at the harbor was a long and hot one for Bruce. He worked harder than he ever had his whole life. Scooping ice cream was easy for the first hour. Then, Bruce's arm began to get tired. By noon, he was exhausted.

But he was selling ice cream! People kept

coming, one after another, and the dollar bills piled up.

Tracy walked by once or twice, but she didn't respond when Bruce called out to her. The last time she passed him, she looked him right in the eye. "Glad to see my grandmother's recipe is helping you to win your contest, Bruce," she said.

Bruce didn't respond. He would try to explain when he had more time, he decided. For now, he had ice cream to sell!

The only time Bruce took a break the whole day was to visit Roger's booth. Jim was helping Roger. The two boys had agreed to share expenses and split all the profits between them. Each photograph, which had been matted, cost six dollars.

"Roger," Bruce said in a low voice, "I'd like to buy one of your photos."

Roger stared at him, clearly stunned. "You want to buy one of my photos? Are you serious?"

"Yeah," Bruce muttered, shoving a few crumpled bills at his cousin. "I'm serious."

"Well, why don't you just take one," Roger said awkwardly. "Jim and I could each have an ice cream cone in exchange."

A relieved smile broke across Bruce's face. "That sounds like a good idea. You must be pretty hot," he said.

Roger gave him a slow, unsteady smile. And then he put his hand out to shake.

"Truce?" Roger asked.

"Truce," Bruce said, taking Roger's hand and shaking it hard. He felt better than he had in weeks, since before the whole stupid contest had started.

"Well, guys, how'd we do?" Elizabeth asked the others, who had just finished tallying up their earnings from the two Harbor Days. It was Saturday evening, and the group had been given special permission to meet in the school.

Lisa frowned. "We wanted to raise five thousand dollars in all, to add to what the PTA is raising. Unfortunately, it looks like we're only a little more than halfway there."

"You're kidding!" Tracy cried. "How much did we make?"

Lisa sighed. "Only three thousand dollars. Remember, we had to split profits with the boothkeepers."

"Some people still haven't given us our half of their earnings," Tracy reminded them.

"Yeah, but who knows if they ever will?" Lisa said.

Tracy was quiet. Lisa was right. Who knew? They had worked on an honor system, and that meant they had to rely on people to be honest. Tracy had found out the hard way that that was assuming a lot.

"I guess it's back to the drawing board," Lisa said and sighed. All of the reps were tired from the long hours they had put in for the past few weeks, and it was discouraging to think they hadn't reached their goal yet.

Elizabeth got up from the desk to stretch. "Listen, you guys," she said, "we're obviously all tired out. What do you say we head home? We'll meet again on Monday to come up with some new ideas."

Everyone slowly got up and gathered their things. When Elizabeth opened the door of the office, an envelope that had been propped up against it fell across her feet.

"Hey," she said, "what's this?"

"That's strange," Lisa said. "The envelope

has our names on it. But who would know we're meeting here tonight?"

Elizabeth shrugged and started to open it. A puzzled expression crossed her face. "You guys, this is really strange!" she exclaimed. She passed the envelope to Tracy. "Look inside."

"It's—"

"Money," Elizabeth whispered. "Lots of it."

"But who—"

"Look, there's a note!" Tracy cried. She pulled it out of the envelope and opened it quickly.

"Dear SAVE Committee," the note read. "Please use this money for your project."

That was it. No name, no signature—nothing.

"Liz," Tracy whispered, drawing out fistfuls of money, "there's a fortune here! We're not talking about hundreds of dollars. This is a serious amount of money!"

"Do you think we should report it to someone?" Lisa asked nervously.

"We should tell the head of the SAVE project," Elizabeth said. "But it looks as if whoever made the donation knew exactly what they were doing. They want it to go to the fund." She looked around at the others. "Why the sad faces, you guys?" she asked gleefully. "We may have made our goal after all!"

Tracy could hardly wait to tell her family that an anonymous donor had given a little over a thousand dollars to the SAVE project. But before she could even get the door to the house completely open, her mother called out to her from the living room. "Tracy, it's Elizabeth Wakefield on the phone. She wants to talk to you right away!"

Tracy hurried to the phone. "Liz, what is it?"

"This is so fantastic," Elizabeth said. She sounded dazed and jubilant at the same time. "You know I told you I was going to stop by Mr. Peterson's house to tell him about the donation we got?" Mr. Peterson was the chairman of the entire SAVE project.

"Yeah?" Tracy said.

"Well, when I got there, he told me that the fund had received *another* anonymous donation. Can you believe it? And the strangest thing is, it was for nearly a thousand dollars!"

"Does that mean we've made the ten-thousand-dollar goal? That the school can stay open?"

"That's what it means!" Elizabeth declared. "We raised three thousand from the fair, and the PTA raised a little over five thousand. So this brings us to our goal. Tracy, I wanted you to be the very first person to know: the Nicholson School is not going to have to close down after all!"

Roger took a deep breath. "Well," he said to himself, "here goes nothing."

He knocked on Bruce's door.

It was Sunday night, and Roger hadn't seen Bruce since the previous day at the harbor. He had been thinking about him a lot, though. Since Saturday when they had called a truce, Roger had wanted to talk to Bruce. He wanted to see how his cousin felt about this contest their grandfather had gotten them into. He wasn't sure where Bruce had been—he hadn't been at brunch that morning, and he hadn't been around the pool all day.

There was no answer to Roger's knock, either. That was strange. Where could Bruce be?

"Roger!" Grandfather Patman called from downstairs. "Come down here and help me with the guest list for the party. You know a great deal more people around here than I do!''

Roger went to join his grandfather downstairs. He wasn't exactly looking forward to the party, especially since it was going to end in the moment when Grandfather Patman announced who had won the competition.

But Roger had to remember that he had done the right thing with his money. *An investment*, he thought with a little smile, *can be something more than a plan to get more money as fast as you possibly can!*

He couldn't believe it had taken him as long as it had to figure that out.

Bruce paused uneasily on the porch of the Atkinses' house. He knew Tracy was still furious with him, but he wanted a chance to make up with her.

Tracy came to the door at the second ring. She looked surprised when she saw Bruce, but she opened the door and invited him in. At least she was being polite, Bruce thought. That was something.

"Can we talk—by ourselves?" he asked in a low voice.

"Sure," Tracy said. "Nobody is home anyway. My parents took everybody to the municipal pool to cool off." She led Bruce into the kitchen. "Want some iced tea?"

Bruce nodded. "That would be great." He looked at her for a long moment. "Listen, I don't know how much good this is going to do, but I wanted to tell you one more time that I didn't do anything to Roger's photographic paper."

"I know," Tracy said simply. "He told me so himself yesterday afternoon."

"You knew since yesterday, and you didn't call me up to apologize?" Bruce demanded.

Tracy was silent for a minute. "Why apologize? I wasn't upset because you actually ruined the paper, Bruce. I was upset because you ruined the caps and because you considered ruining the photo project. Because of what it says about you." She shrugged. "Listen, maybe things have been simpler for me in some ways than they have been for you. We all stick together here. Jeremy's problem is all of our problem. Everything's like that. When I saw the way you treated Roger. . . . I can't go back to feeling about you the way I was feeling before I knew. I just can't."

"I'm sorry," Bruce said softly. What Tracy had said about her family had really hit home. He wondered if Roger and he could be that loyal to each other.

"So am I," Tracy said sincerely. "But you don't have to sit there looking like you're getting ready for a funeral. There's no reason we can't be friends." She put out her hand. For the second time that weekend, Bruce said, "Truce."

"But only on one condition," Bruce said. "You have to come to the surprise party we're throwing for my parents on Friday night." He grinned. "After all, you had so much fun at the last one," he teased her. "You wouldn't want to miss another Patman party, would you?"

"Not for the world," she said.

Fourteen

"Can you believe it? Your parents will be home in four days," Grandfather Patman announced cheerfully at the breakfast table Monday morning.

Roger gave him a polite smile, but he didn't say anything. Bruce was buried in the sports section of the newspaper. Alexander Patman cleared his throat.

"Don't you two want to talk over your competition with me before the party on Friday night?"

Roger waited for Bruce to say something, and finally Bruce looked up with a shrug. "Nah," he said. "Let's make it a surprise."

Bruce knew who had won, and he didn't see

any reason for Roger to enjoy his victory one minute longer than necessary. Bruce wasn't looking forward to the moment he found out Roger had won the contest—and control of the Patman fortunes.

He could just see it now. The party was going to be held on the grounds of the Patman estate, and hundreds of the Patmans' friends and Bruce's classmates would be there. Then, at midnight, Grandfather Patman would ask Roger and Bruce to step inside, into the privacy of the library. Each of them would come forward with an envelope containing the amount of money they had earned over the past few weeks. Grandfather Patman would count Roger's and announce the amount in a booming and proud voice. Bruce's parents would *ooh* and *ah*. And then it would be Bruce's turn.

Bruce felt sick.

"I don't understand, Roger. Have you tried making up with him?" Lisa asked.

Roger nodded. "But I think he's feeling uncomfortable about what's going to happen on

Friday night. I feel uncomfortable, too, but I have a good reason to!"

"What do you mean?" Lisa asked. "I'm confused." In order to explain why Bruce had ruined the hats, Roger had had to reveal that he and Bruce were in a contest. But he had filled her in on only a few details. She had no idea what was going to happen on Friday night.

"Let's just put it this way. There isn't a whole lot of suspense for me about who's going to win," Roger said. "I know for a fact that it isn't going to be me."

"Well, you ought to be glad," Lisa said quickly. "It was a ridiculous contest from the beginning, and it was totally unfair of your grandfather to put you two through it. At least, that's my opinion," she added.

"Still, a contest is a contest," Roger said. "It means a lot to both of us. Nobody wants to feel like a loser, Lisa. And to tell you the truth, I feel a little bit like one. I threw the contest away, without even giving it a real try."

"That's crazy!" Lisa cried. "Roger, you tried your hardest. You did a good job of selling photographs at the fair. I bet you earned a lot of money from those."

"Yes," Roger said uncomfortably, "but—"

"But nothing," Lisa said firmly. "You should be very proud of yourself. And even if you don't win the stupid contest, that doesn't change a thing!"

"You're right," he said at last. He'd just seen Bruce walk into the cafeteria. More than anything, Roger wanted to walk over, give Bruce a friendly shove, and joke around with him.

Maybe once Bruce knows his share of the family fortune is safe, things will be better between us, Roger thought wistfully. He didn't know whether he believed it or not.

The student representatives for the SAVE project were sitting in the front row of the auditorium of the Nicholson School. It was Wednesday, the day the committee was to announce the results of the fund drive. Tracy was so excited that she could hardly sit still. She had managed to keep the results of the drive a secret from her brother Jeremy. And she couldn't wait for him to hear the good news; she knew he was going to go out of his mind with excitement.

Mr. Peterson, the chairman of the committee,

got up to make a speech to the students of the Nicholson School. He kept the speech nice and short, which was smart, considering the age of his audience.

"I know you've all been very worried about what was going to happen to your school," he said, smiling out at the rows of students. A murmur went through the room. From the looks on the students' faces, "worried" wasn't a strong enough word. They looked absolutely *terrified* that the news they were about to hear wasn't going to be good.

"Well, I'm not going to keep you in suspense any longer. The fact is, we've managed to raise enough money to keep the Nicholson School open for at least this next year."

For a brief moment, the auditorium was quiet. But then the students started bouncing up and down and shrieking with joy. Tracy felt her eyes fill with happy tears. She located her brother in the crowd, and the look of happiness on his face made all the work she had put into the drive worth it. She knew it was a moment that she would never forget as long as she lived.

Mr. Peterson put his hand up to quiet the audience. "We're all as pleased as you are. And we especially want to thank our student representatives from Sweet Valley High. They raised an astonishing amount of money and came up with the idea for Harbor Days, which was a smashing success!"

There were more cheers from the crowd, but Mr. Peterson held up his hand to quiet them again. "I hate to conclude on a sober note," he said, "but I think the scare all of you faced this year is still a very real one. We've worked hard to raise enough money to keep the Nicholson School open this year. But all of you need to remind your parents that the work isn't over yet. Until we find a permanent means of support, the school will always be in danger."

"Pretty scary thought, isn't it?" Elizabeth said to Tracy.

Tracy nodded. "But look on the bright side. At least we gave the kids another year. And I think that was pretty important to them," she said, gesturing toward the happy children.

"I still wish we knew who our mysterious donors were," Elizabeth said.

Tracy nodded. "Me, too. Whoever he or she or they are, I'd like to give them an enormous hug!"

"I wonder," Elizabeth said, "whether we'll ever find out."

Tracy had a feeling they would never know. But she was happy letting it remain a wonderful mystery.

Fifteen

Mr. and Mrs. Patman returned from Japan on Thursday afternoon. They were full of stories about the exotic cities they had visited and the people they had met. They brought home presents wrapped in exquisite Japanese paper for Miranda, Bruce, Roger, and Grandfather Patman.

"Come here, Bruce," Mrs. Patman said. "Let me get a look at you. You look a little thin to me. Have you been sick?"

"I'm just fine," Bruce muttered. *But I'll be better after this party is over*, he added to himself.

"You don't look well, either," Mrs. Patman added, turning to Roger.

"Don't coddle the boys so!" Grandfather Patman interrupted. "Now, I want to hear all about your trip. George, I hope you learned a few lessons from the Japanese about how to produce."

Mr. Patman laughed. "We tried to have a little fun on this trip, but, yes, I picked up a few tips as well." He turned back to Bruce and Roger. "I imagine you two have learned a few things in the past four weeks as well. What can you tell us about your investment strategies?"

Bruce felt his face turn red. He wasn't sure that you could call a poker game an investment strategy. And then there were the "investments" he had made on his car, dinners out, and concert tickets.

Roger spoke up. "I think we both learned that it's hard to earn money in a short period of time, and . . ." He paused. "Maybe I shouldn't speak for Bruce, but I found it difficult to compete against a relative."

Grandfather Patman frowned at Roger. "Why? That's the nature of the business world, Roger! Competition at every level."

"I'm not sure I agree," Mr. Patman said, to

Bruce's surprise. "I believe Roger has made an important point."

Grandfather Patman was silent for a moment. "*I* still think it's an important lesson," he said firmly.

Nobody said anything for a moment.

"Well," Mrs. Patman said, breaking the silence, "it's good to be home."

"Thanks," Bruce said to Roger after his parents had gone upstairs to unpack. "You could've told them that I ruined your caps, and you didn't."

"Don't mention it," Roger said.

"You're not half as bad as I thought you were," Bruce said.

"And you know," Roger replied, "some of the time you aren't a complete jerk."

"Want to go swim a few laps?" Bruce asked.

"Sure. Just let me go up to my room and grab my swimsuit."

"I bet I can swim fifty laps faster than you can," Bruce said.

Roger laughed. "I'm glad to see that your competitive edge isn't completely gone, Bruce. I'd hate to see you get soft."

"Never!" Bruce replied. He already had his

swimsuit on, so he went right out to the pool and dived in. It would be much easier to beat his cousin if he had a head start.

"Very elegant," Tracy's mother told her from the door of her bedroom.

"Don't tell me you expected anything less," Tracy replied, grandly lifting her nose in the air. Then she giggled. "It really is great, Mom. Thanks for all your help."

"Your chariot leaves in five minutes," Mrs. Atkins said, turning to go.

"I'll be right down," Tracy said.

Before she left her room, Tracy swirled around in front of the mirror so that she could get one last look at her new dress. Her mother had surprised Tracy with the material only two days ago, and they had both worked like demons to get the dress finished in time for the Patmans' party. The dress was fabulous. It had a V in the back and in the front and a flared skirt that ended just above the knee.

Tracy felt so special in the dress that she almost wished things were still possible between her and Bruce; it would have been fun to be in love on a night as special as this. But she had admitted some painful truths to herself over the past week. Attractive as Bruce was, and as flattering as his attention had been, she wasn't comfortable with him as a boyfriend. They were just too different.

But that didn't mean she couldn't enjoy the party! It was a perfect chance to celebrate the success of the SAVE project.

When Tracy's mother dropped her off in front of the Patman estate, people were streaming up the lawn toward the big house. The house was all lit up. Since the sun had just gone down, the light made the house appear magical.

Bruce hurried over to greet Tracy as soon as she stepped into the foyer. "You look terrific!" he said. "And you're right on time. Grandfather Patman smuggled my parents off to L.A. this afternoon, and they're due back any minute."

Roger came up to them. "Do you really think they're going to be surprised?" he asked.

Bruce nodded. "And not just by the party," he added.

"You can say that again," Roger said.

Tracy looked back and forth between the two

boys. Something was definitely going on between them, but she couldn't guess what.

Just then, Alexander Patman hurried in. "They're on their way in," he announced. "Get ready to say 'Surprise!' " he instructed them.

"This is so nice of your grandfather," Tracy whispered to Bruce.

Bruce made a face. "In a way, yes. And in another way, no."

"Hey, there's Lisa!" Roger said. "I'm going to go say hello." He began to make his way through the crowd toward the doorway.

"You see," Bruce told Tracy after Roger had gone, "at midnight, my Grandfather is going to ask Roger and me to reveal our earnings, and then he'll announce which one of us won our little contest."

"Bruce, you're kidding!" Tracy said, staring at him. Suddenly, the full impact of what was at risk for Bruce hit her, and she wanted to ask him a hundred questions. But before she could say another word, the lights dimmed, the Patmans opened the front door, everyone shouted "Surprise!", and the party began. And it was a great party; the food was delicious, and there was live jazz and dancing.

Tracy would have had a better time if she hadn't been so worried about Bruce. She couldn't help but notice that he was quiet for most of the evening. She knew he must be very worried about his grandfather's announcement.

"Ladies and gentlemen," Grandfather Patman said to the guests who had gathered into the Patmans' massive living room, "join me in welcoming home my son and daughter-in-law, who have been on a four-week vacation in the Far East."

Everyone applauded, and Grandfather Patman held up his hand for order. "For me, one of the dividends of their extended trip has been the opportunity to spend time with my two grandsons. I think they will agree that we have all gotten to know one another far better over the course of my visit." Everyone was listening intently. "When I arrived in Sweet Valley four weeks ago, I met my grandson Roger for the first time. It came to me then that there was no reason for the control of the Patman Corporation to go automatically to Bruce—after his father, of course. Why not let Roger and Bruce fight for it?"

A collective gasp was audible in the living room.

"So what I did was set up a little competition," he continued, clearly enjoying the shock he was giving his guests. "I gave each boy a sum of money, set a time period, and determined that at the end of that period, whoever had invested the money and come up with the largest sum would win control of the Patman Corporation. That time period ends today."

The crowd was silent.

"Roger and Bruce, I think the time has come for you two to step up here and present me with your envelopes."

Tracy saw Bruce and Roger exchange glances. Both boys seemed nervous. They walked slowly up to their grandfather, who was standing in front of the fireplace.

"Grandfather," Bruce said in a low voice, "maybe we should do this in private."

"Nonsense!" his grandfather said crisply. "We have nothing to hide! These people are our community, our friends. Now, hand me your envelopes. Both of you, please."

Bruce stared uncertainly at Roger, and Roger back at Bruce. Neither one of them seemed willing to pass his envelope to Grandfather Patman, who was waiting with his hand out-stretched. Both of them started to speak at the same time.

"Grandfather, if you'd just let me explain—" Bruce began.

"This is going to upset you, but—" Roger blurted out.

Alexander Patman interrupted them both. "Since neither one of you seems eager to go first, I'll open both envelopes at the same time," he said. Bruce and Roger handed the envelopes to him, and with a dramatic shake of his wrist, Grandfather Patman snapped open both. His look of expectant pleasure turned to a frown, then a glare, and then an expression of aston-ishment as he examined the envelopes.

"Empty!" he cried. "What on earth is the meaning of this? Would one of you boys please explain what's going on?"

Roger and Bruce stared at each other, expres-sions of disbelief on their faces.

"But—but you made all that money from those photos," Bruce stammered.

"What about you?" Roger demanded. "What about your ice cream?"

"Excuse me," Grandfather Patman said, a note of anger creeping into his voice. "I think I deserve an explanation from you two—right now! I gave each of you boys two thousand dollars. Now, you can't tell me that neither of you managed to save a single penny of that sum!"

"Well, sir, first there was my car . . ." Bruce began.

"He kept running it into things," Roger finished for him.

"I had to get it repaired—twice," Bruce added. "So then I came up with the brilliant idea of poker. I got my buddies to raise the stakes pretty high, but—"

"Poker?" Grandfather Patman repeated with obvious disbelief.

"I lost. Big," Bruce said with a shudder. "It was a terrible experience."

"I know how you felt," Roger put in. "I felt the same way after I lost all that money on my shares of Robotech."

"You were buying stock? In *that* company?"

Grandfather Patman demanded. He was beginning to look a little sick.

"I was sure you were making a fortune on that stock. That's why I ruined your caps for Harbor Days," Bruce confessed.

"Listen, you two," their grandfather said. "Just give me the headlines, if you can manage it. What happened to all that money?"

"Well, sir, we did manage to earn some of it back. I sold photographs at the Harbor Days fair, and Bruce sold ice cream," Roger told him. "Only, the point of the fair was to raise money for a school for special-needs children. We were asked to give fifty percent of what we earn to the school. And something tells me Bruce decided that fifty percent wasn't enough. So he gave them everything."

"And something tells *me*," Bruce put in, "that Roger felt the same way. So we didn't come out with any profit at all."

"That isn't what I'd say," Mr. Patman spoke up from the back of the room. "Wouldn't you all say these two boys profited a great deal?" he asked the guests. "It seems to me that they managed to turn a lesson in competitiveness into an act of giving. And frankly, I'd like to give them both a big round of applause."

The guests responded with cheers. Bruce stepped forward to shake Roger's hand. "I guess this means neither of us won," he said.

Roger grinned. "I think we *both* did!"

"I can't believe you guys," Tracy said happily. She gave first Bruce and then Roger a big hug. "You two were our mystery donors! Bruce, I want to take back every unkind thing I said to you about your refusing to pay us fifty percent of what you made at Harbor Days. I feel so terrible."

Bruce gave her an affectionate pat on the shoulder. "I forgive you," he said with mock seriousness. "After all, what are friends for?"

"Thanks a lot—friend," Tracy said. She gave Bruce a kiss on the cheek.

Put that in the "Bruce Patman Guide to Dating," Bruce thought. *Staying friends with a girl you used to date is definitely cool.*

Mr. Patman was working his way over to them. He seemed delighted. "You two are astonishing," he greeted them. "Here I thought I knew everything about my son and my nephew, and then you give me this wonderful surprise. Just incredible! I'm so proud of you both!"

Bruce was beginning to feel embarrassed.

"You know," Mr. Patman went on, "I've been talking to Mr. Peterson about the fund you donated to, and it sounds like a worthy cause. Did you know that the Nicholson School is going to need a permanent benefactor? Apparently, even after all the money you raised this year, it may be threatened in the same way in subsequent years. So I've decided to follow your fine example and make the Patman Corporation the chief patron of the Nicholson School. From now on, they'll be guaranteed that their doors will remain open."

"Dad, that's fantastic!" Bruce said.

"I can tell you with authority how happy the children from the school are going to be to learn this," Tracy said sincerely.

Mr. Patman put his arms around Roger and Bruce. "You know something, you boys taught all of us a lesson tonight. But I think you had a particularly special impact on your grandfather. He wants to see you both in the library—immediately."

Roger and Bruce exchanged nervous glances, but the wink Mr. Patman gave them made them feel a little bit better.

"Here goes nothing," Roger said.

"Wish us luck," Bruce said to Tracy.

"I don't really think you need it," Tracy said, smiling broadly.

Alexander Patman was sitting in a big chair at one end of the library. He got to his feet when Bruce and Roger came in. He had a stern look of his face.

"Boys," he said slowly, "I was stunned by what happened tonight. I don't think I need to tell you it was the last thing I expected. I was more than shocked; I was hurt. I felt as though you were taunting me, making fun of the contest I'd taken so seriously." He cleared his throat. "But then I thought about it again, and I realized that you two were right and that I was wrong. When Roger came into this family, he had another name, another identity. Bruce and his parents have tried to welcome you, Roger, and make you feel like a Patman. And then I came along with the brilliant idea of dividing

you boys up, of pitting you against each other."
He shook his head. "Not only did you two
teach me that cooperation is as effective as competition, but you also reminded me that there
are more ways to win than just making money.
You have each made me very, very proud."

"Thank you, Grandfather," Roger said quietly.

"No problem," Bruce said lightly.

"My hope," their grandfather continued, "is
that you two will learn to cooperate, to trust
each other, to share, and to live as true cousins.
I know your father wants it that way, Bruce.
And if I knew your father, Roger, as I think I
did, he would have wanted it too." He patted
each boy awkwardly on the back. "May you
both grow up as wise and as bighearted as you
are now."

For the first time that he could remember,
Bruce gave his grandfather a hug. And then he
even gave one to Roger.

"Of course, if I had really tried, I could have
won this thing hands down," Bruce said as
they headed back to the party.

"No way!" Roger said.

"Piece of cake!"

"Bruce, you're out of your mind!"

Bruce stopped short. "You want to try again? We can set up our own contest—with our own rules."

Roger started to laugh. "Forget it," he said. "I don't think I even want to hear what those rules would be!"

Bruce laughed, too. And then Bruce and Roger went out to join the party, and to tell their friends that the biggest family feud in Patman history had officially been declared a tie!

COULD *YOU* BE THE NEXT SWEET VALLEY READER OF THE MONTH?

ENTER BANTAM BOOKS' SWEET VALLEY CONTEST & SWEEPSTAKES IN ONE!

Calling all Sweet Valley Fans! Here's a chance to appear in a Sweet Valley book!

We know how important Sweet Valley is to you. That's why we've come up with a Sweet Valley celebration offering exciting opportunities to have YOUR thoughts printed in a Sweet Valley book!

"How do I become a Sweet Valley Reader of the Month?"

It's easy. Just write a one-page essay (no more than 150 words, please) telling us a little about yourself, and why you like to read Sweet Valley books. We will pick the best essays and print them along with the winner's photo in the back of upcoming Sweet Valley books. Every month there will be a new Sweet Valley High Reader of the Month!

And, there's more!

Just sending in your essay makes you eligible for the Grand Prize drawing for a trip to Los Angeles, California! This once-in-a-life-time trip includes round-trip airfare, accommodations for 5 nights (economy double occupancy), a rental car, and meal allowances. (Approximate retail value: $4,500.)

Don't wait! Write your essay today.
No purchase necessary. See the next page for Official rules.

ENTER BANTAM BOOKS' SWEET VALLEY READER OF THE MONTH SWEEPSTAKES

☐	27567	**DOUBLE LOVE #1**	$2.95
☐	27578	**SECRETS #2**	$2.95
☐	27669	**PLAYING WITH FIRE #3**	$2.95
☐	27493	**POWER PLAY #4**	$2.95
☐	27568	**ALL NIGHT LONG #5**	$2.95
☐	27741	**DANGEROUS LOVE #6**	$2.95
☐	27672	**DEAR SISTER #7**	$2.95
☐	27569	**HEARTBREAKER #8**	$2.95
☐	27878	**RACING HEARTS #9**	$2.95
☐	27668	**WRONG KIND OF GIRL #10**	$2.95
☐	27941	**TOO GOOD TO BE TRUE #11**	$2.95
☐	27755	**WHEN LOVE DIES #12**	$2.95
☐	27877	**KIDNAPPED #13**	$2.95
☐	27939	**DECEPTIONS #14**	$2.95
☐	27940	**PROMISES #15**	$2.95
☐	27431	**RAGS TO RICHES #16**	$2.95
☐	27931	**LOVE LETTERS #17**	$2.95
☐	27444	**HEAD OVER HEELS #18**	$2.95
☐	27589	**SHOWDOWN #19**	$2.95
☐	27454	**CRASH LANDING! #20**	$2.95
☐	27566	**RUNAWAY #21**	$2.95
☐	27952	**TOO MUCH IN LOVE #22**	$2.95
☐	27951	**SAY GOODBYE #23**	$2.95
☐	27492	**MEMORIES #24**	$2.95
☐	27944	**NOWHERE TO RUN #25**	$2.95
☐	27670	**HOSTAGE #26**	$2.95
☐	27885	**LOVESTRUCK #27**	$2.95
☐	28087	**ALONE IN THE CROWD #28**	$2.95

Buy them at your local bookstore or use this page to order.

Bantam Books, Dept. SVH, 414 East Golf Road, Des Plaines, IL 60016

Please send me the items I have checked above. I am enclosing $_____ (please add $2.00 to cover postage and handling). Send check or money order, no cash or C.O.D.s please.

Mr/Ms _____

Address _____

City/State _____ Zip _____

SVH–6/90

Please allow four to six weeks for delivery.
Prices and availability subject to change without notice.

There Is Really Nothing To Compare To A Grieving Man Whose Grief Is For A Woman.

Especially a woman who is constantly underfoot. And one who doesn't seem to notice the man is suffering. How could she be so unknowing?

Even a half-bright woman would have known Bryan was suffering. Lily ignored his grief and cheerfully chattered and seemed to be around the whole time.

She stretched a man's limits.

But Bryan was silent. He didn't protest. He didn't complain. He was noble. And she paid him no never mind at all. She just went right on like she ruled the place, and no one could lay a finger on her.

This blasted woman was driving him wild.

Dear Reader,

Welcome to a wonderful new year at Silhouette Desire! Let's start with a delightfully humorous MAN OF THE MONTH by Lass Small—*The Coffeepot Inn*. Here, a sinfully sexy hero is tempted by a virtuous woman. He's determined to protect her from becoming the prey of the local men—*and* he's determined to win her for himself!

The HOLIDAY HONEYMOONS miniseries continues this month with *Resolved To (Re)Marry* by Carole Buck. Don't miss this latest installment of this delightful continuity series!

And the always wonderful Jennifer Greene continues her STANFORD SISTERS series with *Bachelor Mom*. As many of you know, Jennifer is an award winner, and this book shows why she is so popular with readers and critics alike!

Completing the month are a new love story from the sizzling pen of Beverly Barton, *The Tender Trap;* a delightful Western from Pamela Macaluso, *The Loneliest Cowboy;* and something a little bit different from Ashley Summers, *On Wings of Love*.

Enjoy!

Lucia Macro

Senior Editor

Please address questions and book requests to:
Silhouette Reader Service
U.S.: 3010 Walden Ave., P.O. Box 1325, Buffalo, NY 14269
Canadian: P.O. Box 609, Fort Erie, Ont. L2A 5X3

Lass Small

THE COFFEEPOT INN

SILHOUETTE *Desire*®

Published by Silhouette Books

America's Publisher of Contemporary Romance

SILHOUETTE BOOKS

ISBN 0-373-76045-0

THE COFFEEPOT INN

Copyright © 1997 by Lass Small

Printed in U.S.A.

Books by Lass Small

Silhouette Desire

Tangled Web #241
To Meet Again #322
Stolen Day #341
Possibles #356
Intrusive Man #373
To Love Again #397
Blindman's Bluff #413
*Goldilocks and the Behr #437
*Hide and Seek #453
*Red Rover #491
*Odd Man Out #505
*Tagged #534
Contact #548
Wrong Address, Right Place #569
Not Easy #578
The Loner #594
Four Dollars and
    Fifty-One Cents #613
*No Trespassing Allowed #638
The Molly Q #655
†'Twas the Night #684
*Dominic #697
†A Restless Man #731
†Two Halves #743
†Beware of Widows #755
A Disruptive Influence #775
†Balanced #800
†Tweed #817
†A New Year #830
†I'm Gonna Get You #848
†Salty and Felicia #860
†Lemon #879
†An Obsolete Man #895
A Nuisance #901
Impulse #926
Whatever Comes #963
My House or Yours? #974
A Stranger in Texas #994
The Texas Blue Norther #1027
The Coffeepot Inn #1045

Silhouette Romance

An Irritating Man #444
Snow Bird #521

Yours Truly

Not Looking for a Texas Man
The Case of the Lady in
    Apartment 308

Silhouette Books

Silhouette Christmas Stories 1989
"Voice of the Turtles"
Silhouette Spring Fancy 1993
"Chance Encounter"

*Lambert Series
†Fabulous Brown Brothers

LASS SMALL

finds living on this planet at this time a fascinating experience. People are amazing. She thinks that to be a teller of tales of people, places and things is absolutely marvelous.

To Indianapolis, our new home

One

It was Lily Baby's own father who firmly decided to name her Lily after his grandmother.

His two-year-long bride, Susan, was shocked. She was a Davie born and bred. Over the years, she had clashed with the directions issued from her husband's grandmother. That woman was a thorn in Susan's side.

None of the families' men appeared to notice what a witch the original Lily was. They couldn't do anything about her anyway, so it was easier not to mention how difficult she was. Susan had thought for sure the old lady would last forever, and she almost did.

In all those years, Susan had had a series of cats named Lilly with two *l*s. It had been revenge because the catty old lady had been a raw sore of a witch.

With a series of cats so named, Susan had always innocently said that adding the Baby part to the great-granddaughter's name was to distinguish whose name was Lily.

It took some time before Lily Baby understood she'd not been named for one of the cats. She was disappointed because she'd liked the cats.

It was Susan who had vigorously backed her husband to transplant them from TEXAS to Indiana. And at Susan's contrivance, they had put a trailer in the small yard behind their small house. They had not only used it as a vacation vehicle, but when the great-grandparents had visited, they'd been housed there. So had other guests, but the trailer was a godsend at various family visiting times.

By now, Lily Baby was just barely twenty-three. She was a slender five feet four, with a mop of raven black hair and blue eyes. She was a crippling combination for vulnerable male endurance. She didn't notice.

She had graduated from Ball State University and was restless about the future. That was when her great-grandfather Trevor joined the original Lily. One can only assume it was in heaven. And Lily Baby was Willed the Coffeepot Inn. It was located southeast, down just past San Antonio, TEXAS.

Her mother said a careful, "Yes." Then she'd asked her Lily Baby, "Are you interested in it?"

Being a Trevor, and her father's daughter, Lily Baby decided, "I'll go look." That was when she decided she could do without the Baby part of her name. She was grown.

Her mother had nodded thoughtfully. Her daddy had been very touched his daughter had been Willed the inn. Her father had never run an inn and had no idea how to go about it. "I suppose you just go down there and open it up?"

And since she was also her mother's daughter, Lily nodded. "I'll find out."

So having mostly grown up in Indiana, but raised by two TEXANS, Lily drove herself down to San Antonio and on to the southeast edge of it. There, San Antonio was gobbling up a little town that had once been quite a ways outside the city. It had been named Quatro for some reason long lost.

With the map provided to her by her mother, Lily knew to go on out beyond the southeast edge of what was Quatro. And there, just off the highway and rising from a green sea of lacy mesquite trees, was the Coffeepot Inn.

It was not only called the Coffeepot Inn, it *was* a coffeepot! It had to be at least thirty feet high, with a handle on one side, a lid roof on top and the spout (chimney) facing the gasoline pumps.

From the lip of the spout hung a sign made like a flat cream pitcher that named it rightly. The Coffeepot Inn.

The door and windows were tall and wide, and they were rounded on top. The upper narrower and shorter but also top-rounded windows indicated there was a second floor.

The big surprise was that on beyond in back, in a half circle, were six large, straight but round, overturned "Cups" on "saucers" that were flat cement foundations. They were cabins for travelers. Amazing.

Each Cup had a handle, a door and windows. One of the Cups held the inn's laundry. From the lawyer's papers, Lily knew that in a portion of the laundry Cup was a workshop.

Lily got out of her car and looked around. The weeds were out of control. The place was...casual. The mesquites needed to be trimmed up.

When and *how* had her great-grandfather ever come into this gem of a weird place? And Lily Baby smiled. It was perfect. All it needed was a little tidying up.

"Looking for a place to stay?" A slouched man stood in the doorway to the inn. He probably hadn't shaved in a week. Like his beard, his hair was black and tended to curl. His eyes were brown. He was so serious that his eyes' squint-wrinkles were pale.

A toothpick was in one side of his mouth. He wore an undershirt that was really clean, and the black curly hair on his chest peeked over the top of it. He had a square, cotton cloth tea towel tied around his waist. It was folded diagonally.

She asked, "Who are you?"

"I'm the cook."

She smiled. "I'm Tom Trevor's great-granddaughter."

He hedged, "Who's he?"

She gestured to indicate the whole layout. "He Willed this place to me."

"How do I know you're telling me the truth?"

"I have the papers."

"Come in and have a cup of coffee—are you old enough to drink coffee?" He came out onto the one-step-up cement square.

She stayed the step down but replied, "Yes. However, I prefer tea."

He asked, "You a Brit?"

"No. " And she went on to give the ancient identifying comment, "I'm a TEXAN, born and bred."

"You don't talk like one."

She was still just looking around. So she readily replied, "I mostly grew up in Indiana."

"You'll die of the heat down here."

"I haven't heard my TEXAS parents complain about growing up down here."

"They probably want you to run this place and support them."

She smiled a little. "They aren't needy."

Just those last three words were a clue to her youth. No alert person reveals anything to strangers.

He held open the screen door and got to watch her walk past him into the inn part of the downstairs.

She looked around. The place needed to be painted. The floor was dim but clean. Set in the middle of the ceiling, a fan was revolving slowly.

There was a counter with six stools. Each stool was supported by a single rod. There were several small four-chair tables. All that took up most of the ground floor. Cleverly, an open stair curled up inside of the outside wall to the second floor.

The cook gave her hot water in a cup, and he put a tea bag on her saucer. She sat at one of the tables, and he sat across from her. He had coffee.

"Do you drink a whole lot of coffee?"

His eye crinkles hid the whiteness as he almost smiled. "Pots."

She told a man who was some years older than she, "Coffee isn't good for you. You ought to drink some cranberry juice instead."

"Yes, boss."

"Good attitude."

That finally made him smile.

He had good teeth. He had a great smile. She asked, "Are you a good cook?"

"I don't get no complaints."

She watched him watching her. She smiled a little. "Is that because anyone can see the muscles in your arms and shoulders?"

He was surprised and asked, "I got muscles?"

She just laughed.

He confided, "It's from flipping them there eggs. I can do it with a flapjack turner in either hand, therefore my muscles match."

"How clever." She noted his grammar changed. But TEXANS tended to do that naturally. That way they proved their Good Old Boy status.

So she asked, "Do you have anyone to help you?"

"Teresa's son spells me during the afternoon. Teresa comes to tidy any of the cabins that need it."

She echoed, "The cabins that . . . need . . . it."

"Yeah." Then he found himself asking, "You gonna move into one of the Cups?"

She asked with interest, "Are they livable?"

"Yeah. Most of 'em."

So she questioned, "Which is best?"

He sprawled and sighed before he observed, "How like a woman to want the best of whatever."

She had a male chauvinist there. And he was the cook. He was clean, he appeared to know the place well enough. He was not in charge of anything but cooking. "Do we have very many people stop to eat?"

"Our share."

"Is it profitable?"

He hedged, "Barely."

She looked out of the low window and over at the upside-down Cups. They were tall and had handles. They were simply a delight to her eyes. She smiled at them. Then she asked, "Can both of us make a living here?"

He evaded any real reply, but he said, "We can try."

That was encouragement enough for the neophyte. She was charmed to find the Coffeepot Inn was built the way it was, with the Cups as cabins. She was ready to try to make it work.

Actually, since the Pot was still open and in business, it must work to a degree. She inquired, "Do you have the keys to the cabins?"

"I'll show you."

However, he took Lily Trevor on a tour of the Pot first. She noted that he kept an eye on the gas pumps and on the door to the inn. He showed her the whole place.

The Coffeepot had a basement! Very unusual in that area. It was neat and clean. It held the staples and there was a large, walk-in refrigerator! He explained, "I stock the fridge upstairs from here. They deliver as I call."

She nodded.

"We get milk delivery every day, the quantity depending on how we need it. They aren't far, and they can send some over if we get a crowd of kids in here."

He took her up the sharply rising, curling stairs, which clung to the outer wall to the first floor, and on up the stairs to the second floor. That floor held a fair-size office, two small bedrooms and a very small bath that held only a shower, no tub.

She was exuberant.

He said carefully, "You can't live here—with me—in this building."

That surprised her. "We'd not be sharing the same room."

The very idea shivered his sex. Earnestly, he told her, "The gossip here is basic and old-fashioned, and you'll never in this world believe it. You can't be around here and live alone. You might rent a room in Quatro. Ask Teresa. She'd find you a safe place."

"Why don't you rent a room, instead, and leave me here? It *is* mine."

He was logical. "You can't be here at night with the inn empty. You could get caught by some really nasty guys. Nobody is interested in me."

She looked at him carefully. He was diminishing himself. Or he had hidden flaws. Awful genes? Some ghastly genetic strain like a weakness for a variety of women?

She ventured, "I own the place."

"You can stay with Teresa. You'd even have a whole room."

"Why not in one of the cabins?"

"Maybe. Ask Teresa."

"Does she make the rules?"

And he replied distantly, "She knows them all—for this area."

Lily Baby considered. Then she commented, "Different places do have different rules."

"I'm glad you realize that."

"Tell me about you."

"I'm Bryan Willard." He looked at her. She was so young. He told her gently, "I'm thirty years old. I'm a good cook."

"Your—wife?"

"No wife." He didn't breathe. She was going to say, *Well, then, we'll just sleep together!*

She gave an edict. "If you were married, your wife could protect your reputation."

"I'll look around."

She looked down, and in spite of her effort to be cool, her smile was very amused.

He watched her. She was something to watch. If she decided to stay around and have a hand in the Coffeepot, he was going to go through a knife-bladed wringer. She was too young in experience. She was an innocent. In her first week, she would set the whole, entire male population of Quatro on their ears.

After that, the craze for her would spread into the southeast side of San Antonio. It would go on from there. In two months even Corpus would be aware of her.

She was a disaster for Bryan Willard. She would become a terror for the male part of the southeast side of TEXAS within the next three months.

And just then the door opened and in walked a young man, also about thirty. He was dressed in a dark suit and wore a white shirt with a discreet tie. Only actual businessmen ever wore ties. What was such a person doing at the Coffeepot Inn? He was probably lost.

The man smiled. He had a good smile. He had blue eyes and his hair was a rusty blond. He looked at them both as they sat at the table. He discarded Lily as being a guest of the undershirt-clad man who was obviously the cook.

The intruder said, "Good morning! I'm Tim Morgan." He said that in the courteous way of a man who knows himself. He then assumes you know him. He was being charmingly modest in that he mentioned his name.

Before they could respond, Tim explained, "I was wondering if you know the owner of this place?"

And because of her tender age and lack of experience, Lily Baby proved Bryan was right in his evaluation of her as she said, "I'm the owner."

Tim was obviously surprised. He hid it immediately.

However, Bryan had seen the eye flash of Tim's shock. But the intruder's interested smile quickly covered it all. That confirmed to Bryan that Tim was some sort of salesman.

Tim was then saying, "Good! Are you free? I would like to see the inn from this side of the hill." Then he bit his lower lip.

Bryan didn't rise or smile or anything. To protect the neophyte, he said, "Why." No question, just the word.

Tim was not a neophyte. He smiled at Bryan and held his hand out to Lily to encourage her in rising from her chair. Time is money.

Again, Tim told only Lily, "I need to consult with you?" The TEXAS questioning statement.

Lily didn't move, but she considered Tim with some interest. However, Bryan slowly rose to his full height. In that undershirt, all his intimidating muscles showed and his look was deadly serious.

Lily didn't notice that part. She was just fascinated by Tim. She said, "Have a glass of orange juice."

"Thank you. I'll have it later. I've a client I need to see in exactly one and a half hours. That gives us time for a good conversation and an exchange of ideas about this area. Will you step outside with me so that I can show you what I mean?"

Bryan told the neophyte Lily Baby, "Don't go anywhere with him."

And Tim was astonished. "Here's my card."

Bryan was not impressed. He retorted, "You can have 'em made at any print shop."

At that, Lily Baby turned and looked at Bryan. She finally understood that Bryan was suspicious of Tim. She told Bryan, "I went through four years at Ball State University in Muncie, Indiana. I know how to handle this."

Bryan silently sucked in a deeply shocked breath and held it. It kept his chest awesomely inflated. He was breathing in little tiny air sips on top of the held breath.

Lily Baby understood he was protecting her, and on such a short acquaintance that was dear, but she didn't understand it. Having never been aware of all the males who'd stood up for her—in chancy situations—and controlled other males for her safety in various crises, Lily Baby rose from her chair.

Bryan knew she had always ignored the threatening impact of the males who had guarded her, just as he was then doing. They'd put their chins on the line for her and stopped some idiot male's maneuvers in possessing her. She really was a neophyte.

Tim told Bryan nicely discardingly, "We'll be back shortly. I just want to explain myself."

Sure. Bryan's eyes were deadly. He told Lily Baby, "Don't go any farther than the Cups."

With endurance learned from just such male communications all her life, Lily Baby replied very sweetly but with the dismissive eyes of a woman in control, "I realize that."

So Bryan looked Tim right in the eyes and told him, "I'll be watching you."

Tim grinned at the cook. He was showing how completely harmless he was. He said to the cook, "You ought to come along." He gestured to the Pot around them. "You could learn a lot."

"I already have."

But Bryan followed the two out the door, and he stood on the slab of cement at the entrance that was the step up from the ground. Bryan put a toothpick in his mouth and he watched Tim from under his eyebrows.

As the pair walked toward the hill in back of the Cups, Tim grinned at Lily Baby and said, "Where'd you ever find that escort?"

"He came with the Pot."

That amused Tim, who was a cheerful man. He looked at Lily Baby in another way. He took her elbow to help her along the weedy, sandy ground.

He asked, "Where'd you actually find that bodyguard?"

"I just met him."

"Tell me about it." And he stopped to listen.

"I own this place. My great-grandfather Willed it to me. Mr. Willard is the cook." She considered Tim. He could listen quite well, if it was something he wanted to know. She asked, "Why am I out here?"

"And just graduated?" Tim asked.

She'd told him that. So she just looked at Tim with an elan Tim hadn't expected.

"You sound like the new women who've been instructed to think that way." Tim smiled kindly. Then he proved how clever he really was. He said, "We're very lucky men to have such women around us. I believe I've heard you want to sell the Coffeepot. What is your price?"

She slowly shook her head in denial as she said, "I just got here. I don't know the books, or the traffic or the potential."

Tim sobered, nodded and walked about slowly as he looked carefully at the hill on beyond the Cups. Then he seriously studied his feet . . . and considered her reaction. "After you've read the books, would you call? Here's a couple of my cards. Put them in various places so you don't forget me."

No woman would ever forget Tim Morgan. But she looked at him as if she was considering remembering him. Women aren't that dumb.

He had a great smile. His eyes danced with lights. He would not be dull to know. But he would be busy. He was different. He was a doer. Could she trust him? Ah, there was the rub. For whom did he plot? Why would anyone want the Coffeepot Inn?

She turned and looked at the place. It all needed help of some kind. Why would anyone deliberately want to put money into the Coffeepot Inn? Out there alone on a road that was two-laned. Who stopped at the Coffeepot? Who would bother?

Tim said, "I think we could decide on a fair price."

"I'm not ready to deal. I just got here today. I didn't know it existed." And she repeated it, "My great-grandfather Willed this to me."

"You've never been to see it before? No old feelings of nostalgia? You didn't grow up visiting here?"

She just said, "I have no idea what it's worth. I'll have to look at the books."

Tim smiled and his words were kind. "You'll understand, almost right away, what a relief it would be to get it off your hands, now."

"I'll . . . see."

So Tim told her very gently, "I don't know how long they'll keep the offer open."

She looked at him.

He smiled just like he was on her side.

"Well, we'll see." That nothing reply was so common to TEXANS. If they're a little hostile, they add to it, "We'll just see about that."

Tim walked alongside her, back to the Inn. He spent his time turning his head and visually inspecting the grounds, the cabins and that Coffeepot. He was then casual as if buying it didn't matter . . . at all.

The really interesting thing to Lily was that Tim didn't ask to look inside any of the cabin Cups.

Back at the Pot, Tim reached and held the door for her to enter, then he followed her inside. He smiled even at Bryan as he asked, "Any good doughnuts? I missed breakfast."

Bryan took a waxed paper slip from a slitted box and reached under the counter for a big squishy doughnut. He put it on a large plate. He drew a cup of coffee and set those on the counter for Tim.

That suited Tim because if Miss Trevor didn't sit with him, he wasn't alone at a table. At the counter, he was available, not isolated.

Tim bit into the squishy doughnut and closed his eyes to make long *mmm* sounds. He opened his eyes and looked at the indifferent man who was busy elsewhere. He asked his hostess, "Where did you find something like this doughnut?"

She questioned, "Bryan?"

"I make 'em."

"Do you come with the Coffeepot?"

And Bryan said, "No."

"Will you sell your recipe?"

"No."

Lily Baby looked over at Bryan thoughtfully. She didn't say anything.

"May I buy a dozen to take home?"

Bryan silently got a sack, snapped it open with obvious practice and put in a dozen. He folded down the top of the bag and put it beside Tim with no comment.

Tim finished his doughnut and opened the bag for another. "I'm hooked. How can we get you to sell doughnuts in our building downtown in San Antonio?"

Bryan shook his head. "I work for Miss Trevor."

"How do we get you involved in the realty business so we can get the doughnuts?"

Lily replied, "Not me. I have no interest at all."

"You'll have to," Tim chided with charm. "You need to sell this place. How many offers have you had in the last five years?"

Lily considered his words. He was very clever. Just "need to sell," not "we want this place" as a bargainer. He was trying to get them to cave in and accept any price with this opportunity to get rid of it.

Interesting.

She didn't reply. That was even more interesting to Bryan.

When Tim took out the third doughnut, she mentioned, "You'll get fat."

Tim reminded her, "I didn't have breakfast."

"You need grain cereals instead of those wickedly perfect doughnuts."

Tim laughed out loud! He said in Bryan's direction, "A woman sells doughnuts as a business and she recommends cereal."

"She's right."

That got another genuine laugh from Tim. "Why do you sell doughnuts that wickedly delicious, if you think clients should eat something else?"

In a level voice, Bryan replied, "People ask for them."

"I see." Then he said, "As a buyer, I ask for this place. How about bending to that?"

Both observers said, "No." But the female voice yet again said the revealing comment, "I haven't looked at the books."

"Let's get them out and look at them now."

Both of his audience said, "No."

And a truck driver walked in. He greeted Bryan heartily and wanted to know if the little lady was waiting for a ride.

All three witnesses said, "No," right off.

Lily was matter-of-fact, but both males were alert and watching. Their "no's" had been instant and positive.

The truck driver laughed.

Lily ignored him.

When the truck driver left, he took a sack of the doughnuts along.

Tim asked with interest, "How many of the doughnuts do you make each day?"

"Depends."

Tim smiled. He was so amused by Bryan's hostility because he understood it exactly. And he figured Miss

Trevor had no clue to why Willard was so hostile. She would glance at the man in a way that revealed she wondered why he was acting as he did.

Women aren't very cognizant. Especially about men.

When he could extend his visit no longer without seeming dumb, Tim shook hands with them both, gave Lily some more of his cards, and he left.

As he went to his car, he took another doughnut from the bag.

In the Coffeepot Inn, Lily told Bryan, "We ought to call this The Doughnut Shop."

"It's a Coffeepot. What'd that guy tell you outside? He was talking the whole entire time. What'd he say?"

"Just that he didn't know how long the offer would last."

"Did he say how much?"

"No."

"Then it's bigger than we think."

"Or smaller?"

It was only then that Bryan finally smiled.

Two

It was as Lily and Bryan sat again at the counter that Bryan advised, "You need a lawyer before you do anything at all about this offer. Since Morgan didn't give you a bid of some kind, he's being too sly."

"I have a cousin over in San Antonio who is a Realtor. I'll ask her."

"Do it."

As she rose from her chair, she inquired, "Where are the books?"

"In the office, upstairs."

Lily grinned at her cook. "Logical."

And Bryan added, "Since San Antone is taking over all this territory, they're trying to make us feel a part of them, and they've taken over our telephone system. You can make a local call to your cousin."

"I'll go up to the office."

"You got Morgan's card?"

"I have—" She took the cards out of her pocket and counted them. "Five."

"He's buying. He's got a reason to push. I just wonder if—" But Bryan stopped and just looked at the morsel who was Lily Trevor.

She wasn't conscious of his implication, she said, "I'll go call my cousin right now."

So she went along the back of the counter to the stairs and went up the curving steps to the upper floor and into the hall there. She automatically went into the first door, and it was Bryan's room.

Since she was alone then, she looked around more carefully. There was nothing outrageous like pictures of naked women or anything like that.

Then she turned away and crossed the hall to the office.

Downstairs, Bryan mapped her movements by the sounds of her steps. She'd gone into his room and stopped dead. He wondered why she had stood there that long minute. What had she seen? He would have to wait to go up there and look at his room from her point of view.

He tried to remember if his bed had been made. It had. He'd shown her his room. Why had she looked there again? And Bryan gazed out of the window and he was lost in foolish imagination.

Upstairs in the office, Lily called her cousin, Marly Foster. She was with a client. She would return the call, please leave name and number.

So having done that, Lily hung up the phone. She looked at the row of books on the shelf above the desk. Probably the biggest surprise of the whole day was the neatness of the office. Was it Bryan? Or was it the mysterious Teresa?

The black books held the costs and profits of the years. The years' numbers were in gold. That year's book was neatly kept and up-to-date. There was a surplus, which startled Lily.

How could the bank have that much deposited, and none had been used to tidy up the place?

Lily had thought she would have had to spend days figuring and sorting and seeking. It was all there in tidy, updated neatness. All she had to do was open the book at the marker. And there it all was.

He certainly was honest. His salary was quite good. The business was quite good as well. How amazing. And even as she thought that, a school bus came and a noisy, cheerful bunch of kids was released to flow over the whole place!

Lily closed the book and went out of the office and down the stairs. She said to Bryan, "How can I help?"

"Wash your hands. Pour milk into glasses. Get out the spoons and napkins."

She did that while he did everything else. How interesting to watch skill. There are all kinds of things people do who know what they are doing. Bryan knew how to feed thirty-some-odd kids without seeming to be hassled.

To a neophyte, as she was, it was astonishing. Remarkable. He certainly earned that salary.

The locusts, who were schoolchildren, were everywhere. They ate and were gone in a very brief-seeming time. Time goes quickly when one is very busy. The two servers had been that busy.

All the doughnuts were gone. There had been exactly enough. She exclaimed over that.

And Bryan replied, "I was told they would be coming. We were ready."

"You did well."

He was already making up another batch of dough. She asked, "You'll need more?"

"I'll make some now, the truck drivers come along in an hour or so. And the dough will be just right early tomorrow."

"Should I do anything to help? Dishes?"

"We got the automatic washer."

"That was a good idea. Yours?"

"Your great-granddaddy was bendable. He—admired me. It was him that raised my salary."

"My daddy loved his granddaddy. Daddy said his granddaddy was a good man. I didn't know him very well."

"Neither did I. I met him a time or two. He sent me notes. He came and looked at the books, or he sent someone. He was an easy boss."

"Do you plan to stay here?"

His eyes were down as he kneaded the dough. "That'll depend on what kind of boss you are ... and what happens."

"What ... could ... happen?" She asked that with attentive curiosity.

"We'll see if Morgan comes back and what his next move is."

"You think there's something going there?"

"We'll—see."

* * *

Her cousin Marly called. "So what's the beauty want of the beast?" Marly was gorgeous and so secure in herself that—to another woman—she could rag herself without any problem.

"Who is Tim Morgan and why would he want to buy the Coffeepot Inn?"

Unexpectedly, so it was shocking, Marly drew in a quick, audible breath. "Tim?" Her voice was soft and vulnerable. "He's seen you?"

"He wants the Coffeepot Inn."

"What did he offer?" Her voice became businesslike.

"Wasn't it you who got it for our great-granddaddy?"

"Yeah. And he gave it to you."

Lily sighed with exaggeration and suggested, "Okay, now tell me what you got."

"Their house."

Lily exclaimed, "The one in town?"

"Yeah."

Lily said a soft, impressed, "Wow."

"I'll trade you even."

And Lily laughed. "Tell me about why Tim wants the Coffeepot Inn."

"So you call him—Tim."

"He insisted."

Sourly, Marly advised, "He's selling."

"That's what Bryan says."

Marly asked softly, "And who is this Bryan?" Then more quickly, she asked, "Is he the undershirt-wearing cook?"

"Yeah."

"My God."

"Marly, I get the most amazed impression that you *still* cotton to—men!"

"What else is there?"

"You do have a point."

Marly then said, "I'll snoop around and see if I can find out anything. Keep your hands to yourself, you're too young to deal with either the cook *or* Tim. Got that? I'm older and wiser, so you should listen."

"Baloney."

"As I recall, that's one of your mother's favorite words?"

Lily responded kindly, "It's brief and says it all."

"For a wet-eared kid, you come on very smooth and knowing."

"I graduated."

Marly sighed into her phone. "So I missed the last year. There weren't nothing more, no-how, they could cram down my craw."

"I believe it."

Marly laughed. "I'm glad you got some sense and came home. I'll be out with whatever gossip about Tim I can find... and I'll tell it all to *Bryan*—in one of the cabins, without lights. That's just so as we can be private with no eavesdropping, snot nose kid around."

Lily Baby responded, "With a phonic listener, I'll be against the wall, ear first, and I'll take notes."

"You would do that. I recall you as a child."

"And you were a gloriously budding *woman*. I remember you well."

Marly remembered, too. "You had such big eyes. But your ears were bigger."

"It will comfort you to know I've learned to be discreet."

"I see. That's why you said you'd stay outside the Cup when I was interviewing Bryan?"

"Of course."

Marly laughed. "I believe you've grown up enough to be tolerable. I'll check out what Tim's up to and let you know. Eat a dozen doughnuts for me."

"When did you find out about the doughnuts?"

"When I had the inn surveyed for the Will. At that time, I surveyed Bryan." Marly's sigh into the phone was very like the top of a tornado.

"That's what I really remember about you. You're so marvelously dramatic about men. I've never seen anyone who could collapse and roll her eyes the way you did."

Lazily, Marly admitted, "I'm more subtle now."

"That's probably good. Men can't really handle drama. At least not in public."

Marly inquired, "Now, how did you find that out?"

"Research."

Marly replied, "I always knew you'd get to be one of us."

Gently, Lily Baby responded, "I'm my own woman. I'm not 'one' of anything."

"Wow!"

"Come on out and let me visit with you. Bryan's doughnuts—"

"I know all about Bryan. I'll be there." And she hung up.

* * *

As Lily came down the curved stairs, two of the customers were leaving and three were still eating. The leaving two carried boxes of doughnuts.

Lily considered whether the people came there because of the coffeepot building, the food...or the doughnuts.

How did Bryan make them? She would have to snoop. It could take a while.

She stacked dishes in the washer and cleaned the tables. She listened and paid attention.

Bryan was really good at his job. With food, he knew exactly how long to cook it and when to turn it and whatever. And he was clean. He swept the floor before it really needed it. And he washed his hands.

He wiped the counter with a clean cloth...every time. He changed his towel apron if it showed one stain. He changed his undershirt to a pristine white shirt with the sleeves rolled up. He was a stickler. He'd always worn a pristine undershirt, but now a lady was there.

Teresa's oldest boy came to help out for two hours after school. In the afternoon especially, truck drivers were tired and needed a stop, and they stopped at the Pot. The youngster was very quiet but watched and concentrated on helping. Bryan called him Joe. Bryan was a good, patient teacher.

They were very busy until just after ten that night. Bryan had made Lily sit down and drink some orange juice. He'd used a juicer. The pulp was in the fluid. It was delicious. The oranges had been cold.

She was exhausted.

She'd chewed and licked off her lipstick. Her hair was neatly behind a band. She asked, "How do you survive?"

"I've been doing it since...for a long time. Your great-granddaddy double-crossed me when he Willed the inn to you. I thought he was going to let me buy it from the estate."

"So. You want the inn, too?"

His brown eyes widened and his face was vulnerable. "Too?"

Not paying any attention to what was obvious, she replied, "So does Tim Morgan."

"Oh."

It was so late, and they'd been so busy, that it was too late for her to go to Teresa's. So Bryan took her to the best of the Cups. It was neat and clean.

Very kindly, Bryan told her, "It'll be easier with each day."

She nodded.

He put her overnight bag onto an opened folding rack, and he stood there looking at her. How could he be so lured? She was too young. Probably most of her lure was that she didn't yet realize how alluring she was?

He even tested the shower. When he had no other reason at all, he said, "Good night. I'm just over yonder if you should need anything."

"Thank you." She then yawned so that she bent her head forward and her lax fingers went to her forehead. "Give me a call when you get up. I need to understand this place."

"Ummm." A nothing reply.

* * *

Lily slept dead out, unmoving, dreamless. She finally moved about ten the next morning. She was a little while in puzzling out where in the world she was and why. She looked at her watch and saw how late it was. She decided it wouldn't change the world that she wasn't up and doing.

She stretched and gently rolled one side to the other to see if everything still worked. Her body was reluctant and a little cross.

The world wouldn't stop if she didn't get right out of bed. It would go on. She didn't need to be that alert and ready. She lay there thinking the mattress was okay, the pad and sheets were pristine. The room was sparkling clean.

It was a nice place.

The shower was exactly right and the stall for it was spotless. Everything glowed. Teresa must be a paragon. What was she paid? She probably ought to have a raise.

Lily put on light blue, cotton trousers and an elbow-length dark blue cotton pullover. Her muscles were a little sore from the long drive from Indiana. And there was the different response from the muscles she'd used in helping Bryan though the evening hours the day before.

She'd kept the floor clean, and the tables wiped. Bryan wouldn't let her use the same cloth to wipe a second table. The laundry must be something! Where was it sent?

She went over to the Coffeepot, and Bryan put down his newspaper as she came into the inn. He looked at her with a small smile.

She chided, "You let me sleep."

He was startled. And through all her gasps, he asked, "You don't remember me stripping your nightgown off and dressing you and carrying you over here at five this morning? You cooked the eggs and poured the cereal!"

"I did not."

"Well," he agreed slowly with a fake frown. "You were a little dim, but you did try. I had to keep you from pouring honey syrup over the eggs."

In a deadly, dramatic voice, she told him, "I haven't yet eaten breakfast."

"We were kinda busy."

If his eyes hadn't sparkled so, she just might have believed him. "I want cereal with pecans, raisins, apricots and grapes."

"The raisins are grapes. I can find the pecans and we do have dried apricots."

"Good. Now. I'm starved. I don't remember eating last night."

Bryan assured her, "You ate supper at seven-thirty and you had a doughnutS at ten."

"A...doughnutS?" Lily inquired with a puzzled frown.

Bryan replied with earnest kindness, "I was being subtle in minimizing how many you ate."

"Is that why I feel so loggy?" she gasped. "I can hardly move."

He was kind. "It's muscle. You haven't done anything like that in a long time, if ever. You were remarkable help yesterday."

With his wordage, Lily slitted her eyes. He was saying in a polite way that she'd been a nuisance and underfoot. She told him in a deadly firm voice, "I helped."

"You certainly did."

She began to smile.

Bryan's eyes danced. He licked his lips. He shook out the morning newspaper and organized it as he handed it to her and said, "Read the paper. I'll get your cereal."

"Did you ever get to sleep?"

"I had no trouble. Some fairy godmother came and waved a wand to make everything neat and orderly."

"It was I."

"By golly, you're right!" Then he told her, "You had a call from your cousin. She has a very sexy voice. I don't believe I've ever heard—"

"Marly. Watch out for her," Lily warned the thirty-year-old man. "She'll eat you alive."

"Wow."

Lily Baby looked up with partly squinted eyes as she considered Bryan. She shared knowledge. "Men are very strange. You should be terrified."

He told her softly, "*You* terrify me."

"Baloney."

After Lily had demolished the entire bowl of cereal and drank her milk with satisfaction, she went upstairs to the business phone where she put in a call to her cousin, Marly. As was predictable, Lily had to leave a message.

So it was past noon and in the premidafternoon doldrums when Bryan was cutting out doughnuts and dropping them into gently boiling oil when Marly called. "Nothing, yet," she told Lily, "but something doesn't ring right. I'll be in touch. Tell Adonis not to do anything I wouldn't do."

So with interest, Lily Baby inquired of her cousin, "What wouldn't you do? About what sort of thing did you have in mind?"

Marly laughed and hung up.

Lily went back downstairs. Teresa was there. She was scrubbing the floor. She banged chairs around like a ferret after a mole. When Lily got to the counter, Teresa stood up and smiled at her. "Welcome to your own house."

"Ah, Teresa, you are a wonder. That cabin is so spotless. And you do such a good job here."

"So does Bryan."

Lily frowned and said, "Hush! Don't tell him he's a genius. You'll ruin him."

Teresa laughed and shrugged as she generally did. "He is a genius."

"You are right. His doughnuts! Ahhh."

"I take home the ones not perfect."

And Lily gasped. "He makes doughnuts that *aren't* perfect?" She took a step back and put her hand on her nice chest as if in shock to hear such words.

Teresa loved it. She laughed and went back to attacking the floor's surface. She worked furiously.

Apparently, there'd been other overnight guests. How amazing that even with the carelessly kept outside, there were visitors. Then she considered. The people who came there knew the place, and they knew how clean it was inside. It was the food that lured them to the big Coffeepot Inn. It was unique.

With Teresa there to holler if a guest arrived, Lily took Bryan up to the office. He'd been so sure that she was taking him to his room and with Teresa aware of them! So when she went into the office, he was very disappointed. However he would have been some shocked if she had accosted him with Teresa just downstairs.

Men have it rough.

Lily opened the books, with which he had to be familiar, and she said, "We can afford to have the place spruced up."

He nodded, but he told her, "It's your money now."

Her eyes got quite large. "Mine?"

"Actually, the profits were yours—to your great-grandfather. He never touched it. So it's accumulated."

"You should have taken some and had the grounds trimmed."

Bryan watched Lily. Then he replied softly, "Let's not do it—yet. Let's wait to see what Morgan has in mind."

She considered Bryan, as he looked back at her. She said a nothing, "Ahhhh," of understanding. "We don't need to be bought, and you're curious why he wants the place, so you want me to back off and let him sweat."

"It's just that I wonder, why a Realtor? He seemed interested in the hill in back of us. He mentioned the hill. Why would he say anything about the hill? There could be a testing about building something back there."

She scoffed. "Ahhh. But this side of the town isn't that great. It's neat and tidy but it's modest."

"We are on beyond the town. He could be feeling you out." Bryan said those words and the reality of the try hit him so he then said, "Don't let him get close to you."

"You think he will lure me in order to get the Coffeepot?" She couldn't not laugh and she did.

"I haven't touched you."

That surprised her. "No. Why should you?"

"You've only been here about twenty-four hours." It was as if he was reminding himself of that fact. He went on, "You need to look around and you need to absorb what all it takes to run this place. You might want to sell it to me."

"To you?" She looked at him rather startled. He wanted the place for himself and her out of it? That disappointed her somewhat. Her spirits dampened. She was silent.

Bryan went on, "If you need to sell, sell to me. That guy could put anybody in here and the place would collapse. Teresa and I have kept this place going. The traveling people who stop here, come back.

"We got a good reputation among the salesmen and truckers. They like this place. People stay here. They take pictures of it. It is different from what they generally see.

"We got reservations for the Cups for a coupla months ahead. There's the reservation book by the phone. Look at it. If Morgan comes back, be careful. Keep what you know to yourself. Don't give any promises. Wait."

Lily Baby told him, "I'm listening. You know more about this place than I. I'll do as you suggest."

He warned her, "Your cousin could convince you to sell. Watch yourself with her."

She agreed, "If there are any meetings, I'll include you. This is your place, too."

Bryan shook his head. He was very serious. "It's all yours. I just work here."

But she said seriously, "I need your input. You know more about the place than I."

"You saw the books."

"There's more money here than I would have believed."

And Bryan told her again, "Your part is an accumulation. Remember that your great-grandpa didn't take out any of the profits. He left them to you."

"We can get the yard tidy."

He watched her seriously, then he began a slight smile. He said, "Teresa's husband can do that."

"How do I contact him?"

"Ask Teresa who you should get and how much you should pay."

"Ask . . . her?"

"She's so honest, she'll see to it that you get it done reasonably."

"Ah, Bryan, what would I have done without you?"

"Your great-granddaddy did it all."

So curiosity made Lily ask, "Were you here when he bought the place?"

Bryan nodded. "He tried the doughnuts."

"And that did it?"

"Yes. All the rest of his life, the several years, he had our doughnuts every single day. That's why he lived so long. They're good food."

"You wicked man! All that grease and sugar?"

"It's invigorating."

She laughed and her eyes sparkled.

He warned, "Play your cards close to your chest." And he prevented his eyes from doing more than a split second checking of her sweet chest. He told her, "Be careful even with your cousin. She's a business-woman. You look beyond that relationship to what the world is."

She narrowed her eyes and guessed, "You don't want me to sell this place."

He slowly shook his head. "I've been saving up, but I couldn't counter a serious offer."

"We need to paint the Pot."

He watched her seriously as he said, "It's your place. Morgan will think you're trying for a bigger bid."

"We don't mind. He can think what he wants!"

And it was Bryan who laughed softly in his throat as he watched the budding woman.

So Lily Baby went out to the Cups and sought out Teresa. She helped make the bed and got in the way so, that she finally stepped back and left the woman to do it her way. But the entire time, Lily Baby was telling Teresa about the weeds and the limbs on the trees and how were they to find someone to handle it all?

Teresa stood up straight and eyed the neophyte. "My man does such. I tell him to come here."

"Thank you." Lily Baby smiled.

Teresa pushed up her bottom lip as she regarded the budding woman. "You let Bryan handle this. You leave my man alone."

Seriously, then, Lily said, "Yes, ma'am."

"Don't you tell him jokes or laugh around him or wiggle or talk to him or ask him questions or directions or anything. Hear me?"

"Yes, ma'am."

"Bryan tell him what to do."

"Thank you."

"Stay out of his way."

"Yes, ma'am."

"Your momma taught you manners."

"She worked hard at it."

"I believe that is so. Behave. Be careful with Bryan. He is the—vulnerable."

In surprise, Lily Baby asked, "Of me?"

Teresa stopped and sucked in the corners of her mouth. "Are you dumb?"

Lily frowned in puzzle. "How...dumb? About... what?"

And Teresa turned away in disgust as she told the Cup walls, "She is dumb!" Then she told Lily Baby, "Go, scoot, vamoose!"

So Lily Baby was ejected from her own Cup. She went back to the Pot puzzled and frowning.

Bryan asked, "What's the matter?"

She looked up and said in puzzlement, "Teresa told me not to speak to her husband and told me I'm dumb and to vamoose."

Bryan bit into his lower lip, but his eyes danced with humor. Then he had the gall to say, "That sounds normal for Teresa."

"She's like that all the time?"

"She scolds everybody, but you'd better stay away from Juan. Tell me what you want him to do, give me

a list and I'll tell him. That ought to ease Teresa a little. Stay out of her husband's way.''

Lily Baby became somewhat hostile. "I don't interfere! But I *do* know this place is *mine,* and I *ought*
to be able to direct what is *done* here!"

"You're right. But if we want either of the Lamars
to work here, we'd better do it Teresa's way. Tell me
what you want done, and I'll direct them."

Lily Baby turned to the stairs and she flung out her
arms and told the ceiling, "I don't believe this."

Three

So the next day, Bryan gave Lily a long, jointed bamboo pole. Bamboo is light and strong. At one end of the pole, he cut off the sturdy joint, split the cane and inserted a marking chalk. Then he bound it tightly. With it, Lily was set.

The pole made the whole nuisance of specifying which of what was to be trimmed much easier. With the marker, she could indicate where branches needed to be cut off.

She was diligent.

Bryan watched her from the Pot windows. She was so earnest. She charmed him. Not trying at all, she still charmed him. That realization made Bryan falter.

He had never met a challenge that he hadn't won, in some sense. Probably the only "winning" in this situation would be that Lily would be satisfied.

Tim could possibly be the man for her. Bryan needed another evaluation of Tim Morgan. Bryan didn't *want* Tim to return for an evaluation. He wanted Morgan gone. Out of there. Never to be seen again.

Outside, among the lacy, mean, thorned mesquites, Lily was completely concentrated on what she was doing. She was doing it very well. But she was something to watch. She stretched and reached and considered. But she was completely unaware of herself. She was concentrated on the tree limbs.

Maybe, what Bryan meant was that Lily was completely unaware of herself as a woman who attracted attention. How had that happened? What normal woman didn't realize she caught male attention?

Bryan turned from the windows and saw the male customers who were serious-faced as they, too, watched Lily.

That underlined what Bryan thought. Other men wanted her. It was in their faces. They were reasonably civilized, so she was relatively safe. With him. Lily was safe—with Bryan Willard? Not likely. His own daddy would split his gut laughing over Bryan being the protector of a woman.

That it was true was a sobering thing for Bryan to consider. He wasn't sure why his protection of Lily was so. It could be that he was mentally marking her for himself, or he could be mature enough that he valued women. Which was it for Lily?

And he decided it was her age. As young as she was, he was a good seven or eight years older than she. If she was then thirty and he thirty-seven, it would have been different, but she was only, just barely twenty-three. A neophyte.

The phone rang up in the office and Bryan picked up the extension. "Coffeepot."

"You must be Bryan. Hello!"

"Who's this?"

"I'm the baby's grown-up cousin, Marly Foster."

"Yes'um. What can I do for you?"

And *she* asked, "How much time do we have?"

Bryan replied, "None. She's out marking the trees to be trimmed. I'll ask her to call you." And he hung up. He was irritated with himself. He'd held women off before then. He'd been kind and subtle and withholding. How come Lily's cousin annoyed him that much?

Most men would rather make the first move. His response to her move is what's important. But there were no rules against him being aware of Lily, talking and looking, if he was discreet enough.

He looked out the window at the earnest Lily who was too young for him. He wondered if she'd make a move to tempt him. And his body groaned. Well, not his entire body. Just parts.

As he cooked, he knew he shared the earnest view of her with the clients who chewed, swallowed, drank and watched along with him. She was surely something. They'd all be back to look again. Most were earnest men who were married and committed. But they could look.

It wasn't until the trucks and cars were gone before she came to the door and leaned her pole against the outside of the Pot. She came in and went to wash her hands.

She needlessly said to Bryan, "I got some of it marked. Could you go out sometime and see if I'm doing it right?"

He admitted, "I saw you studying it. I think you're doing okay."

"I'd feel better if you would check it all out."

He was unreasonably pleased that she asked his opinion. His ego was stroked. What did he know about trees? Not one damned thing. Well, he knew they grew out of the ground and were different types. Some gave fruit, some nuts and some gave nothing. Mesquites gave out beans for likker and thorns that are nasty. That was about the whole shebang.

Lily drank a glass of water and sat down for about five minutes. Then she went back out with the arrival of several men and one woman customer for the Pot.

The men all stepped aside and got to watch Lily go down the steps and on out into the mesquite. One man stood on the cement step for a while and just watched until the door opened and his wife told him, "They said it's okay for you to come inside now."

The man raised his eyebrows just a tad, spit off to the side of the block as if he was having tooth trouble, and he went inside.

Somewhat gloomy, Bryan also watched Lily as he efficiently organized the orders. But he thought: Why her? Why this innocent who, just yesterday, had landed on him so casually? His feeling of protection for her was weird. He'd never felt responsible for any woman in all his life, not even for his mother, wherever she might be.

But this fluff had come in, and he'd felt all the vibrations thrumming through him. She was just lucky this wasn't a caveman time or guess where she'd be.

Then even as he watched, who should show up and find her out there all by herself, but Tim Morgan! Well, hell.

So Bryan saw as Tim Morgan strolled out toward where Lily was reaching, marking and not aware of the picture she made in men's minds. What was Morgan doing back there after approaching her about selling the Pot to him only yesterday?

What was pushing the man that he'd be so blatant as to show up again so soon? It was obvious. He was after that fluff. That innocent child-woman.

Bryan tensed. He glared down at the various foods he was preparing for those waiting, watching men. And Bryan was trapped inside only able to watch as Morgan gained on an unsuspecting woman.

Morgan took his own sweet time. Obviously, Morgan didn't call out. Lily Baby wasn't even aware of his slow approach.

Of course, she wasn't aware everybody in the Pot was watching her, either. Nor was she aware that Bryan Willard was one of the watchers.

Outside, Tim Morgan stopped near her and obviously asked what the he-heck she was doing out there?

Bryan knew Tim had asked that because then she gestured and explained and twisted and pointed and replied.

Any man wanting her attention would ask her questions. Then he could watch and listen. But he would mostly just watch.

Actually, Tim Morgan didn't give one hoot in hell what she was doing. Of course, maybe he thought she was improving the place to get a better bid? Not with mesquites. Even trimmed, they were still thorny and nasty. Nobody walked barefooted under mesquites.

Bryan saw that Tim stood and listened to her, giving her his full attention. She had no protection from a skilled man. Tim would have her in his car and off to God-only-knew-where in ten minutes.

Tim would say, "You need to see the area." He would say, "Being an alien, you ought to know the territory." He would say, "I have something interesting you ought to see."

That's what Tim Morgan would say, and he'd get her into his car and take her someplace else where Bryan Willard couldn't help her.

The hamburger on the grill burned. He scraped it off over the far end of the grill and slapped another raw round on to cook. He squashed it with a spatula with some deadly force.

Bryan noted nobody else had noticed the burned meat, which proved his own distraction. They, too, were all watching outside.

Along with the rest, Bryan looked out the window. Tim was taking off his suit jacket and loosening his tie. He took up the bamboo stick and tested it. He looked around as he obviously inquired which she needed marked.

Bryan turned over the hamburger patty. Then he got the other things off the griddle and onto plates or buns. He served those quickly. And he hustled the hamburger along.

One customer said, "I didn't get any coffee."

So he was served two cups.

Another said he hadn't gotten his milk yet.

And Bryan fixed that up, too.

One of the five asked, "That guy out yonder rattling you, Bry?"

And Bryan asked, "What guy?"

One of the others supplied, "The one's we's all watchin'?"

Bryan scoffed, "Him? She can handle him."

That got guffaws.

So the entertainment turned to baiting Bryan. He didn't mind. It took their minds off— No. They were still watching her. They were hoorawing Bryan, but they were watching on out beyond.

One said, "Maybe you just ought to go on out there and tell that city slicker to run along home, his momma's a-callin' him."

"Yeah."

That gave Bryan the excuse to look outside. It didn't help. He slipped the hamburger on its bun and put it on a plate. Then he looked back outside yet again.

Lily was laughing.

It was always irritating to a man when another man could make a woman laugh. It was so...intimate. That Morgan was being clever. He was pretending he had all the time in the world to get her to sell him the inn.

Damn.

But—

The very idea squiggled around in Bryan. Why would anybody want the inn? Why was Morgan being so clever and careful and interested in a nothing woman who had such a nothing inn?

And Bryan looked on beyond to the mesquite hill that rose in back of them.

When Morgan first came, he'd let slip just a word about the hill. Then he'd changed his attention to looking at the inn. Somebody wanted to develop the hill? And they wanted the inn . . . gone.

Yeah.

Bryan's eyes slitted and he considered. She could make a bundle if she just had the courage to wait long enough.

If she could just resist the time Morgan was going to give her, courting her into his frame of mind, she could win.

Morgan could . . . seduce her. Her mind . . . and her body. Then she'd be malleable, willing jelly.

Morgan could make Lily think he cared about her so that she'd give up the inn . . . and then he'd give *her* up. She wasn't in his cards. He was probably seriously courting a daughter of the head of his agency.

Bryan could taste bile in his throat.

How was he going to save her and the inn, and help her through this fiasco? If the situation was as he thought, it could be wobbling for her.

Byran scraped off the sheet of metal, cleaning it. He turned and saw all his customers had left. And each had left the money they owed.

He rang it up. Tidied. And he realized he was suffering for her.

A twenty-three-year-old girl, that young, didn't have the moxie to understand an underhanded man. Underhanded. Yeah. That Tim Morgan would probably handle Lily.

Where the hell was her voracious female cousin?

With everything under control in the inn, Bryan took a toothpick and stuck it in his mouth. He went out onto the slab that was the step up to the door of the inn.

And there, he watched openly.

Morgan saw him and ignored him. He obviously didn't mention Bryan was out on the stoop.

But when Lily saw him, she called, "Bryan! What do you think? Is it too much?"

And he strolled out from the inn and looked around as she waited for his opinion. Bryan told Lily, "You did a good job."

He said that because he figured anybody like Morgan would have to dominate, and he'd probably criticized her markings. He'd do that in a cheerful and teasing way, but he would want it done *his* way.

The two began to walk over to Bryan. She started and Morgan instantly joined her. He even left his suit jacket on a limb. That was interesting. He was either stupid or trusting or he didn't dare allow another man to say anything out of his earshot to this nubile woman.

Which was it?

Bryan said with a brief nod, "Morgan."

"Hi there, doughnut man."

That irritated the very hell out of Bryan. He said, "Hi, dirt man."

So Tim asked, "You talk to her about selling me the inn?"

"No."

"Whose side you on?" Tim Morgan laughed.

He was really selling. He wanted that land. *Was* it the hill?

As they approached the cook, the easy Tim said lazily, "I'm not sure my client *wants* the inn, but it gives me the excuse to come out and visit. How're things going?"

Bryan was stony-faced and didn't reply. But Lily Baby said openly, "Bryan is a genius. He can do anything. He made that marker for me."

That apparently startled Tim and he looked at it with interest. "You made this?"

Bryan saw no reason to confirm it. She'd already said he had.

She came onto the slab and stood next to Bryan. That little happening helped his ego. He looked over at her and she was looking beyond for the markings.

She groused, "You can't even see all the work I've done."

"I did. I saw from inside. The windows are just right." And he bit into his busy tongue. There had been no reason at *all* for him to comment like that to her.

She asked, "Would you call Mr. Lamar and invite him over to speak with you about the tree limbs and the weeds?"

Bryan nodded once as he replied, "I will do that."

And Morgan asked with a twinkle, "Need any help?"

"Not from you."

That caught Lily's attention and she slid a quick look to Bryan to see if he was serious. Since he was, she didn't say anything.

Foolishly that twenty-four-hour-acquaintance's heart was lifted. And he considered that he and Tim were no better than yowling tomcats.

So Tim went inside the Pot and took a seat at the counter.

In a low, intimate voice, Bryan asked the neophyte, "You want him gone?"

She shrugged in that eye-catching manner. "He's harmless."

That reply shattered Bryan's faith in her being an almost adult. He tried to be soberly dedicated. Helping her was all up to him. And he smiled.

He held the door for her, and they went into the Pot. Morgan was cheerfully patient. Did she notice? The buzz of the real estate world was a fooler. He didn't have this much time. He was pretending.

Bryan looked at her—what other her was there?—and she was looking around the inside of the Coffeepot Inn. She said, "Have you taken bids on painting?"

Because Bryan was suspicious anyway, his eyes slid over to Morgan and he saw the slight jolt that went through him. Now Tim Morgan would have to go to his boss and say to him, *Some female kid has inherited the Coffeepot Inn and she wants to spruce it up. It could cost us a little more?* The TEXAS questioning, do-you-understand statement.

But that jolt Morgan hadn't been able to stop gave Bryan a feeling of freedom. Tim Morgan was vulnerable. He wasn't the highflyer Bryan had thought. He was just like all the rest of us.

So it was the ideal time to call Juan Lamar. He didn't go upstairs to the office, he used the phone behind the counter. "Hey, Juan, how're you doing? Yeah. That right? No! This soon? Uh-huh. Hmmm. Uh-huh. Yeah. Well, could you come over and look at some of the trees? She wants them trimmed up. It's practical. Teresa said to call you."

That was the ringer, of course. So Juan was there in no time. He drove a very old and interesting pickup. He loved old cars. It shuddered to a standstill and the area was silent. The rattletrap pickup had quieted the birds and everything else.

Lily said to Bryan, "Find out how much, right away."

Her comment was an apparent show of lack of money that lightened Tim Morgan's heart.

The three trooped out. Bryan was speaker, as directed by Teresa. And with some courtesy, but avid interest, Lily Baby stayed her distance.

However, an amused Bryan moved so that he faced Lily Baby, and he repeated Juan's words and watched her reaction. It was very interesting to Tim Morgan. Communication was his whole life. He was silent as he listened avidly.

In his up-and-down, badly scrambled English, Juan questioned why any of the trees should be trimmed?

That caused Bryan's eyes to sparkle but his face stayed still. He replied in Juan's language, "The trucks are tall. They are harmed by the scrapings of the trees. The mesquites are mean and thorny."

Juan could understand that.

So he went around and looked and spit and blew his nose on a red bandanna. He sighed and squinted and finally said he'd do it for a hundred dollars.

Lily Baby grinned and shifted because that was a lot less than she'd thought, but Tim Morgan quickly took her arm and silenced her. Morgan did that. Bryan saw him.

So they dickered and walked and observed the size of the limbs and the cleaning up and how long it would take.

Bryan once mentioned, "It makes the best firewood. You ought to do it free just for the wood."

In English, Juan exclaimed, "All that work! You kid with me!"

So Bryan gestured openly as he stated, "I will ask Teresa what she told you."

Juan muttered. He paced. He was agitated. He scowled at Lily Baby and the slick man next to her. He glowered at Bryan. In Spanish, he said, "No less than seventy-five."

"Seventy and you clean it all up."

Then Juan cautioned, "You do not tell Teresa I was paid."

Fortunately, being a TEXAN, Lily had taken Spanish all along in her schooling. While she mentally corrected grammar, she did understand the exchange. She tucked her lower lip under her upper teeth and waited with avid interest.

The two bargainers shook hands. It was done.

It was then that Juan told Bryan Willard, "I would have done it for half that money."

"You will tell Teresa you got fifty."

Juan smiled.

The two again shook hands, and Juan laughed.

Bryan's eyes came up to Lily and she mouthed, "When?"

So Bryan asked, "How soon can it be done?"

"Another day."

"Tomorrow or I give the job to Roberto."

"Tomorrow? I have to get into the mood. The day after."

Bryan was firm. "Teresa said tomorrow."

So Juan said, "Half now. Half after."

"All when done."

Juan demanded soberly, "Ten now, sixty later."

"No."

Juan sighed and flung out his arms to flop against his sides. "You are the hard-nosed man."

"Yes." And Bryan looked up at Lily Baby to be sure she'd heard that exchange. He wasn't a man to be used carelessly.

But Tim Morgan took Lily's elbow and shifted her so that her attention could come back to him. He told her, "You'll need a little house to rent before you find the one you want. There's one near here in Quatro. Want to see it?"

"Well, I might."

"I have the time, right now."

"Okay. Should I change?"

He had been freed to actually look down her body. He did do that. He smiled and said, "You'll do."

"Your suit coat is still in that tree."

"Right." Tim went over to fetch it back and was putting it on when he noted that Bryan was talking to Lily...just that quick! He made his steps longer.

Bryan Willard was saying, "—not yet."

"I'll just go look. Is there anything we need in town?"

"No. You don't—"

And Tim took Lily's arm and asked, "Ready?"

"I probably need to brush my teeth and freshen my makeup."

Tim had sisters, so he understood she wanted to go to the bathroom. He smiled and said, "I'll wait right here."

Bryan was disturbed. He asked calmly of Lily, "How long will you be?"

She looked at him with some interest. Why did he want to know? So he considered Tim? He was harmless. What was the problem? She said, "When do I need to be back to help?" That was a clever signal to Bryan to give her a limit she could use with Tim.

But Bryan didn't know what to say to that. He was baffled.

So she asked Tim, "Will it be over an hour?"

And Tim said, "Maybe a tad."

She then smiled at Bryan and told him, "I'll be back before then."

Then she went to her Cup room and closed the door after her. She tidied herself and put on some lipstick, before she went back outside.

Bryan called, "Your cousin's on the phone." He'd gone inside and called Marly. She was not in her office. It was a clever ruse that *never* works. Lily was so amused.

She went to the phone and picked it up. The dial tone was patient and continued. She said to the dial tone, "Marly! I'm just leaving. I'll call you back in—" she looked at her watch "—almost right away. I'll be back in about thirty minutes to an hour. Bye, cousin." And she hung up.

She smiled at Bryan and said, "I'll be back soon."

But Bryan was sober-faced. He said, "Take the portable phone from your car. Call me if you need me."

That made Tim smile.

So in Tim's elegant car, they drove to Quatro, and the cross-country phone was plugged into the car's lighter as it sat on her lap.

Quatro was a bypassed town. There were charming, long-ago built houses and those that had been there since the multibuilding after World War II. But there hadn't been any building since then. The yards were nice, the trees were grown, and it was all settled. Accepted. Known.

There were three rental houses Tim had been given to show for that day. He knew the guy who had them for rent. Tim took her to each one and appeared to have all the time in the world for her to see the houses. He was charming.

So as they went through one of the houses, she asked Tim, "Why do you want the Coffeepot Inn?"

Dismissively, Tim shrugged. He told her, "I'd take it off your hands. I think we could resell it. I know someone who might be interested."

"Why?"

"Why are you there?"

She told him again, "It was Willed to me by my great-grandfather."

"You've only been there two days, why not pass it along to somebody who wants to work that hard?"

"I haven't said I didn't want it." She observed Tim. "Why do you want it? Who is your client?"

Good questions from the neophyte. He smiled. "I'll check to see if my client will name itself."

A slip. The "client" wouldn't have a name, it would be something larger to be termed "its self." Maybe Bryan was right in being suspicious? So being also a

TEXAN and with college shine, she asked, "What's going on?"

Tim raised innocent eyes and asked, "Where?"

She smiled a little and replied, "In your head."

It was not a question. She knew he was involved in something. She was suspicious of him. The tilt of her head and her level look made it obvious.

"I'll see what I can do to define this whole thing. Please don't mention any of it to anyone. This is between us. All right?"

"Okay."

And Tim cautioned, "Just give me a little time."

So they looked at the houses and all were fine. She just preferred to live in one of the Cups until she was used to the whole routine. She said, "I'll need some time."

"Well, if you're planning on selling, then you're absolutely right in this delay. There are great places handy in San Antonio. Want to see some of them?"

"Not now."

"How about dinner tonight?"

"I have to spell Bryan."

"You can cook?"

"Brilliantly."

"I'll come by after supper time."

"Not tonight. I'm exhausted from marking the mesquites. And tomorrow I have to discreetly watch Juan cut which branches. Bryan has to be involved because Juan's Teresa won't let me actually speak to her husband."

Tim loved it. His eyes sparkled and he grinned. "I'll come by and see how you're doing."

"If you come clear out here, you're losing valuable time from your work."

Tim assured her, "I can handle it. I want to be around you."

"That sounds flattering. Why do you want the Coffeepot Inn badly enough to waste time on me?"

Tim laughed. He tried not to, but he had to bite into his lower lip. As his eyes watched her, they danced with his humor.

She said, "Right. You can't tell me as yet. It must be interesting."

"Everything just about is, if you're curious. I'd like you to find me curious."

Without any rancor at all, she told him, "I think you're only briefly distracted."

And her words made him watch her differently.

Four

The fact that Tim Morgan was interested in that TEXAS tulip, Lily Trevor, who'd grown up in Indiana, was one thing; but for him to suddenly see her as a real person who was savvy was another thing entirely. Especially for such a knowledgeable man, she was a surprise.

So after Tim had delivered her back to the Coffeepot, he returned to San Antonio. There he logically asked his senior boss, "If a woman is savvy and expects me to be truthful, what should I do?"

The older man looked over at the agent who had his daughter mesmerized, and he asked cautiously, "Who is 'savvy' in the female division?"

"You know that Coffeepot Inn out yonder on the other side of Quatro by the hill? The owner just inherited it from her great-granddaddy. She's curious as to why we want such a place."

"She thinks it's tacky?" His voice went up in surprised delight.

Tim shook his head once as he replied, "No, sir, she smells a mouse."

"Uh-oh. How'd any woman get that smart?"

In a soft voice, Tim warned, "Careful, this is a new age. We can't speak out our minds no more, no how. She's equal."

The older man snorted.

Tim went bravely on, "This Lily Trevor is logical. You know her mother is a Davie? Yes. She is. Her partly Davie nubile daughter squints up her eyes just a little bit and asks, 'How come you want the inn?' Now what am I supposed to reply to that?"

"What did you reply then?"

"I said the buyer was anonymous, and I'd check to see if the identity can be made public."

"No."

"I doubt she'll be interested if she doesn't know what's happening. That old Coffeepot's been there a long while. She's already attached to it. She has plans for it. There are old customers who still come there. You do know about the cup cabins?"

"*Cup*—cabins?"

Tim nodded wearily and replied, "There are six cabins that are contrived to look like upside-down cups. It's really neat. People love the place."

"We want it—gone."

"I know, but what if they won't sell?"

Rather aloofly, his boss replied, "I'll probably fire you."

Tim gave no indication of alarm. He was so good at selling that nobody would be stupid enough to fire him. They'd adjust to what he didn't like. The older man considered. Could they move the project to another hill? How weird to even consider it.

Meanwhile, back at the Pot, Lily Baby was asking Bryan, "Would it be selfish of me to keep one of the Cups as my place?"

And he replied logically, "We can always rent that one room upstairs here in the Pot."

Disgruntled and chiding, Lily told her cook, "If you weren't such a stickler, I could have that room myself."

"*Teresa* would *throw* a screaming FIT!" He said it like it was the very *worst* kind of gossip *ever!*

Lily was patient. She said, "There's a bolt on my door upstairs."

He smiled as he licked his lips discreetly. Then he told her, "My door has a bolt . . . too."

"There!" she exclaimed. "You'd be perfectly safe! I'll move upstairs."

He held up his hand like a traffic cop. "You have to get Teresa's okay."

"It's *my* inn!"

Bryan shook his head once and enunciated, "That don't make no never mind."

Lily made an exasperated throat sound as she looked at the ceiling and she said, "There is *nothing* worse than a small town!"

"Honey, we're a part of San Antonio now? We're a city? Muncie, Indiana, don't hold no candle to San

Antonio? You do understand that fact." That last wasn't a question, it was a firm assumption.

And Lily Baby remembered her mother talking to her about men. It was unsettling to finally know one's mother could be right. Lily said, "Balderdash."

"Now where did you find that there impressive word and get it dusted off at just the right time?" He pronounced "just" as "jes."

"My grandmother on my mother's side. She was called Elizabeth? No nickname at all. And she didn't cotton to *any*thing. She questioned *every*thing. She was an out-and-out nuisance. My mother loved her."

"Now why would your gentle momma love an obstinate old lady like that?" Bryan asked as he studied the neophyte.

"Because after she left our house, my daddy thought my momma was superb, perfect, easy and nice. All the good things."

Bryan considered as he eyed the neophyte. "Your momma is a smart woman. I'd bet good money, those two were in cahoots."

"In cahoots?"

Bryan nodded. "The old lady pretended to be difficult so your momma could bask in the sunshine of peace after the old harpy left?"

"You scare me a little. I would *never* have questioned either of their behaviors. But now that you mention it, I do remember Momma and her mother softly laughing together like they knew a secret."

"Uh-huh, just like I thought."

She inquired, "How come you know so much about people?"

"I see them all the time and I listen."

And speaking of strange people, the very next day, Lily's cousin Marly Foster came in the door. Just Lily and Bryan were in the Pot.

Being the darling she was, and still so young and uncritical, Lily Baby jumped up and hugged her cousin.

Her cousin gave her an air kiss as she asked, "Where'd he go? I swear I heard his voice."

—and Bryan had disappeared! Vanished.

Like Alice in Wonderland, Lily Baby blinked a time or two and looked around. What had happened to the ratty-furred Cheshire cat? How'd he do that? She even discreetly looked at the floor for a trapdoor. None. Not a sign of how he'd managed his vanishing act. She'd have to find out how he'd done that. It could come in handy.

She poured a cup of coffee for Marly, and they sat at one of the tables.

Marly said, "I'm hearing questions?" The TEXAS questioning do-you-understand statement. "It seems like everybody knows something is going on around in the real estate area, but nobody can nail it down as to who or what all."

Marly lifted her eyebrows and went on, "It is fascinating! Thank you for calling me. I feel like I'm in on the cutting edge, but I haven't found one clue as to what it is or how I'm going to find out."

Lily commented, "Stimulating."

"Especially at this time of the year when it gets so boring."

"Right."

So Lily's cousin asked without any pauses, "How're you doing? Who is that gorgeous guy out yonder with the crew trimming your trees?"

"Trimming? Now?" Lily got up and went to the window to look out into the lacy trees. The ground was already littered with tree debris. Lily gasped, "Today?"

Her cousin looked at her with some concern. Marly said the obvious; she said, "Obviously."

"He wasn't to do it until tomorrow."

"A day early... and you're complaining? You baffle me. Lets go see if they're doing a good job."

"We might get in their way."

Marly scoffed, "You own the place. You can be wherever you want. We can go look in one of the Cups as if I'm thinking about buying the place."

Lily suggested, "How about pretending you want to spend the night?"

Marly smiled. "Who'd keep me warm?"

"A hot water bottle?"

Marly sighed hugely because she could do that so well, and her bosom lifted beautifully. Marly knew that, too. But she said, "Let's just view what's happening on the grounds and examine one Cup."

So they went outside.

Bryan came out of the drop under the counter that led to the basement—and to the shotgun down there. He stood back from the window and watched as his bird girl went with the buzzard out across the yard, watching and picking their way.

Lily was looking at the trees. Marly was looking at the men working with their shirts off.

The men looked back.

Lily had never before seen Marly so dainty with her steps. When she finally noted the men, she was laughingly disgusted. She growled to her cousin, "For Pete's sake, Marly, behave!"

And Marly retorted gently with big eyes, "I *am* behaving like a lady."

"What sort of—lady?"

"Hush!"

Juan had a chain saw working and was cutting up the fallen limbs into firewood for his wife. Teresa was there! She was directing the men. She was making two piles of wood.

In a growl, Lily told her cousin, "Straighten up, there's a wife here. She'll knife you if you look at her husband or brothers. Behave."

So Marly took a measuring look at Teresa and changed. She was convinced. She went into the Cup and looked around. She said, "Nice." And she was out and walking around outside of the busy area to her car as she called, "Gotta go. I'll be in touch."

And she was gone.

Teresa came over like a thundercloud and asked, "Who was that hussy?"

"Now, Teresa, she's my cousin."

"Keep her out of here." And with that Teresa turned away and left to go back to supervising the woodpiles.

It turned out that one pile was for next winter's fireplace in the inn. The fireplace was small and the smoke went up the chimney and out the coffeepot spout. It was clever.

With Teresa's good eye, there were some of the marked branches that were left on the trees. It was not their time to be cut. And Lily agreed. She even told Teresa with candor, "You're right about those branches. They do need to stay there a while."

Teresa looked at Lily observing the whole of the yard, and Teresa blinked.

After that, Teresa would tell Lily Baby what was being done and why. She still didn't ask permission, but she did speak to Lily and she did explain what was to be done.

Lily would nod. She would say, "Um-hmm." She would say, "That's logical."

And she said that last so much that Teresa took it up and used it, too!

Gradually Lily's San Antonio kin found out she was there and visited. Especially the Davie branch of her mother's family told Lily, "Your mother said you were here!" They would come to the Pot and they left with doughnuts. And Lily was included in Davie family doings. The packed days passed.

And in that time, Tim would drop by to see Lily. He'd have a doughnut and he'd visit with whoever was there. Sometimes Lily was with kin in San Antonio. And hearing it, Tim wilted a little.

Bryan didn't mention the wilt to Lily, but Teresa relayed that observation. She did that deliberately because she wanted to see how Lily would react to Tim wilting.

Lily didn't appear to notice the wordage. She just said, "Umm." And then she'd ask what Teresa was doing. And she'd hunch her shoulders a little to withstand what in hell the woman was doing *now!*

Teresa said, "We need flowers." She gestured. "There and there and over there."

The proposed places were odd. Lily said firmly, "I'll draw up a plan." But while she was drawing, Teresa had her husband planting. It was a done deal.

So Lily asked Bryan, "Do you ever have the feeling you're not in control here, and Teresa is?"

"Yeah."

Crossly, Lily Baby complained, "Why don't you assert yourself?"

Quite smoothly but with a suspicious deepening of his eye crinkles, he replied, "I'm waiting for you. You're the owner—and boss."

And Lily Baby got testy.

As the days passed, Lily was still sleeping in the best of the Cups. One night when all five available Cups and her empty room in the inn were filled, two men slept on Scout bags in the inn's basement.

Lily told Bryan, "I ought to have my own room. Those two could have slept in my cabin. Did you charge them?"

Bryan nodded, "Half."

"That seems greedy."

"They were safe, slept hard, and they stole about a dozen doughnuts from the cooler down there."

"How shocking." The tone was all wrong.

He scoffed at that. "You can do better."

So she looked at her hand before she curled her fingers in a varying sequence, then she put the back of that hand to her forehead with the curled fingers out and she said again, but flatly, "How shocking."

He sighed and looked out the window as she went back to placing doughnuts in a box.

He told her in exasperation, "You can do that better."

She looked up at him and raised her eyebrows.

He directed, "Drama. If you're going to put the back of your hand to your forehead, just so, then you have to follow up with body language and *drama!*"

"Oh, hell." She moved her mouth around and her whole body made little jerky movements of disgust. Then she rearranged her fingers to curl just so, with the index finger straight and the other three curled in steps. She put the back of the hand to her forehead. She tilted her head back, bowed her body and closed her eyes.

Bryan said suspiciously, "You've done that before."

She calmly went back to boxing doughnuts. "I have my cousin Marly who knows all the tricks. Then there's Lucille, Anne, Ellen and Rose." She soothed him with the gentle fact, "I'm actually a Davie. I take after my mother's side of the family."

"As I recall, there was your sneaky grandmother on your mother's side?"

Lily explained, "My mother's mother was not a Davie. What they did was playacting for impact." And she added with impatience, "The others are simply useless attention-getting drama."

He watched her. "You're not dramatic?"

She shrugged in that fascinating, although minimal manner. "I would be, if I knew how."

He said admiringly, "You curl your fingers quite well before you lay the back of your hand to your forehead."

She shook her head once as she explained, "My real problem is that I have to place them first. If I had the talent of the others, then I could just put the back of my hand to my forehead and the fingers would know to correctly curl, on their own."

She was still just communicating, and putting doughnuts in the box. So he could bite his lower lip to control his laughter and watch her. She was a gem.

Another day, Bryan came back downstairs from his nap and found Lily looking out into the trimmed and neat mesquites. He asked, "What's wrong?"

"It doesn't look natural. It's too neat. Teresa made the flowers look deliberate."

Bryan spoke slowly to comfort her, "For a coffee party, which this place implies, the flowers wouldn't be—strewn—across the table."

She considered the area. "You're right."

How amazing that she could give in and not argue for her way.

Then she said sadly, "I rather liked it tacky."

His smile was tender, his throat a little rough as he said, "A nature girl."

She sighed. "I suppose."

But she wasn't adamant about it. She was again packing doughnuts. She finished a box and began another. She asked, "How many doughnuts do we actually sell?"

"I don't keep track. I just make more when we run low. I'll put a paper on the board and mark them, if you'll remind me now and then."

She looked at him. "You work hard."

"I'm not bored." He smiled and he heard the clack in the back of his throat. It was revealing. Had she heard it?

She commented, "I should think the doughnuts would finally start marching past in your dreams, row on row."

He held up a hand. "Don't even *say* that! It'll start!" Then he put his hands to his head and his face became alarmed and stark. "It's starting! It's *starting!* All because of *you!* You had to go and say it all!"

She was laughing, and he was still being dramatic when Tim came inside. He didn't like what he saw.

Through her laughter, she was pulling down Bryan's hands and saying, "It's all right. I'm here, and you're okay. Don't be afraid."

Bryan had looked at her and his face had changed as he—

And Tim asked, "What's going on?"

It was obvious that Tim's voice was a little hostile and he was intense.

Bryan became still and stony.

Still laughing, Lily Baby told Tim, "All those millions of doughnuts he makes are beginning to march row on row though his mind."

Tim was watching Bryan but he said, "Yeah," in response to Lily's comment.

Tim sat on one of the stools near to where Lily had been working. He was still watching Bryan, whose hands were in his pockets under his pristine bib apron.

Lily moved the doughnuts to another counter. In the odd silence, it was Lily who asked, "Coffee?"

"Lemonade."

Bryan got the pitcher from the refrigerator and poured the glass. He rang the price on the cash register, and set it and the glass in front of Tim.

Lily smiled and picked up Tim's bill. Then she went over and took the charge off the register. She then asked Bryan, "Did I do that right?"

"Yeah."

Sassy and grinning, she told Bryan, "I'm getting good at this stuff. If I could just do your doughnuts, you could have a day off!"

Bryan breathed again. For that split second, he'd thought she was going to say she could do without him. But she'd said he could have a day off. What would he *do* with a day off? Sit at one of the tables and watch her? Probably.

Why her?

And Bryan looked at Tim with hostility and compassion.

What a mix.

Bryan hated the guy for being there, yet he understood why Morgan was there. And Bryan understood why Tim looked—mussed. Obviously, he had put his hands in his hair in despair, and he wasn't paying attention. Tim was different from when he'd first come there to encounter the deadly neophyte.

That was when Bryan realized he was a contender. He wanted Lily. So did Tim. One would lose. Which of them would be the loser?

It would be . . . Bryan Willard.

There was no way he could compete with such a setup as Tim had accrued. And Bryan knew that he should give up on Lily, now, before the whole thing got out of his control. He would lose anyway. Now was the time to back off.

Could he?

He looked at Lily with clear eyes, and she stood in a halo of magic. Her movements were perfect. Her humor. Her modesty. Her lack of the need to take over and rule. No woman matched her.

And Bryan knew that he could catch her attention. She was interested in people. He'd watched her with their customers. She had exactly the right interest without being luring. She didn't think about her own self. She would see his own regard for her and it would touch her. She wouldn't want him to hurt, and she'd be torn.

He could love her enough to give her up. He could save her that hurt, that anguish. He was that noble. Well, damn. He looked at Tim and saw that he would probably be a good husband. He would be distracted, but he obviously was reluctantly drawn to her.

Bryan's eyes slitted. Did Tim think this was just physical and a tussle in the hay would solve it? There was no way Tim was going to have such an opportunity! Not even if Bryan had to get Teresa to go along with them anywhere Tim wanted to take Lily.

Now, how would Lily take the idea of having Teresa along on a date?

Not too well.

Then, maybe, *he* ought to go along? She would probably accept that. She wasn't yet snared. However, Tim would more than likely find some way to lose Bryan somewhere along the way.

By then, Bryan had made another batch of doughnuts and was mixing the dough for yet another. They didn't *need* any more doughnuts. Bryan knew that! He was losing his control. She was rattling his brain. Why had her great-grandfather done this to the vulnerable bystander who was Bryan Willard?

And his squint-wrinkles became white. What if the old man had set this whole thing up and left the money in the Pot to lure her there so they could meet? Had that old coot been a . . . matchmaker?

What if— What if the old man had planned that Bryan Willard was to be her husband? Couldn't he at least try? The old man had raised his salary to that of an owner. Had that been to keep Bryan there? And he looked on Tim, then, as no different than any other yahoo who walked around in pants that needed a fly.

Tim wanted Lily to go with him and look at some apartments for rent.

"I can't now. Bryan's made more doughnuts. I have to wait until they are exactly cool enough before I box them."

Tim said in a serious way, "I'll buy the whole batch, if you'll go with me now."

Bryan's heart beat in thuds that moved up near his Adam's apple. Adam's apple. Adam had taken a bite of the Forbidden Apple and the bite was eternally caught in men's throats. Why did God punish all the men in the world for one man's foolish sin? Well, maybe that's why men still did forbidden things? They already were marked as sinners by the Adam's apple, so why not?

But Bryan was watching Tim in such a way that when Lily glanced at Bryan, she knew he didn't want her to go. So Lily Baby replied, "You can have all the doughnuts for a two percent reduction in price! But I can't go anywhere now. We're going to get another load of kids in ... Oh, I didn't tell you, Bryan. When you were napping some driver called and said they'd be here in one hour. He said he'd contacted you."

"Yeah."

So *then* Lily smiled at Tim and asked, "For two free doughnuts, you can stay and help with the kids." She was testing him. Would he stay for her? Or would he slip away and avoid being involved?

She watched Tim.

He wasn't thinking straight and said, "I've got to see about a house we sold that has no water as yet."

Kindly, Lily mentioned, "They must be irritated."

Tim shook his head. "They haven't moved in as yet." He pushed up his lower lip and looked at Lily. He almost shook his head as he sighed. He got up and said to her, "Come with me."

She smiled. "The kids'll be here in about—" She looked at her watch. "Twenty minutes."

That was too long to wait. And she would be too busy after the kids got there. Very serious and rather sad, Tim said, "I'll be around."

She smiled kindly. "We'll have fresh doughnuts."

Tim left the Pot, went to his car and drove gently away. It was as if he thought she would come running out and go with him. She did not.

Bryan said it. It shocked him even as his mouth said the words. "Tim has a crush on you." At least he'd avoided the word *love* in the blurted statement.

Lily Baby scoffed. "He just wanted to take me to that empty house. There, he'd want us to compare naked bodies to see how different we are."

In actual shock Bryan asked, "Who tried that?"

"I was about six."

"And the other tries?"

"They were all clever, but I did understand. Just like now. Tim thinks he has a crush on me."

Bryan's words, "He...thinks...he has?" were said in shocked surprise.

"You probably haven't noticed, but he's been coming out here when he really doesn't have anything to say and he has too many other things to do."

Bryan was asTONished. "You know that?"

Openly, as to a friend, Lily explained, "Females learn about males long before males even notice us. Of course, there *was* Billy D. He was eight."

Tension stopped ebbing from his distraught body, and Bryan asked, "What did Billy D. do?"

"He kissed me."

"That wicked, wicked boy!" It was only then that Bryan found he could smile again. He asked, "How old were you?"

"Six."

"So you started your scarlet career at... *six?*"

"I thought the kiss was sloppy and I wouldn't allow another for a long, long time."

Bryan sighed rather gustily for his own relief but he made it appear to be compassion for his gender. "Clumsy males ruin women for the rest of us."

"You are astute."

And he volunteered quite kindly, "I can show you that kisses can be very nice."

"Not now. It's almost time for the kids."

With her reply his whole nervous system shivered and bumped into each other and ran wild.

Women ought not do something like that to an almost innocent man.

She was a neophyte. That was the most dangerous thing a grown man could try to deal with . . . and survive.

Five

The bus that arrived wasn't filled with children as Lily had told Tim. And Bryan wondered why she had lied to Tim. The very idea of a busload of children was probably what had driven Tim into flight.

Instead of active children who needed control, it was a bus trip of retirees. Looking at the Pot, they came slowly from the bus as they looked around, gestured and exclaimed.

Everybody loved the Coffeepot Inn. But probably the older people were the most charmed. Seeing the Pot took them back to remembering another time.

The meal was a half sandwich, a salad and a sliver of pie. That day, the dessert was Bryan's custard pie, and it was perfect.

One of the Cup cabins was open for investigation. That lured most of the group. And of course, the circle of the drive through the mesquites was available for a walk. The guests loved Teresa's flowers. And they exclaimed over the Coffeepot and the upside-down Cup cabins.

They took pictures.

Inside the Pot, Lily said to Bryan, "We need some benches out yonder."

"Um-hmm."

She nudged, "Some wooden ones."

"Yeah."

"With slats."

Bryan looked over at Lily. She was at a window, watching outside as their guests strolled around and discussed . . . whatever.

Lily Baby said, "Let's buy that hill back yonder and build retirement homes on it."

Bryan guessed, "And all the retirees would come for lunch here."

"Yeah."

But Lily's suggestion wiggled around inside Bryan's brain. Again he wondered at Tim's tongue-bitten mention of that hill. Had it been a slip? Or had the vista been as charming to Tim as it was to everyone else?

Tim had never said another word about the hill. He just wanted the Pot.

Why would anyone want the Coffeepot Inn? Bryan did wonder who Tim was representing. And again, he wondered who actually owned the hill, which rose behind the Coffeepot.

Of course, Bryan had been over there, looking around like men do in order to judge an area. He'd been there fairly often. It was good exercise and it was quiet. There were armadillo, fox, turtles, rabbits and a skunk or two.

He'd also seen the laughing, sneaky, actual coyotes.

Occasionally there was a dog. The dog was courteously territorial and curious about an intruder. He never barked. He watched and kept his distance.

Cattle were periodically moved into that area to graze. The people at the Pot could hear the beeves sometimes in the day, or late at night if a coyote was prowling around.

There was a fresh spring on beyond. It gave enough water to start a flow even in parched weather. It was pure water. To begin with.

One night it was very late after there'd been a big celebration party at the Pot. Everyone was tired. The Lamars had helped out. They had enough relatives around that could be tapped for just about anything. They were all good workers.

The party had been an anniversary. The couple were now grandparents, and some years ago they'd first met there at the Coffeepot Inn. The group had driven down from Austin for the celebration.

The couple couldn't get over the fact that the Coffeepot was still there. They rented the third cabin for the big night. And after their Pot celebration dinner, the two had retired to their Cup.

The rest of the visitors were raucous and hilarious. They'd brought along horseshoes and banged them on garbage lids and hoorahed. The guests had sung and laughed, and finally they had all left the celebrating couple alone.

The Lamars all helped with the cleanup, and they, too, went home.

There were just the two left. Bryan and Lily. They saw the other guests tiredly walking off, to their own cabins, to their cars to drive home. All were sentimental and lighthearted. Some celebrations were that way.

The new bench the Lamars had made was sitting empty. So Bryan and Lily sat a while to catch their breaths and listen to the quiet with still-ringing ears.

Bryan looked over at Lily and said, "Now, *that* was a party."

She grinned with cheeks tired from laughing. "Having family around and supportive is primary."

"Yeah."

Lily asked with hardly any curiosity, "Where's your family?"

His slow reply was delayed. "Around." A dismissive reply that avoided any real comment.

That reply caught her lagging attention. "Around and about? Or around here?"

"Mostly around and about." Bryan was still avoiding any actual reply. "I hear from them now and again."

With some drollness, she commented, "How casual."

He agreed. "That about says it, all right."

After a silence, she was forced to ask, "Do you . . . miss them?"

He shook his head and shifted on the bench. "I'm too busy."

So then her curiosity pushed her into asking, "Would you make a good husband and father to your own kids?"

He couldn't move but his eyes shifted to her. He inquired softly, "In what way?"

"Would you be there for them?"

He took a while before he told her, "I never had that backup, and I got along okay."

She considered his words. Then she observed, "So you don't know how to nurture people?"

After some time, he replied, "Probably not."

And she said, "Oh."

He turned his head slowly and looked at her for a while, then he asked, "What's that 'oh' mean?"

"That I understood you." She stood slowly and stretched discreetly but not the way he would have liked to watch. Then she said, "You did a magnificent job of the party. Everybody had a great time." Then she asked with interest, "Where did you get those records?"

Bryan replied readily enough, "They'd said it'd been forty years ago. I just went to Pete at the record place, and he had tapes."

Still standing, Lily smiled down at Bryan. He hadn't risen. She told him, "It was very thoughtful of you to think of getting those tapes."

"I surprised them." And he was just a tad smug because they had been so delighted.

"You pleased them immeasurably."

"We got a good tip. I marked it in the book."

Lily suggested, "You take half. You worked the hardest. And give the rest to Teresa. She's the one who herded that bunch up here and controlled them.

Without Teresa, those Lamars would have taken over the party!"

His throat chuckle was very masculine. "They're a party bunch."

Still standing, she considered, "You're right. We should throw a party for Teresa."

"She'd cry."

"But she'd have a good time."

He considered before he agreed, "She might if she didn't take charge and run everyone around and about and nail people down to doing things."

"Maybe." Lily looked around the area. Then she suggested, "We could have more elaborate chairs for her and Juan."

After a silence, Byran asked curiously, "Why are we having this party?"

"For Teresa," Lily explained kindly. Then she went on, "She works hard, and she makes her family fill in for us."

He mentioned, "We do pay them."

Lily was sure. "It's still a generous and family push she makes for us."

Bryan shrugged. "Just tell her thanks."

"I've done that."

Positively, Bryan told the neophyte, "That's enough. Believe me. Give her a party and she'll drive you crazy paying you back and being grateful."

Lily laughed deep and quietly in her chest. The intimate sound was lethal to a susceptible male. His breathing changed and was noisier. He shifted on the bench and put one ankle on the other knee.

She was still standing. He was still sitting. She said, "Good night."

He sat there and replied, "Good night."

She turned and walked away with her remarkable feminine walk, which was straight and without any wiggles.

He shifted enough and watched after her. So he also saw that she got to and into her cabin alone.

Then he sighed, rose stiffly and pushed his hands into his trouser pockets. He hunched his shoulders and squinted his eyes. Then he breathed for a while.

Being a man was tough.

The next day, Tim came by yet again. He scolded, "What kind of party was here? How come I wasn't invited?"

While Lily Baby smiled, it was Bryan who replied. "You weren't a member of the family."

Directed, emphatic, Tim announced, "I saw all the Lamars here. If they're family, then so am I!"

Even Bryan smiled.

Lily explained kindly, "It was a fortieth anniversary of a couple who had their wedding breakfast here all those years ago. They just found out last year the Coffeepot Inn was still here. So we had the reception. The Lamars were servers and cleaner uppers."

With his lower lip out, Tim scowled. "I could have helped." Then he complained, "Everybody was laughing and having a good time."

"We'll give a guest party."

"We?" Tim asked cautiously.

"The Coffeepot will. We'll go through the receipts and see who are our most frequent guests."

Tim was emphatic. "I'm one."

Bryan denied that. "Lily gives you a free cup of coffee every time."

Tim asked, "How come you noticed that?"

Bryan went on complaining, "She's on my back about every penny!"

While Tim nodded in agreement, Lily objected and threw a dishcloth at Bryan's stomach.

Softly, Byran cautioned, "Be careful what you start."

Lily's eyes got big and she said to Tim, "Is he threatening me?"

Quite sassily, Tim replied, "You need a paddling and I'll hold you while he paddles . . . with a paddle."

She said, "No way," just as Bryan said a very serious, "No."

Tim frowned. He asked Bryan, "You don't believe in chastising sassy women?"

And Bryan's stern reply was: "No."

"Ah, heck, you're no fun at all."

Bryan was serious still. He told Tim, "I get my fun another way."

Lily said, "That again."

Tim got very serious and hostile. "Just what do you mean by, 'That again'?"

And Lily said, "His idea of 'fun' is cleaning the frying sheet and emptying the gutters. It's a *mess!*"

Tim's "Oh" was bare-eyed and sober.

And Bryan smiled at him in a one-upmanship.

But then Tim told Lily, "Don't let any man or woman ever abuse you. Tell me if that happens, and I'll take care of it for you." He was very serious.

But Lily Baby looked surprised. She replied, "No one has ever abused me." Then she added with a lift of her chin, "And no one ever will."

Tim said, "Good girl."

And Lily turned to Tim and put in quite sassily, "I'm a woman."

Tim grinned at her and said, "Good." Then before anyone else around could put in any word, Tim said to Lily, "Come with me today." It wasn't a question. It wasn't a command, either. It was an invitation.

She asked, "Where are you going?"

Tim rose and said seriously, "I have a couple of places to check out, and the ride is long between them. You can talk to me."

Lily turned to Bryan and gave him a level, studying look. "Am I busy today?"

But he didn't say that she was and would be, he said seriously as he watched her, "No. It's all done." He meant that she was indeed free. She controlled her own life. Would she understand that?

Or would she think he was rejecting having her around? Would she go with Tim?

She looked at Bryan with her head tilted just a tad and she studied him.

He very seriously watched back at her. What would she do?

And Tim was rising from his chair as he said, "Good, get a jacket. The air conditioner is a little chilly."

So then, Lily turned and looked at Tim. And she smiled the slightest bit. "I'd be delighted to go along." But she warned, "I don't care for smutty jokes."

Tim looked up with naked eyes and said, "I've never heard any, so I don't know any."

Even Bryan had to smile but it wasn't much of one. She was going with that guy. She was going to be alone with him. Without questioning, Bryan wondered: What would Tim do to her? What all would he say? Tim was a seller, he'd try to sell himself...to her. That Tim wanted her was obvious by his repeated, useless visits to the Pot.

Byran asked his neophyte woman, "How long will you be gone?"

Instead of replying, she turned to Tim and raised her eyebrows.

Tim said, "Don't expect her back until late. There's a great place for a perfect supper."

Tim said that to a man who was a cook.

So she took off her apron, and as she walked past Bryan to go around the end of the counter, Bryan growled at her, "Behave."

She paused that very brief almost nothing time to just look at Bryan with wide-open, innocent eyes.

It was a miracle Bryan hadn't swatted her sassy backside.

She said to Tim as she passed by him, "I need to change. I'll be right back."

With her gone to her Cup, Bryan took advantage of the time alone with Tim. He said to Tim what any contender says. He told Tim, "You leave her alone."

Time expressed surprise. "I have to be in the same car. I drive."

In a deadly voice, Bryan warned, "You know damned good and well what I mean."

Tim watched the hostile cook as he said, "I'm serious. I need time with her to understand if she could be as serious about me."

"Leave her alone."

Tim repeated, "We'll be in the same car."

"Don't you touch her."

With impatience, Tim complained deliberately. He told Bryan in and up-and-down voice, "I *may* have to hand her out of the car and be *sure* she's *secure* going up steps—"

"Steps . . . to what?"

"A front porch?" Tim never smiled or looked other than earnest. He was probably a superior Realtor.

"Don't you dare to harm her. If you do, you answer to me."

Almost gently, Tim explained to Bryan, "I know her family."

That only slitted Bryan's eyes as he asked softly, "What do they think of you?"

Tim shrugged like any vulnerable man and he told Bryan, "They don't avoid me."

And Bryan snarled, "Do they know you've been out here panting after her?"

"Yes. Her cousin Marly, whom you've met, has spread the word that I've been around here. You can depend on her telling." Tim added, "They also know about you."

Bryan frowned. "What'd'ya mean they *know* about me?" And he leaned forward with his jaw and put his thumb to his own chest.

"That you're of an age and looks that might lure her." Tim watched the expressionless cook. "Is she lured?"

"No."

Tim grinned widely and relaxed. "You've scared the spit out of me. You give me nightmares."

Bryan frowned. "Why?"

"You could have any woman you wanted." Tim explained that openly. "There's something smoky about you that is almost mystery." Tim gestured widely and added, "Women want to smooth out your life and make you happy."

"Who in *hell* told you *that?*"

"Her cousin Marly. I hadn't actually slept at night until Marly told me that. I talk to her about Lily just about every day. Marly gets bored fast."

And Bryan gave up on Lily. He said with a stony face, "Just be sure you're serious enough to be permanent."

"I think it's that way now."

The door opened and *she* came into the room, making it magic again. Both men's faces turned to her as weeds turn to the sun.

Tim rose as he felt his tie to be sure it was okay. He smiled without meaning to, and he said to the neophyte, "You're worth any wait."

She curtsied, pulling out the skirt of her dress just a tad. She didn't change expression. Then she looked at Bryan and she smiled just the barest little bit. She told him, "You get tomorrow off."

"No," he replied soberly. "I never know what to do—away from here."

Lily said airily, "We'll figure out an agenda."

And Tim laughed in his throat. He told Bryan in an aside, "I'll try to block that." And he took Lily's arm and eased her carefully out of the Coffeepot as he told her, "A man Bryan's age knows how to entertain himself. He doesn't need any help."

But back from the window, Bryan soberly watched as Tim carefully put Lily into his neat car before he went around to the other side, got into the driver's seat, in control, and drove them away.

A dead quiet fell on the Coffeepot. Bryan lifted his head a little to consider that. Before she'd come there, there'd been peaceful quiet times. He'd had the radio on and read the paper. It had been a hiatus for him. Why was he now aware...of silence?

As Tim drove Lily along toward San Antonio proper, he pointed out places he'd shown or sold. He talked about her family and those he knew. He was courteous about Marly in a distancing manner, which amused Lily.

He asked her questions.

She was so amused by Tim. He had either a book of questions or he'd been writing them down and memorizing them. He knew quite a bit about both sides of her TEXAS parents' families, and he shared information about his own.

Lily remembered a cousin of his from kindergarten. The cousin had been incorrigible. She didn't mention that part to Tim.

But Tim said, "A hitch in the Marines helped him quite a lot. Those Sergeants just don't fool around. You won't recognize him when you see him again."

"They battered him?" She asked that with some blankness.

Tim shook his head and explained, "The Marines never touch the recruits, but they can really yell, and there are the marching with equipment times that are very sobering, he says.''

"He's a first cousin of yours?"

Tim explained kindly as he withdrew from the kinship, "He's his father's child." The mother was his cousin.

She loved Tim's distancing the genes and laughed.

He glanced over to see that, and his own eyes were filled with delight. "Anybody in the family who doesn't behave is always traced to the nonrelation of the pairing."

"We do that in our family."

"Is that how you explain Marly?"

"I love Marly."

"Oh."

After some silence, Lily turned her head and inquired, "What's the—Oh—mean?"

So he replied logically, "I've just realized that I can tolerate Marly."

Her laughter bubbled, and Tim was delighted.

They had a very nice day together. Their interests were opposite and stimulating and strange to the other listener. So there were debates and explanations and nods.

They could talk. He did listen. And he added and divided and multiplied all the conversations. He was a good communicator.

In turn, she examined the houses they were to inspect. She saw flaws, and he wrote those down. He didn't mention that he'd seen them right away. He was tactful and took good care of her. But the prime thing was that Tim was a good communicator.

Their dinner was at a very well-appointed place. She exclaimed in some surprise, "You're a member?"

He explained, "The real estate group has a membership for specific things. That way we can boggle a client. Are you boggled?"

"We have a country club up in Muncie that is just about this good." She was firm.

And he was charmed.

Her manners were those of a lady, and his were more than just adequate. She asked, "Who taught you knives and forks?"

"My momma is a stringent worrywart."

She nodded. "I have a mother just like that!"

"Your momma grew up in San Antonio. My momma knows your momma."

"How'd you sort that out?"

"I asked her. She sat down and wrote your momma a letter." He reached into the inside pocket of his suit coat and brought it out. "We need the address."

He gave her a pen, and she addressed the letter.

He loved it. His eyes sparkled and he smiled.

But Lily Baby recalled that Tim Morgan was also a salesman.

He asked, "How about Saturday night? Can you get away? There's a party at one of my friends' houses. We dance and talk and the gang is a nice bunch."

"I'll see if I can get away."

He instantly pushed, "Try."

She grinned.

After the elegant dinner, there was dancing in another area. The music was live and good. Tim could dance. He showed her off and knew the steps and was quite skilled. How unusual.

"When did you learn to dance?" she asked Tim as he twirled her with smooth skill.

He sighed as if forbearing. "Mrs. Gates's classes from age twelve."

"We did that, too!"

"I could tell." Tim smiled. "You can follow. Most women try to lead."

"Nonsense!"

He grinned. "You are really easy to dance with. You have a natural rhythm."

He gave her other compliments. It wasn't just how she looked or how she acted, it was in other ways. He was clever. But he didn't overdo it. That showed he was smart. Anyone would assume his mother had helped heartlessly or that he had earnest sisters.

The talker coaxed her to talk. He listened. He gave opinions. He didn't always agree with her.

And Lily began to compare him to Bryan.

It wasn't too late when Tim took Lily back to the Coffeepot Inn. He drove to her cabin and got out to open her car door. He offered to unlock the Cup's door for her. So she handed him the keys.

From the darkened Coffeepot, Byran watched. He girded his loins and temper to watch Tim kiss her. His mouth was bittered by such a happening.

Tim did not kiss Lily.

He said, "I'll see you Saturday about six? Will that be okay?"

"Probably seven would be better."

"Okay." Tim grinned. "Thanks for the day. This has been good."

And she said, "I had a nice time."

He advised, "Work at getting used to me."

She laughed softly.

In the Coffeepot, Bryan could hear that soft laugh. He turned away so that he wouldn't see the good-night kiss. But as his body turned, his head stayed steady and his eyes stayed glued to the pair.

It would be now. Her Cup's screen door was open, the door was unlocked. Tim handed back her keys. But he moved aside.

She said something to Tim, then she went inside and closed the screen door.

Tim said something else, then he lifted his hand in a brief wave of goodbye, and he went back to his car.

That shocked Bryan. They'd probably spent the whole day somewhere in bed. Tim hadn't kissed her goodbye. They'd laughed together.

Bryan went up the stairs to his room slowly. He felt drained.

And Tim drove away with a high heart. His momma had told him how to act with Susan's daughter. And Tim wondered if Bryan had sat up waiting for them to return. If Bryan had witnessed that chaste good-night, he would be sure they'd spent the entire day in bed and were so exhausted that a kiss would have been redundant.

As he lay in his bed, Bryan was thinking just about along those same lines. He looked at the clock. It was only ten o'clock.

He took two aspirin and finally slept. But he wakened when he generally did. He took another shower and dressed. Then he went down the stairs to start the day. It was only six o'clock.

And there Lily was, alert, dressed and making the coffee. Bryan was shocked. He bit his lip so that he wouldn't ask what had happened with Tim in all that time they'd been together.

Had he... Had Tim... What all had they done in all that long, long time they'd been together?

Lily smiled at Bryan and said, "Good morning."

He replied a somber, "'Morning."

She didn't say anything else. He waited and watched her, but how could *he* ask, when she wasn't going to say anything?

He blurted, "How was it?"

She said, "I haven't eaten yet."

Bryan stared at her in shock. They hadn't even had supper? They'd been in bed the whole, entire time?

She asked, "Want a perfect doughnut? A friend of mine makes them."

She was being sassy.

She asked, "Bad night?"

He nodded rudely... once in a jerk.

She looked at him and he looked back, somberly. She frowned. "Are you all right?"

"Why." Not a question.

"You look strange."

"This is what I wear about every day." His words were like slapped down cards.

"Has someone been nasty to you? Who all should I stomp on?"

She said *that!* So he said, "Where did you go last night?" Then he bit his lip because he had sworn that he was not going to ask *any*thing about what all they'd done last night.

She supplied the information quite readily, "We went to some of the places which Tim is trying to sell. It was interesting. He wrote down the flaws and I found some for him. And we went to dinner. His mother knew my mother back in school. And we talked families. He can dance, and we went to the same kind of dancing school when we were growing up. I was in Indiana by then."

The two were of the same ilk. Bryan Willard was an outcast whose relatives didn't keep track of one another. He had no backup. No acquaintances to dust off. Or even one to show off. None qualified as being special. Bryan was a loser in this competition.

He was competitive in snaring this nubile woman? When had that happened? My God, was he in *love* with her? Surely not.

Six

So Bryan Willard went into a blue funk of grief. He didn't understand it. The reason he didn't was because he'd never known anyone well enough to find out their feelings against which he could judge his own.

As the time passed, Lily Baby asked Bryan, "What's the matter with you? Why are you so grumpy? Are you trying to catch my attention?"

His eyes hit on her in shock. She knew! But she was frowning at him and her hands were on her hips. Again, she asked, "What's the matter with you? Do you need some vitamins?"

And he replied crossly, "No."

Then Lily went to get Teresa. And right there in front of Lily, *Teresa* asked Bryan if he needed a cathartic!

A man never had a peaceful minute when there was a nosy woman around. Bryan got cross and hostile.

So Teresa got Juan, and they sat Bryan down and asked what sort of complaint was bugging him?

He said in a narrow-eyed, nasty way, "I'm all right. Leave me *alone!*"

Teresa hit her palm to her forehead and said to Juan, "It's that Lily. She went out with the Tim. Bryan's into the decline!"

Bryan yelled, "I am *not!*"

Juan grinned and nodded. They patted Bryan on his shoulder and told him how to handle the situation. Juan asked Teresa, "The flowers I present?"

And she giggled.

Bryan had never known that Teresa could giggle. He stared at her.

Teresa added, "And the candy."

So Juan brushed off the old "Candy's dandy but Likker's quicker" saying, which probably crossed all language barriers. It was somewhat altered by Juan's Spanish.

But the reference set Teresa off, and she laughed and laughed.

Bryan narrowed his eyes. Just why had Teresa laughed? So Bryan asked, "What's so funny?"

And Teresa told her husband, "You tell him. He be moist behind the ear." And she swished out, but at the door she turned back and gave her husband a lascivious look with heavy eyelids, and she gave him a really naughty smile.

Bryan told Juan, "She's luring you."

And Juan said, "*Sí.* She do so after she needle me to do the terribles. Women are so." He sighed with the burden. "She worth *pena,* uh, the troubles."

Bryan said, "If you're going to tell me how to court a woman, just go on home. I'm not interested. I don't want a woman. They only complicate a man's life— and they tend to have snotty, bawling kids."

Juan sat down and scratched the back of his head. He agreed. "Yes. There is truth, but ah, there be benefit."

"I don't need a woman."

And Juan asked, "Why you say serene but you *enojo*—angry?"

Juan observed Bryan with interested compassion. "You should have experienced as did I in Teresa. Women are the trial."

"Then why in hell are you here now?" Bryan shouted at Juan.

"To comfort. I know what you feel." Juan shook his head. "Even you now know no-thing as horrible as it was to Juan with Teresa."

After a long while as Bryan deliberately kept silent, Juan sighed and settled to cheer up Bryan. "Winnie, she like sugar." Juan tilted his head at Bryan and smiled. "Teresa scratch Winnie's *carne,* the flesh."

Curiosity wins over almost anything. Bryan asked, "What did Winnie do to Teresa?"

"She fight. But Teresa, hah, she win." He looked out the window and smiled. Then he told Bryan, "She win *me!*"

And Bryan was kind enough to say, "She was the winner. You're a good man."

"*Sí.*"

So Juan sat and read the paper from Mexico, the Spanish one printed in San Antonio, and he look at the one from Corpus. He made no other comment. He would look at Bryan and evaluate him, but he made no other conversation. Bryan had been told the facts of life, now it was up to the woman to decide.

Ah, *sí*. It is the woman who decides. Juan smiled at his newspaper.

It was that night that Tim took Lily to an opening of a building his company had managed. She wore a dark suit that was elegant and a satin blouse was under it. The suit was black, the satin was pearl colored. The top of it was in a fold over her breasts.

Tim drove along the highway and he looked at Lily several times. Finally, he asked, "Do you just have a wide ribbon wrapped around your...chest? It's great looking, but I need to know if it might slip down."

With a large, patient sigh, Lily leaned forward in the restraining seat belt. Then she pulled down the sleeve of the jacket so that he could see the sleeve of the blouse. With her movements, and not knowing what she might do, Tim had trouble watching the road.

She raised her eyebrows in a questioning manner and asked, "Okay?"

Very seriously, Tim told her, "You just about gave me heart failure—there." He was, again, back to mostly watching the road.

Lily looked down at herself. In some indignation she retorted, "I'm perfectly decent!"

"I think if you were wearing a floor-length veil, you'd rattle me still."

"What a charming compliment."

Tim shook his head seriously. "It isn't a compliment. It's the truth. Haven't you noticed how much I've been out there to the Coffeepot? I was trying to give you enough time to get used to me."

So Lily reminded Tim with some drollness, "You hardly paid any attention to me when we met."

"I was sundered," Tim said earnestly. "I got one glimpse of you and didn't believe you were real." He glanced over at her, then he looked back at the road. "I had to stop myself from spending all my days out there just watching you. You're magic."

"You're getting a-way ahead of all this," Lily cautioned instantly. "Don't rattle me."

He was a little indignant. "You've rattled me! It's only fair for you to share the rattling. Do you find any...bad...flaws in me?" He turned for a glance to her and his eyes were stark.

"I'll pay attention." She smiled.

He complained, "This time, in knowing you, has ruined me. I can't pay attention to anything." He breathed out in an impotent puff. "My mother said I'd better take you out a time or—"

"Your *mother*?" Lily was astonished.

Tim admitted soberly, "I was just as surprised as you are now. Mother wasn't so much surprised as she was startled. After she understood why I was there to talk to her, her hair never quite lay back on her head. And her eyes stayed open. Really open. I have no explanation as to why it was so, but, yes, I talked about you to my mother."

Lily asked cautiously, "What did you say—to your mother—about me?"

Tim's reply was quick and logical, "That you're perfect."

"Good heavens! Now what will she think of me?"

Tim assured Lily, "Mother nodded." He considered in the silence of Lily's shock. Then Tim mentioned, "Come to think of it, she never did say much."

"I'm not at all surprised."

Tim expanded on the commitment. "I told her what I told you. That I ought to see you and see if it's real. I'm not ready for anything serious."

She was very quiet and very positive, "Neither am I."

He just went on. "I'm trapped. If you turn me down, I'll go into a serious decline. I'll mope and lose my orientation and quit eating."

Lily exclaimed, "All that? On a second date?"

He chided, "You forget all the days I was out there making myself known to you?"

"This is entirely too fast."

He was silent for a space. Then he guessed, "You need time."

"Yep."

Tim nodded slowly. "Yeah. Mother said you would want some time. She knows your mother."

"You told me."

Tim said logically, "That's about what all I've been doing lately. Even my boss asked, 'Who is she?'"

"What did you say?"

"I asked, 'Who?'"

She waited but she finally nudged, "And what did he say?"

Tim blinked once and looked at Lily. "He said, 'The woman who's distracting you from your business.'"

Again she had to nudge, "What did you reply?"

"I said, 'What business?' He thought I was being clever and slapped me on my shoulder. He's been trying to pair me up with his daughter. He thinks I'm still free." He sighed hugely but with contented commitment.

Lily tilted her head and lifted her eyebrows. She urged quite clearly, "You are free."

He assumed a defeated look—without looking at her—and said, "I'm zonked."

Lily shook her head as she told him earnestly, "It's much too soon for you to be so blatant."

Quietly, he admitted, "I know."

So she inquired, "Well, if you *know,* then why have you said all that?"

Tim slowly shook his head as he watched the highway. "I don't know. That's why I told my mother. And she just listened. She's already called *your* mother."

"Good gravy."

So he kindly explained to Lily, "You got that expression from you paternal great-grandmother. Mother knew her, too. She says that on occasion."

Lily instructed Tim, "My mother avoided her grandmother-in-law."

"Everybody knows that." He grinned at her. "And they know why." He laughed out loud.

She asked cautiously, "What sort of mother-in-law would your moth—"

"You give *in?* Well, hallelujah! Things are finally going my—"

"Hold it." Lily put up a stopping hand. "You're entirely too far ahead of where we are."

He looked around avidly asking, "Are we *there?*" Then he grinned. "Where are we?"

Snippily, she retorted, "We've met. We've had A date. One. This is only our second date."

He slid his eyes over to look at her. He told her smokily, "I get a kiss. On a second date, the rules are that the guy gets a kiss."

"I'm not at all sure of that right now. I'll see. I doubt it."

Tim sighed as if he was settled somewhere nice. He told her, "I'll convince you."

In a spooked voice, Lily warned her escort, "Don't rattle me."

But Tim just grinned over at her and then looked back at the highway.

The evening was interesting. All those there who were a part of Tim's real estate office already knew who Lily was. They said, "Well, hello, Lily."

So she never found out who *they* were. She felt swamped by strangers who knew her warts and moles by heart. But she hadn't a clue as to who they were. It was unsettling.

Tim held her hand in his warm hand and he smiled. He smiled at everyone and he smiled at her. His eyes sparkled and his grin was perfect. His hand around hers was perfect. He was about eight inches taller than she and that was a nice match.

Everyone spoke to Tim, and he called each one by name. There were too many names for her to remem-

ber them all. But Tim resaid their names every time.
And she began to sort a few of the people from the
avalanche of others.

"How come you know so many people?" she asked
Tim rather late in the evening.

"It's the business," he explained. "We buy and sell
and trade." He shrugged over reality. "So we know
the whole town and everybody in it and what they paid
for what place."

"Wow."

He looked over at her and his grin widened. "It's
interesting."

"Are you planning on running for some political
office?"

"Naw." He discarded that without any regret.
"That's beyond me," he said; then he added, "But I
have helped a few. Ricardo over yonder by the door?
I helped with his campaign. He's a winner."

And Lily considered. "So you help." Then she
added, "But it's with somebody who's bound to
win?"

He guessed, "You want me to tell you all the losers
I've helped? Okay. There was Ja—"

"No. No. I just asked." She was serious. "I only
wondered if you just rode the wagons of the win-
ners."

Tim expanded his involvement. "I get in early on
and I stay. And I do talk, but I mostly listen. It's interesting. And to me, it's important for citizens to be
as involved as the politician."

"Are you going to eventually run for office?"

"Nope." He shook his head emphatically. "I'm not
the type."

Of course, there's always a flaw in any perfect evening. A slinky vampire woman came up and put her body close to Tim's as she said to him, "Well, hello, darling. Did you miss me?"

Tim laughed and extracted himself, never letting go of a fascinated Lily Baby. He backed off with some tact and said, "This here's my dream woman?" It was the TEXAS questioning statement. "Her name is Lily." He lifted their clenched hands and with them, indicated the siren. "That one is Winona Harding."

Being her mother's daughter, Lily said, "How do you do?"

And the Harding woman said, "Get lost."

So what did Tim do? He held up his free hand like a traffic cop and said, "We're leaving! We're outta here! Don't push."

That made the siren indignant. It was then that Lily Baby thought how young Winona was. As Tim hurried away, and over her shoulder, Lily said, "Sorry to leave so abruptly. He isn't a Davie, you know."

The siren gaped. "You're a *Davie?*"

But Tim took Lily into a crowd and Winona was lost in people before Lily could reply.

Tim asked, "How could you be courteous to a woman who was trying for me right in front of you?"

Lily replied, "I had it ground into me to be courteous at *all* times and under any circumstances."

He grinned with hilarity. But his words out of that grin said, "That shows moral strength. That's another plus. Do you have any minuses?"

Lily suggested, "Talk to my mother."

"Naw." Tim discarded the suggestion. "She's probably a stickler and would say you'd wrongly used the soupspoon after your teaspoon fell to the floor."

"Exactly."

He sighed with fake guilt. "My mother is a whole lot that very way. Another stickler. Are you going to hound our little ones like that?"

She slid her eyes over to him and said with some terseness, "This is our second date."

He readily agreed. "I know, I know. But we got to plan ahead. Are you gonna raise our youngsters like our mommas did us?"

She just lifted her eyebrows as she responded, "We'll see if we get that far."

And he admired that. He said, "Now *that's* just exactly what our mommas would've said back when they were your age. I can see it all happening. And our little kiddies'll come to me and say, 'Papa, why is Momma saying we have to do things her way?'"

Lily waited. Then she had to ask, "And what would you say?"

"I'd sigh and say, 'It'll give you some city shine if you listen to your momma.'"

She had to laugh.

Then the people around them noticed her trying to be silent *and* laugh out loud, so they wanted to know, "What's so funny?"

"I just told her we'll have a whole passel of little kids all clinging to her apron."

A female voice questioned seriously, "A passel of kids?"

And Lily Baby supplied, "He's dreaming."

The woman looked at her steadily without expression, but the men all laughed and clapped Tim on his back.

Lily felt the need to mention, and she did it rather stridently, "This is our second date."

And the men hooted. One said, "Get 'em young and raise 'em right."

Since Lily Baby had been in Indiana most of her life, until just recently, she was only gradually learning the ramifications of the Davie kin. There were people who came to her and asked, "Who's your momma and papa?"

"Why do you ask?"

"I'm a Davie, but I've never met up with any Davie like you." That was a male who naturally then tried to be a kissing cousin.

The female parts of the family were more curious than anything else. No Davie ever felt diminished no matter what happened or who showed up. They validated Lily and then included her.

So eventually Lily Baby was taken back to the Coffeepot and to her little Cup. It was late. Who would be up and watching at a time like that?

Guess.

So he saw the two kiss.

They stood together. Bryan could see that Tim's feet were braced and since he had good-sized feet and wore the wide solid men's shoes, Tim could keep their balance as they kissed.

Bryan saw only that Lily gave no resistance. How could he rescue a willing woman? His soul groaned in agony. But he watched.

Lily didn't pay much attention to balance. Her body had never been that excited. The stirring of sexual lust was surprising. At times in her life she had felt flickerings of desire. Being a female Davie, she was brought up to avoid such lure.

But now. With Tim. How strange.

She was so fascinated by the squiggle inside her, that she set Tim on his ear and his breathing was just about ruined. Fortunately, he was young enough that such strain to his libido was mendable.

It was Tim who released her by first leaning his head back, then taking a small step back before he found the backbone to release her. It was a tough thing to do and he felt very noble, doing it.

Released, Lily Baby went into her Cup and softly closed the door.

Bryan watched with snarling envy as Tim leaned his hands on the side of his car's hood and hung his head down as he tried to push the car over. He knew that he couldn't, so it was a safe thing to do.

Then Tim stiffly got into his car and gently drove away.

With him gone, Bryan could breathe again. His face was gaunt and his eyes naked and vulnerable. He watched the Cup that belonged to Lily...

And her Cup door opened!

It was just a little bit and she apparently looked around to see if anyone else was anywhere around. The place was deserted. She came slowly outside into the night and just stood there.

Why?

Bryan's breathing picked up markedly. He watched avidly. Would she come to...him? Would she use *him* for surcease after kissing another man in that way?

He would allow it. He would! He'd let her use him. It would be better than nothing at all.

He grabbed a glass and snapped on the faucet so that he could get enough water into his mouth to rinse it around quickly and spit it out. He slammed down the glass and went to the door. He tore it open and erupted onto the slab step.

Then he looked over to see if she had seen his foolish hurry...

But she was gone. Her door was closed.

Bryan went slowly back into the darkened inn. He was sundered. Tim's kiss had disturbed her so that she had had to come out of her Cup and breathe the night air. She was attracted to Tim.

Where had they been that whole long time?

Did he need to even ask the question? Tim had had her alone since just after six and now it was midnight. In six hours, what all had they done?

Yeah.

By the time the sun rose, Bryan had had about an hour's sleep. He got up grumpy from his disheveled bed. Grimly, he tore the sheets free and, disciplining himself, he carefully remade the bed into the neatness it required.

She might come up the stairs and see the wreck she'd made of that bed by just dating Tim. Bryan admitted he'd have to get used to seeing her leave with Tim...and watching her brought back to her Cup...by Tim. And Bryan would get to witness other kisses.

He considered leaving the Coffeepot, going somewhere else. How would it be to go again as a stranger? If he left, he'd even miss Teresa's sharp tongue, and Juan's amused interest.

But he couldn't leave Lily. He couldn't be beyond her radius. He couldn't not watch her.

If she married Tim, she would leave the Coffeepot, but she was still the owner, and she would come occasionally to check the books and to talk to him.

And she would get pregnant by Tim and she would show off their children.

Bryan knew then he would never marry. Nor would he leave the Coffeepot. He would have to be content to live on the edge of her life. A shadow man. One who wasn't whole.

While it *does* happen, and there *are* men who think that way when they have a crush on a woman, it doesn't last long. Any woman charmed by a dedicated man, other than her husband, is startled that the declared lifetime devotion is so brief.

There's a weirdo occasionally who actually clings to the premise she's the only woman. But the rest are practical and know there's always another woman somewhere findable.

That morning, Tim came by, sleepy-eyed and smiling. But Lily wasn't up then. Even Tim knew better than to waken a nubile woman too early. He had two cups of coffee as he watched out through the Pot to her door, but after that Bryan gave him ginger ale or orange juice.

Tim finally left a note in a sealed envelope for Lily.

With all that coffee, ginger ale and orange juice, Tim probably sloshed when he walked.

When Lily Baby finally came hurrying to the Pot, she was appalled by the time. "My alarm must not have sounded. I slept like a *log!* Why didn't you call the cabin? You did all this by yourself!"

Rather bitterly, Bryan reminded her, "I managed before you got here."

"Ah." She lifted a finger which she shook. "Now I'm an active participant."

So Bryan asked, "What all did you do last night?" And the question was a sneering one.

Quite honestly, she replied. She told him where the party was, who was there, the cousins! It was such a surprise to run into so many more of them. She'd known them through the earlier years. It had been such fun to meet them again and to find out where everyone else was!

And Bryan knew he could never be a part of her life. She was beyond him. How could she introduce a fry cook to a bunch of people like them? And his mind withdrew from her—as close as she was, that did happen. He could see the flecks in her blue eyes and he discarded their beauty.

She had put a wide white band on her dark hair to hold it neatly back. And she chatted like he was her college roomie and interested in such talk. He couldn't have cared less.

But he watched her. She was talking to him. She was sparkling eyed and laughing. She gossiped as if he was her sorority sister, for God's sake!

She slitted her eyes and told of a couple of pushy men who'd wanted to know her and wanted her phone number. She laughed as she told him she'd given them Bryan's number.

Coldly, he asked, "What'da'ya want me to do when they call?"

She tilted her head in a sassy manner and suggested, "I'm busy?" And with that, she wiped the clean counter with a new cloth, and then she went to do the tables.

With Lily in the Pot, Bryan's body knew exactly where she was all of the time. That was interesting. He knew where she was when she went outside or if she went down the stairs into the basement. And he knew where she was when she went out the door.

And she would do that if someone couldn't fill her own gas tank.

At the pumps, most people put in their own gas. Juan was available if there was something wrong with a car. He knew cars. Bryan helped if someone needed help. And even Lily was skilled if someone needed something done about his car.

Once he asked her, "How did you learn so much about cars?"

"My daddy. He didn't ever want us alone and vulnerable on a highway. My sisters and I can fix anything."

Hearts? Could she fix his heart? He watched her sadly.

Seven

There is really nothing to compare to a grieving man whose grief is for a woman. Especially a woman who is constantly underfoot. And one who doesn't seem to notice the man is suffering. How could she be so unknowing?

Bryan considered Lily was so stupid that she didn't even know what she was doing to him...to his ego...to his faltering feeling of self-worth.

Even a half-bright woman would have known he was suffering. Lily ignored his grief and cheerfully chattered and seemed to be around the whole, entire time.

She stretched a man's limits.

What man hadn't run into something like this blasted woman who was driving him wild?

But he was silent. He didn't protest. He didn't complain. He was noble. He sighed. He stood limp. He put a hand to his bent down forehead.

Did she notice? No. She chattered away about her cousins and about her sister's coming visit.

Her *sister* was coming to visit?

Bryan's brain shifted. Her sister could be used as a lure to distract Tim from Lily!

But then he looked soberly at Lily and realized no hooked man would be distracted from that fatal woman. So Bryan girded his loins to suffer.

He did it well.

He would straighten as if he was a hundred years old and put his hands on his back as if it had been rolled on by a horse. He sighed. He would move and gasp quietly.

Not once did she ask what was wrong. Not even one little time did she notice him. That infuriated Bryan. What sort of mother would she make if someone was suffering *within arm's reach,* and she couldn't even tell there was anything wrong?

She paid him no never mind at all. And she just went on around doing things and talking and living on her own safe little island.

At night, he'd stand in the unlighted Coffeepot and watch her go across the ground under the thorny mesquites. She never once asked him to escort her. Nope, not her. She just went right on out there like she ruled the place and no stupid ass could lay a finger on her.

So Bryan had to watch her into her Cup every single damned night. Well, not the nights she went out with old What's-his-name. Then *Tim* took her to the Cup door and *he* kissed her good-night.

Bryan stood in the dark that one night when Tim must have talked fifteen minutes about going into her room...coaxing, cajoling, pleading. That was a riveting time for Bryan. He breathed in stress from the tops of his lungs, but he breathed fire. He could feel the fire all through him.

He hyperventilated. He was on his way to the Pot's door with the baseball bat from under the counter, and he reached for the door as Tim drove away.

Was she with him? He became frantic! He ran outside and watched after the car. It turned off toward San Antonio.

Bryan stood there, breathing. He wasn't sure what he ought to do. She wasn't yelling as they went by. Tim hadn't had time to wrestle her down and throw her back into the car.

She'd gone—willingly.

The bile in his throat was like acid. His eyes were moist. It wasn't tears or anything. Nothing dumb like that. There was just moisture there. But he was bitter.

He heard a sound and turned as she came out of her Cup and walked to the bench. There, she sat and leaned back with her arms along the back of the bench.

She was there.

He walked quietly over to her to scare the hell out of her and give her a good reason to be more careful. She had no idea who might be—

She asked, "Is your nose bent out of shape?"

He was shocked. She *knew?* He said, "How'd you know I wasn't some rapist stalking you out here all by yourself?"

"I saw you move inside the Pot when you came to the door. I knew you weren't in bed as yet. Why wouldn't you date my cousin and go with us?"

And he told her the truth, "I don't want to date your cousin."

"You don't even know her well enough to be that negative."

"She's a nice woman."

"She's almost your age."

"I'm ancient."

"No." She sighed with endured patient forbearance. "You are maturing... in some aspects. In others you're an irritating subteen."

He sat down on the bench, and she didn't move clear away from him but she stayed on her side. She didn't move closer and complain about the chilly night.

Of course, it wasn't chilly. It was the usual perfect TEXAS night.

He asked, "You like Tim?"

She sighed again. Then she said, "He knows everybody in the state of TEXAS."

He waited, and she added nothing more. So he asked again, "You taken with him?"

From the corners of his eyes, he saw her turn her head slowly. She told him in a patient, adult manner, "You're a dead bore. You are so stupid that it's no wonder your family abandoned you."

Hotly, he retorted, "They did not! We still see each other, on occasion."

So she inquired with some snotty irony, "When was the last—occasion?"

"I don't remember."

She pushed. "Was it this year?" And she waited for his reply.

"No." It was too abrupt.

"Last year?" she asked in a rather chili pepper manner.

And he snapped back, "What the hell difference does it make to you?"

So she replied in a charming, fake smiling manner, "I'm just making conversation. It matters not at *all* to me whether or not you've been kicked out of your family."

"How'd you know?"

She gasped, "You *were?* Are *you* the black-dressed stalker everyone was talking about two years ago?"

He groused, "Oh, hell."

"You *are?*" she gasped.

And he was honest to her. "Lily, my family isn't like your family. We don't depend on each other or need each other. We don't need to talk all along the way. What we do is what we do. That's all it is."

"It's weird."

"You have a friendly family. You probably weren't *told* you ought not talk to strangers and—"

"No." She was a stickler. "The parents insist on that one."

"You talk to me." He scowled at her.

"You're not a stranger," she retorted. Then she added with an emphatic sneer but her voice was proper: "You're only strange."

"I am not!"

She snapped at him, "Not even my mother would sit in the Pot thataway and wait for me to come home on time."

He was infuriated that she would know! "I was *not* waiting for you to come home!"

"Then why do you go to bed just after I get home every time I date Tim?"

He hesitated, then he asked, "How'd you know that?"

"I can see you walk through the Coffeepot and up the stairs as soon as I've closed my door."

Lamely, he replied, "We just happen to go to bed at the same time."

She wouldn't leave him be. She pointed out, "The hours vary in the time I get home. That's another black mark for you on St. Pete's log up by the pearly gates."

"You think I'm *lying?*"

And she replied easily enough, "Yeah."

He stood up and said, "I'm offended you'd think such a thing of me."

She looked up at him and asked, "Why do you watch me?"

He was at least six years older than this fluff. He was not committed to telling her anything. He said, "I feel responsible for you. I knew your great-grand-daddy."

She made a puffing sound. "That sort of reasoning won't even get off the ground, much less fly."

"Fly?" He jumped on the change of subject. "Your daddy fly in Nam?"

"Yeah." She frowned. "My momma still has to put her hands on him to be sure he's real."

As a kinship happening, Bryan told her, "My grandmomma marched in the protest with me. I wasn't sure what was going on, but now I brag about being there.''

And Lily said, ''I'd like to meet your grand-momma.''

He promised, ''She'd be nice to you. She likes ladies.''

''What about your momma?'' Lily asked. ''Would she be nice to me?''

''My momma took off with a ranchman when I was just a tad. We ain't never seen hide nor hair of her since then. One of my brothers went looking for her, and he never came back, either. We get cards from him on Christmas. He never gives us any address.''

''You left home.''

''They know where I am.''

She nodded slowly.

With hooded eyes on her, he asked, ''You ain't been back home since you been here.''

She gave him a slow turn of her head and formed the word carefully, ''No.''

''See? Even you.''

''I've been visiting with all my kin down here. My family talks with me on the phone. I just haven't been back up yonder.''

''You're getting more TEXAS shine saying 'yonder' thataway.''

''Perhaps you've forgotten both my parents are TEXANS?''

''So you aren't visiting,'' he said thoughtfully. ''You've just come on home?''

''Right.''

Sitting beside her, he stretched out. His ankles were crossed and his arms were along the back of the bench.

His one hand could almost touch her shoulder. He said, "That's the way we think in our family. We're home. We don't need to meet and celebrate that. It's just a simple fact."

She stretched.

That was eye-catching for any man.

She said, "I believe I'll go take a shower and go to bed."

He let that go on by so as not to antagonize her. Instead, he told her, "You owe me a good-night kiss."

She was astonished. "Now why would I do that?"

He explained, "I've been out here on this hard bench, entertaining you, all this while, and you owe me a kiss for that effort."

She scoffed, "Sitting out here? This wasn't anything *near* a date!"

"Oh, yes. We've been out on this bench together. The moon is clear over yonder. We've had a long conversation. You owe me a good-night kiss. And I'll let you kiss me good-night, and then I'll see you safely to your door."

"Bushwah!"

"Nope. It's genuine, honest to goodness protocol in these here circumstances. You've had my protection and company for this date together—"

"This was not a date." She told Bryan, "I was here, and you came out and joined me."

He rebutted, "While I wasn't actually out on this bench thisaway, I was already here. I planned to sit out here alone and meditate, but you came along and sat down. I was kind enough to come out and welcome you to share this time and talk with you."

"How kind."

"Yes'um, my momma would've been proud of me."

"Why?"

"In all this time, I haven't laid a finger on you... yet."

"You may—"

"Good!" He reached over, turned the gasping neophyte adroitly so that she was lying across his chest and then he kissed her. He really kissed her.

She made little sounds and wiggled somewhat at first, then she settled down and just waited it out.

He was good.

He knew how to kiss. Who'd taught him all that? He was a little careless with his hands. She smacked one and then put her hand back on the nape of his neck.

He could really kiss.

When he let her breathe, she asked, "Where'd you learn to kiss like that?"

"I practiced on my hand."

She'd never heard that old saw. "Your *hand?*" Her tone was unbelieving.

"Yeah." He demonstrated. "You put your thumb alongside the bottom of your hand thataway, and then you can kiss that there crack. See? And you can even wet kiss it and slide in your tongue!"

She chuckled and looked up at him. "Now *that* is desperation!"

He sighed hugely. "Men have it rough."

Lily made a disbelieving sound. "Why would you say *men* have it rough? It's women that have to fight men off. Men try every time!"

"Has Tim—?"

"Of course not," Lily exclaimed. Then she told Bryan, "He's a gentleman."

Bryan was indignant. "I'm a gentleman!"

And she said, "So far."

He turned a slow head and his eyes were almost screened by his eyelashes. "You waiting?"

She held up a traffic cop hand as she said, "Not at all. I'm out here for peace and quiet. I'm waiting for you to leave me here by myself."

In a smoky voice, he told her, "You've kissed two men today, that I know about. How come?"

She considered rather elaborately. "Nobody else offered?"

She heard his smothered gasp. She felt reckless. She knew she ought to get right up, and go back to her safe Cup over yonder.

But she sat there in the tense silence. She could hear his controlled breathing. It was loudly stifled and moderated. He didn't move. He was tense. And she was just real curious what he would say—or do—next.

So he inquired, "Want me to go run out the local men to line up? Or would you be more . . . selective?" He quit breathing entirely as he waited for her reply.

She shrugged in that way of a young woman whose breasts are eye-catching. She casually gestured with the farther hand in a careless manner and said, "If you can't handle *mmmmmmm*—"

It was still only the second man who was kissing her, but he was doing a very good job of it. Yessss.

When he lifted his mouth from hers with myriad soft sounds, she said through puffed lips with her eyes closed, "You are one of the same men who did this before. So there're still only two for today."

Bryan made a growling throat sound and his strong arms squeezed her closer to him. Possessively. He said, "And I didn't even have to take you to a movie."

With her neck limp and her head lying back, she had the gall to say, "You didn't even take me to supper."

"I fixed you doughnuts."

"True." She strived slowly to release herself and stretched. "You have to quit doughnuts. I'm gaining weight."

He put both hands around her slender waist. "Not yet."

She mussed his hair as she told him, "I have to get to bed—"

"Let's go to my room."

She laughed in that soft way of women who tease or are amused by a man. She said, "You know better than that."

And he said, "Your bed? Mine's better. Narrower."

She snorted marvelously, "A *narrow* bed?"

He agreed logically. "I'll be on top." Then he added, "Or you could be." And he assured her, "I'm comfortable to sleep on."

"Oh? Who—"

His reply came hurriedly, "Our cat."

"Feline?"

"Of course!" He faked being indignant. "I'm a nice TEXAS boy who needs guiding." And he suggested quite earnestly, "Tell me how to seduce you."

"Darned if I know."

Earnestly, he told her, "We can learn together."

She grinned. "Go to your room and recite one hundred times—I shall behave."

So he wanted to know, "How does that help?"

She did that fantastic shrug again, and she echoed his own words, "Darned if I know. It's what my parents demanded."

He gasped in shock, "What on this earth did you do?"

"I cut my sister's hair. That was bad enough, although she didn't mind at all. But I shaved the cat. It was such a hot summer, and the poor thing panted. I was trying to help. My parents were appalled. The cat got sunburned. The vet was very serious."

He asked rather cautiously, "How old were you?"

"Six."

He was firm. "Don't become a nurse."

"How odd!" Lily exclaimed. "That's what Mother said."

He kissed her again, holding her close, not crushing her but firmly hugging her to himself. His. And the kiss was enflaming.

She was limp when he lifted his mouth from hers. He didn't loosen his arms. That was probably good since she was so zonked.

He told her with a very husky voice, "You're so soft."

That startled her. No other male had ever said anything about her body against his. None had ever made such a comment. So she'd never once considered how her body would feel against a male's surface. She blushed.

Because she was cool and in control, she didn't consider that Bryan would notice she was blushing. It was dark. The inn lights were at a distance, and the lacy stupid mesquite leaves filtered what light there was.

Being in control with a man is a lot like not seeing mice. If a woman ignores mice, they don't exist. Men aren't that considerate. They're greedy. When they're hungry, they like women close. Closer. At least until they're replete. And during all that while, women get to pretend they're in control.

When men watch a sleepy-eyed woman, she thinks they're thinking how nice it is to be around her. The men are probably judging how soon they can do it again.

But Bryan wasn't replete. He was on the razor's edge. His breathing was unstable, and his muscles were all hard. He was triggered.

She knew it. She undid his embrace and almost got away. But he realized she wasn't shifting into another position, like being on his lap—she was escaping. He couldn't allow that.

She didn't curl back down when his hands and arms suggested that was what he wanted. So she wiggled a little and tightened her lips.

For women, that's enough of a suggestion for a man to cooperate. It never occurred to her that he might not. His grip was strong.

Lily Baby had to bow her back and put her head back to look him in the face and she said, "Let go."

That was clear enough.

He made relishing sounds as he hugged her closer. He moved his hard hands on her back, and he breathed. That is, it was obvious that he was breathing. It was rather labored and quickly done. He wasn't panting, but he sounded like he'd been doing something trying and he'd been tried.

She said it again, "Let go."

"I've only just started."

But she said, "No."

He heard her and was then still. He breathed. But he did begin to release her. He groaned and suffered to move his hands from around her. He said, "You ought to give me a sweet kiss since I'm minding you exactly."

She chided, "You take too long doing what I said for you to do."

"You don't want my arms empty and useless, do you?"

"Yes."

He labeled her, "A hard-hearted woman."

"Yes."

"You surprise me. I'd always thought you were compassionate and kind."

"I'm not."

He considered her soberly. "I suppose you're this mean to Tim? Or do you—"

In a rather deadly manner, she encouraged him, "Do I... what." And it wasn't a question. It was a nudge for him to just go ahead and put his head in the noose.

And he said readily, "Do you straighten him out?"

"I don't need to 'straighten him out'! He isn't as bold as you."

"I'd've never guessed that was so. You do surprise me, but *his* picky conduct is a shock!"

And she lifted her nose as she declared, "Tim is a gentleman."

"Glory be." His tone was all wrong.

She told him, "You're really rather tacky."

"I was raised thataway." But his words were stiff. He was pushing for a quarrel? Why would he want her to get mad at him? Then he'd have an excuse for being discarded? She didn't like him enough? He said, "I beg your pardon. I didn't mean to push."

She considered him silently for quite long seconds. Time is odd. It wasn't long, but she appeared to thoroughly study him. Then she said, "I'll see you in the morning."

She moved easily from his arms. He felt abandoned. His arms were empty. He slowly rose to his feet and he just looked at her.

She was still regarding him. She said, "Good night."

Somberly, he replied, " 'Night."

Then she turned slowly away and began to walk to her Cup.

He found he was following her. Why? And he understood that he wanted to see her to her door. He didn't touch her or say anything. He gave her room. But he walked her to the door of her Cup.

She opened the screen and turned the knob of the door. She looked back at him.

He said, "It wasn't locked!"

"No. It was. I unlocked it when I came home."

Some portion of his mind heard her call the Cup "home." And that eased him. He said, "Let me just check it out. We've been distracted. Somebody awful just might be inside."

She looked at the Cup in surprise. It was true. That could be so. She said, "I can screech like a banshee."

"What a talent! I'll have to hear that sometime. It must be awesome!"

She preened a bit and admitted, "It is." Then she had the gall to ask, "While you're looking under the bed, will I be safe out here?"

"Yes."

"How do you know that?"

"I've been looking around while you were fooling with me."

She gasped, "I did *not!*"

And he was sure. "Somebody's got me all stirred up."

"Well, it wasn't *me!*"

"You're supposed to say it wasn't 'I' because you reverse it to I wasn't."

"Yes." But she made no comment on his knowing grammar. Poor grammar shows the good ole boys are right there with all the rest of us.

He grinned at her. Then he said, "Stand over there so you're not in the way if I have to run out of there."

"If *you* have to...?"

"I just said I'd look! I didn't say nothing a-tall about actually doing anything about anything. I'll just look. But get out of my way. I'd be irritated if you tangled me up and some yahoo would get a poke at me."

She took a bracing breath and told Bryan, "You stay out here, and I'll go look."

"No. This-a way, if I'm apprehended, you can still call the cops."

She inquired, "Haven't you conquered the telephone as yet?"

"On occasion."

How like a man to reply in that manner. He didn't for one minute think there was anyone in her Cup. He was just being cute. She watched his careful approach to her door. She licked her grin. He *was* cute. He was also amazing. Clever. And a really attractive man.

He could kiss like nothing she'd ever witnessed. That was practice. He—

He bolted from the door saying softly, "Run!"

She gasped. Her eyes had to have bulged. And she said, "What?"

He took her arm on the way past and was still whispering, "Run!"

Probably the thing that caught her attention was that he didn't yell. His voice was ordinary and the word was soft.

She was being hustled along as she tried to look back. She asked, "What was it?"

He stopped. "Nothing."

She pushed her flopped hair back off her face and stared at the man. "Nothing? Then why—"

He grinned. "Didn't that stimulate you? Are you sleepy now?"

And she lifted her arms out and said to the night sky, "For crying out loud!"

He guessed, "I'll bet Tim never got you that alert."

"He's an honest, normal person."

Bryan declared, "I'm honest."

"No. You said—"

"But I didn't raise my voice," he lectured. "My momma once told me that a gentleman never shouts."

She watched him. "You never shout. Not even when that trucker insisted on taking me along with the doughnuts."

Bryan was honest. "I was scared pea green."

She scoffed. "I could handle him."

And in a level voice he promised, "I would have."

"No. I can take care of myself."

And he said a strange thing. He said, "See to it." His face was serious. His eyes were firm.

She guessed, "I quit kissing men?"

"No, no. You have to keep in touch and in practice. You can kiss me now and then. But you have to quit kissing Tim. I can't allow it anymore."

With indignation, she retorted, "I'll kiss whoever I want to kiss."

"Not Tim. I'll listen to any other candidate and advise you as we go along."

She declared, "No one, no how, in no way, can tell me what to do or how to act."

He soothed, "We'll take it a day at a time."

She reminded him, "You're not my guardian."

"Just about. I'm going to see to it that you marry the right man. Tim isn't the one. He's in a courting slot, right now, and he's giving you all his attentions. He wants you. But then he'll put you in a house and give you kids and a car. You'll be lonely and frustrated. You won't like it."

So she inquired, "Then you plan on finding me the perfect husband?"

"I'll see what I can do. Uh, I've forgotten what sort of kisser you are and that's primary when a man is selling a woman's *premise*... Fooled you there, didn't I?"

So while she was still gasping with indignation, he stepped close and wrapped her arms around his neck and then he pulled her body over against his and he really, really kissed her.

Then he sassily patted her bottom and said, "Dream of me."

She was still getting her body in balance as he walked off, whistling through his teeth.

She watched him to the door of the Pot, then she looked around trying to figure out why she was where. She sorted that out, went to her cabin and opened the door.

She went inside, looked around, squatted down, looked under the bed, and went over to check out the bath. She glanced about. Everything was serene.

As she went to lock her door, her phone rang. She picked it up and put it to her ear.

His voice said, "Is that you, Lily Baby, or is it the Creature again?"

She hissed into the phone and put it back in the cradle.

She smiled into the bath mirror. She stripped and showered. Then she went to bed without any night-clothes on. She dreamed erotica.

Eight

The next morning, Lily went into the Pot, humming. She looked at Bryan, who was fixing breakfast for about ten drivers. Two were female. They all looked at her, but she hadn't really noticed them.

People are seldom actually looking at anyone else. Anything that moves around in a waiting place draws eyes but not necessarily attention.

Lily didn't feel she was the object of their regard. She told Bryan, "Need any help?"

His quick smile flicked over her. "Pour the coffee and see about juice?"

So she did that.

As the time passed, some of the people left, more came. For the size of the Pot, the turnover was just right. All who came had a place to be seated. And there were those who preferred tables. Almost all of them left with boxes or bags of doughnuts.

And Tim came to the Pot.

Lily smiled at him and said, "Hi." But Tim was so tired from lying awake all night thinking about her that he didn't notice the difference in her. He said, "Good morning." And his eyes were kind and vulnerable.

Of course, Bryan was riveted. His breathing was high in his chest and hostile. His movements were slow and careful so that he would be braced when Tim attacked him.

Tim didn't attack. He didn't eat, either. He sat with brooding suffering on his face and watched as Lily moved around.

That very morning, Tim had again been accosted by his boss, who wanted a solid commitment to getting the Coffeepot Inn demolished and out of there. Then there was the boss's languishing daughter—

Tim had nodded as his boss went on in his hard-nosed grilling. "Tim...you got that damned Pot torn down yet?"

"I'm working on it."

His boss had ground out through his teeth, "I've got to commit on this deal. Either you get this done, or we'll have to find somebody who can do it."

Tim had tilted back his head and explained slowly as to a man who hadn't had the experience to know, "It's a delicate maneuver. I need some time." Tim's controlled manner was soothing. "I'm working on it. I'm going out there this morning. I'll be in touch."

That had sounded committed.

He was, but it was to the Pot's blue-eyed, black-haired vision. He watched the graceful movements as she went about the Pot, pouring coffee, being sure everyone had what they wanted . . . for breakfast.

His body hungered. His mind was in a fog. Since his body couldn't, his eyes feasted on Lily. Men have it rough.

As Bryan took the orders and skillfully filled them, he noted Tim being ignored by Lily! She didn't want Tim. That put Bryan in shock. Gradually, Bryan found he was feeling sorry for Tim. Now when had Bryan *ever* felt sorry for another man in the winning of a woman? It was part of living. No big deal.

But it did come to Bryan that he'd thought *he* was the odd man out. Tim would soon have to face the fact that Timothy Morgan was out of the running.

As Bryan prepared all the various foods and kept track of what he was doing, he finally came to the understanding that Tim was really zonked.

Right away, Bryan found he'd need to consider the idea of explaining to Tim that Lily was not Tim's. She belonged to Bryan. Tim would be appalled and not understand at all. He'd probably argue. He might take a swing at Bryan. Okay, Bryan thought, he could handle that.

But Tim had never been a totally calm person. Mostly lighthearted, he could be argumentative and tenacious. Tim would lose his temper and create a ruckus. He'd be angry. He wouldn't give up until he got Lily back.

Then Bryan realized he wasn't compassionate enough to give Lily back to Tim. However, with some reluctance, he *did* understand the jolt that would be coming to Tim. How was he to tell Tim that *he* was the odd man out?

And just like that, Bryan figured it out! He'd let Lily handle it.

The morning advanced. Lily was serene. She smiled. She used the phone and she got doughnuts packed. She took change and pocketed tips. She floated. She touched Bryan. She replenished Tim's coffee. She was everywhere.

And in that entire time, she was never out of Bryan's sight. Well, once when she went to the basement for more of the doughnuts.

That had caught *every*body's attention, for while she was down there, she had *shrieked!*

Most of the men got caught up in the jam at the top of the stairs, but Bryan had put a hand on the rail and jumped exactly to the fifth step down.

It wasn't a mouse. Women seldom see mice. There was a snake curled up comfortably on the floor drain.

Bryan picked it up behind its head and carried it carefully out of the Pot. Most of the men laughed as soon as they saw it. It ate mice and was a pet?

It *was* a pet ... but not then and not there.

Bryan was thwarted when he tried to comfort Lily. But while she rebuffed Bryan even *touching* her with his snake-polluted hands, she wouldn't let Tim touch her, either. She said, "Quit that."

She said that while she made Bryan wash his hands first. She went with him and frowned as she supervised the washing. With that done and his hands dried, she allowed Bryan to comfort her.

Tim saw it all. Seeing it sobered him. Well, he was still dating June. And there was his boss's eagerly languishing daughter.

Bryan was telling Lily, "Its name is Slippery. He swallows mice and rats. Unfortunately, he ignores cockroaches, but he does his share with the rest. He comes out so seldom that I forget about him."

Lily Baby breathed. She was white-faced and brave. An almost hostile Tim came over, horned in and again tried to comfort her, but she said, "Get away."

He was shocked.

She then said to Tim, "Go sit down over there. I want to show you something in just a while."

Tim stared at her in some surprise. He obeyed her and went carefully over to his table and sat down with equal care. He was alert and watched everything, especially Lily when she wasn't looking his way. It was then that he discovered that she only looked to be sure his water glass and coffee cup were filled.

That was automatic. Lily did exactly the same to all the other people who came to the Pot to eat. He was just another customer. The only difference was that she didn't charge him for anything.

So. Why was Timothy Morgan sitting there? That was the next thing that entered his mind. And he mentally chewed on that. She was kind to the cook. Tim watched her touch that man. And he saw the man's subtle reaction. The guy's name was Bryan Willard.

As Tim had faced the simple fact that he was wasting time there, the door opened and a shockingly beautiful, young, slender, dream woman came into the Pot. She was alive! She exuded vibrations of energy.

She and Lily laughed as they hugged each other in greeting.

Gesturing, Lily said things rapidly to the grinning woman. The woman looked over the Pot and her eyes landed on the watching Tim. Her eyes stayed there...on him. It was unsettling for a man committed to another female to be looked at, in that way, by such a vibrant young woman.

The watching Tim saw Lily gesture, and then she brought the newcomer over to Tim's table. Being a gentleman, Tim stood up, and he lost no time in standing.

Lily said, "This is Tim. Tim, this is my cousin, Joyce Davie."

That was apparently enough, for Lily then left them. She just walked on off. She'd left her cousin with Tim, and he was supposed to host her? He put his hand on the back of a chair. He didn't move it as yet because he could pull it out, and she could just walk on off.

But Joyce said, "Thank you," and she waited for Tim to seat her.

Tim did. He was careful. He smoothed his tie. His hair. He glanced over at Lily. She was explaining something to Bryan. Then Tim looked at Lily's cousin. And he thought, *That family is something!*

Quite comfortably, Joyce was easy and didn't demand conversation. She made comments and was amazingly cheerful. Her eyes danced. She was amused. About—what?

But while Tim was aware of Joyce's amusement, he was so distracted by Lily that he didn't ask Joyce what was so funny.

The time came when Tim felt he'd been at the Pot too long. He said to his tablemate, "I've enjoyed your company, but I have to get back to the city."

And Joyce smiled. "Lily said you had your car. Can you take me as far as the bus stop?"

"Where're you going?"

"Too far. I live on the north side."

"I'm going that way, I'll take you along."

"Why... how nice of you."

For some reason, the two women laughed almost too much as they said goodbye. To Tim's knowledge, there weren't words exchanged that were funny enough for such hilarity. But Tim took the opportunity to look mean and squint-eyed at Bryan as he said to him, "Behave yourself."

And, relaxed against the counter with one hand on his hip, Bryan had the gall to reply, "I'll see."

As the newly met pair drove to the actual city of San Antonio, Joyce wasn't a chatterer, but she did comment occasionally. Tim responded politely. However, he did ask, "How'd you get out to the Pot?"

And her reply was logical. "A taxi."

Tim frowned. "That must've cost an arm!"

And she agreed airily, "Yeah."

With the silence, he finally asked her, "What do you do, or are you a precious flower who sits and is admired?"

She laughed. "That was beautifully said. I've just completed my master's in business, and I'm looking for a little house out northwest. Know any?"

"It just so happens that I'm a Realtor, and I think I know just the one for you."

"Why, that's wonderful!"

"When are you free?"

"Tomorrow?"

"Great." Then he said, "I'll have to call in." And he did that on his car phone. He got the call-ins listed. He told his secretary who to call back. He drove, doing that, and they eventually got to the northwest side of San Antonio... and he had gotten all his business neat and tidy.

Joyce was nicely named. She was a joy to watch. And she was friendly. She looked at him as if he was something special. As they discussed the size house that interested her, he found that Joyce was almost as special as her cousin. He smiled.

Back at the Pot, there was the midmorning lull. Bryan was making more doughnuts, and Lily was meticulously wiping off the tables and the counter.

Bryan would watch her. She seemed serene and untroubled. She didn't appear curious about what had happened between Tim and her cousin, Joyce. Lily was calm.

Bryan didn't feel at all calm. She had him on his ear. Logically, he inquired, "Why did your cousin come clear out here in a cab?"

Lily seemed open and aboveboard, and she replied readily and without any evasiveness at all, "I asked her to do that."

However, in replying, Lily didn't pause in her work and give Bryan a studying look as she waited for his response or his next question. To Lily, her reply was all he needed.

Bryan was silent for a while. Then he asked, "How was she gonna get back? Another cab?"

"Oh, no," Lily told him, "Tim could take her. He was here and he had to go back to town."

Bryan returned to the doughnuts for a while before he observed, "You set them up."

And she looked at him with puzzlement. "Set them *up?* Of course not!" She lied but she appeared logical. "Tim was driving back to town alone, and Joyce needed a ride. I didn't have the time. She could catch a bus from the edge of town."

Bryan observed slowly, "Since she's your cousin, and he's trying for you, he'd take her wherever she needed to be, and you know that."

Lily was somewhat lofty. "Perhaps." And she added kindly, "It would depend on where Tim had to be. If her destination melded with his route, he could take her there easily. Otherwise, she'd find a bus."

There was a long lack of conversation before Bryan chided, "You set him up."

Lily observed Bryan with such innocence, then she explained kindly, "I never interfere in other people's lives. I do what needs doing." Then she explained more clearly, "We were busy. Joyce needed a ride. I didn't have the time to visit with her, and I didn't have time, then, to take her back home." She considered Bryan with clear eyes, and she said, "Her visit was a surprise."

"Why did she come here at such a strange time for a visit?"

Lily's clear eyes regarded him with earnest communication. And she told Bryan, "I never found that out. I'm curious, too. She didn't mind leaving. So she's probably just restless and thought this was a good time to see where I was working?"

"Did you ask her to come out here and give me a once-over?"

"No. Are you interested in another job?"

He said it flatly positive, "No. You trying to get rid of me?"

"Get *rid* of a man who makes magical..."

He gasped.

She finished, "...doughnuts?"

His body went lax. His head rolled on his shoulders. He strolled over to her and said, "You're wicked."

As she carefully swept the floor with a broom, she denied his comment airily. "Not yet."

Those words jolted through him like a flash of lightning. He sucked in air and his body was out of control...so, naturally, a couple came inside for coffee.

Funning, they said, "A Coffeepot like this seems to indicate you'll have coffee?"

And having heard that from about two-thirds of the people who came into the place, Bryan said, "Why, here's some of that stuff right here!"

The man said, "I smell doughnuts."

So Bryan exclaimed, "There *are* some!"

The two travelers sat at the counter, and Bryan kindly listened to all the same old comments about the place and about the coffee. The guests bought some of the doughnuts. Every bit of the response was predictable.

After they left, and with curiosity, Lily asked Bryan, "Do you get tired of the same old jokes?"

He smiled on her. "I love them all. They have no idea how many others say the same things. They think they are original. I don't mind."

"Do you tolerate manipulation?"

Bryan watched her seriously. "It depends on who's doing the manipulation and why."

Lily thought that was an interesting reply.

So Bryan pushed, "You get your cousin out here to lure Tim?"

And she exclaimed, "That would have been a perfect thing to do! I'll try it next time."

He watched her, but she was sweeping carefully. Her interested attention was carefully on the floor; she licked her lips, but she didn't peek at him.

He figured she was innocent. The pairing of Tim and her cousin had all been happenstance. Tim had just been there, and Joyce had showed up and needed a ride back to the city. That was all.

Bryan asked Lily, "You gonna move into the Pot with me?"

"Why, *Mister* Willard! How you do go on!"

"One of those."

"Worse. My momma *and* my pappa are TEXANS. I was carefully brought up and I have rules about everything."

"Like . . . what all?"

She said, "I always make my dates meet my parents."

"I didn't."

She agreed, "I know, but you will. I've told them about you and what all you do here. My daddy loves doughnuts. I sent him some of yours. He thinks you're probably eighty years old and a genius."

"You didn't tell him how old I am?"

She was logical. "Well, with just the two of us here, I didn't want his imagination to go rampant on us."

"He thinks I'm *eighty?*"

And she agreed, "Well. Yes. It's best he's deluded. Otherwise he'd probably quit his job and come down here."

Bryan smiled a little. "One of those kind of daddies."

"It's been a burden."

His voice got foggy. "So, you're a virgin?"

"Now, that *has* been a burden." She sighed.

He chuckled a little. "How many have you had?"

"None."

"Go on!" Bryan chided her. "You kiss like an experienced woman."

"I was going to mention the way *you* kiss! You ought to wear a warning sign!"

He licked his smile. "So you think I'm pretty good, do you?"

She shook her head slowly as she commented, "I hadn't known a kiss could be like that."

And his foggy voice said, "Let's see if it was."

"Now?"

"Nobody's around. Come over here so I can watch the doughnuts."

She sassily pushed up her lower lip and told him, "I'm not sure a distracted kiss would take the same toll as one of those you gave me out on the bench."

His voice was soft but roughened by his desire as he told her gently, "Come here."

And she swished right on over to him. She stopped and put her hands behind her back and looked up at him. She smiled just a bit. Then she wickedly licked her lips with a quickly done tip of her tongue. It was an outrageous thing to do to such a triggered man.

He did look around. And he took her against him and kissed her witless. He shivered and his hands trembled. His breathing was uneven and harsh. In no time at all, seemingly, his strong hands set her back, away from him.

Her head wobbled and she bumped into the counter because her eyelids were so heavy. Like all other things over which there is no control, heavy eyelids are a nuisance.

His trembling hands steadied her and his face was stark. He had never felt the way he did in all his thirty years. No woman had sundered him like this twig had just done. He felt, if he could just breathe, it would be a sign that he was okay.

He did breathe, but it was erratic and harsh. It betrayed the fact that she'd boggled him.

Fortunately, Lily was also boggled. She was unaware of his own state. She floundered. She was serious-faced and earnest but her equilibrium was shot all to hell.

As with Brueghel's painting of the Halt Leading the Blind, Bryan put out a sustaining hand and steadied Lily.

She didn't notice. She said, "Ummm."

He asked, "You okay?" And even the asking of that, after his kiss, was a stimulation to his sex. She was zonked by him. He smiled a little.

She tilted her head back so that she could see him through her slitted, heavy-lidded eyes and she commented, "How come I could handle you kissing me last night better than I can today?'' Her mind had become coordinated. Her equilibrium wasn't that swift. She waited for a logical reply.

He said, "We'll see."

That could mean—anything. But it was a reply. Whatever she'd said, his reply was okay. His entire attention was on looking hungrily at her. Words really didn't matter. They were together, and no one else was around.

A truck pulled off the highway and swung into the parking area.

Lily didn't notice. Bryan, being male, did. He told Lily, "Somebody's coming."

She turned her heavy-lidded eyes to the window's light and asked, "Daddy?"

How revealing. She knew good and well Bryan had been doing things to her that would shock her daddy.

Bryan smoothed that over. Guilt was harmful to any relationship. So he told her gently, "A trucker's coming in."

And she said, "Oh."

While a woman can float in limbo and be unhinged, a man was doomed to trying for logic and conduct in public. Men have it rough. Ask any of them, and they'll all readily agree to that to you.

So while Lily Baby was pressing a cool cloth to her face, Bryan watched her as he jiggled around and practiced breathing and seeming normal.

The truck driver came inside and immediately paused and considered the two opposite-gendered people who were silent and fidgeting. A dead giveaway.

The trucker moved slowly and sat carefully. The female was pressing a wet cloth over her face. She'd been—crying? So he looked at the male.

He was superhyper and watching everything and hadn't even said hello. Then the trucker relaxed a little. It was love. They'd been doing some serious kissing. He'd intruded. He smiled and told the man, "Sorry."

And Bryan replied the automatically rendered, "No problem."

The trucker laughed. No problem? With a neophyte like that? She'd be a holdout and drive this fidgety guy into stark, staring idiotishness. With droll humor, the trucker lifted his doughnut from the plate and took a bite.

He had the doughnut and coffee because that was an automatic response for Bryan and he didn't even think about doing it. Somebody came inside, he got coffee and a doughnut and whatever else he'd think of to order. But he *always* got coffee and a doughnut.

Being the kind of man who helped others, the trucker told them all the gossip along the highway. The language was cleaned up for Lily's sake but it wouldn't have mattered. She wouldn't have heard. She was still seriously coping with La-la land.

In the meantime, Tim made an appointment to further show Joyce houses that would be available. He delivered her to her family home. Then he went back to his real estate building.

There, he went into his boss's office. No one was there. While he waited, Tim took another look at the vulnerable daughter's picture. He sighed. He knew

that even if he had captured Lily, he would have gradually been distracted from her. He was a real salesman. It took up most of his time.

He looked back at the boss's daughter's picture.
Jerry was an only child. She would be used to a daddy
who was gone most of the time. Therefore she
wouldn't expect to see a husband all the time, either.
It could work. And his time wouldn't be gobbled up
by a siren who thrived on attention.

When had the Lily siren demanded his attention?
And Tim soberly admitted that Lily hadn't been
zonked by him. It was even possible that there could
be other women who wouldn't cotton to him.

Cotton to something was a Southern comment
based on the lint of cotton hand-gathered by the pick-
ers in olden times. Their clothes and hair would be
whitened with bits of cotton. Cotton stuck to everything like glue.

Tim had no question at all that Lily's cousin, Joyce
Davie, was something special. No denying that one.
But did he have the time she'd need from a lover or a
husband? As dedicated as Tim was to his job, he had
no time for indulgence to a woman.

He looked again at Jerry's picture. She was a sweet
thing. He could maneuver her to suit his own time.
He'd see if that would be satisfactory.

Tim felt noble.

So he sat down in the visitor's chair at his boss's
desk, and he used the boss's phone to call the boss's
daughter, Jerry. She was an only child and spoiled
rotten.

Her voice was liquid maple sugar as she said,
"Hello?"

And Tim said, "This is Tim Morgan, and I'm sitting in your daddy's office waiting for him. I've been sitting here looking at your picture on his desk. Are you really that sweet? Or was it the manipulation of the photographer?"

And her sweet voice replied, "I don't know."

The sound of the syrup went around Tim and touched in him. He laughed softly in his throat.

Jerry asked lazily, "Why're you waiting for my daddy? You been naughty and unruly again?"

And he said, "I'm a good man. I've never been naughty or unruly because I don't have a clue as how to act thataway. You want to teach me?"

And she said, "I could teach you." But her voice was smoky like she was lying in a rumpled bed and was stark naked.

Nine

Meanwhile, back at the Pot, people were stopping off like always and the two frustrated, interrupted servers were exquisitely conscious of each other. The other people, who came and went, were shadow people and didn't garner anything but food and something to drink.

There is no punishment that can rival the physical separation of lovers. Especially those who aren't yet lovers but who are willing. Lily would move, and Bryan's eyes were like metal files to a magnet. It's always like that in the beginning. With some couples, it goes on all their lives.

Would it be that way with this strange attraction between Lily and Bryan? Or was their meeting just a chance encounter?

Neither of them wondered. They didn't have any interest in exploring the ramifications of their interest and its longevity. They were so riveted. Without looking, each body knew where the other was. It was as if their flesh was so sensitive that it felt the glow of the other's fire.

It was something like radar.

But why these two? How come they had met and this remarkable chaos now ensued? That old "other half of the orange" baloney? No way.

Or had it been Lily Baby's sneaky great-grandfather's doing? Had he searched out the perfect man in such a way that he'd set Lily up to actually meet him? Had her great-granddaddy been that sneaky? A male matchmaker? Of course not. What old man ever had that foresight? Her great-granddaddy was a male and what male ever helps to entrap another male?

It was Fate.

It had to be. What other explanation was there? None. She came there, they saw each other and that was that!

But she *had* gone out with Tim first. She had even kissed him. Bryan had seen her kiss Tim. Was that to prove to her that not only wasn't Tim the man for her, there *was* no other man but Bryan Willard?

That was beyond all believing. Balderdash. Phooey. It didn't float.

Bryan growled to Lily, "Go take a nap. I'll probably keep you up all night tonight."

She wasn't working on all cylinders and frowned a little in puzzlement as she asked, "Making doughnuts?"

And Bryan said, "Not doughnuts."

She smiled at him in a heavy-lidded, slow blink that set him on his ear. She said, "Bryan is such an odd name for a scruffy man."

He watched her. Did she think she was so far above him that she wouldn't be serious about him? A woman of means who was dallying with the help? He asked her carefully, "So you think I'm...scruffy."

She made a *mmmm* sound before she told him, "I think you're gorgeous."

He chided, "Women don't say such things to a grown man."

And she asked, seriously interested, "They don't? Why not?"

Bryan instructed in a husky tone, "Men are handsome or nice looking or look worthwhile. Men are not gorgeous."

Her smile became wicked. "You are gorgeous." She narrowed her eyes a little as her smile widened. "I want to smooth the hair on your chest. It's wiry and curly, and I want to rub it with my chest. I want to feel it with my own skin."

Bryan gasped, "I may not survive."

She sobered and blinked. Then she inquired seriously, "Survive...what?"

"Until I get you into my bed."

She exclaimed, "You're going to let me go upstairs to your room!"

"It'd be more subtle than my barging into your Cup." He gave her a look that melted her insides. He told her, "If I went to your Cup, Teresa would know in five minutes and she'd be there in two more. That's not long enough for you to rub my—chest—with—"

he gasped and tried to breathe before he finished with "—your chest." And he was already wrecked entirely.

She asked with kind concern, "What's the matter?"

"I'm having trouble breathing."

She asked with earnest concern, "Do you have asthma?"

"No. It was your offer to rub my hairy chest with your gentle—chest."

She took up that idea with earnestness, "I'd like the feel."

He was panting. His voice clogged. He managed to gasp, "So would I."

People came in and acted ordinary and real. The two serving them were in La-la land. They weren't reliable. They smiled. Their eyes didn't really focus. It was just a good thing that Bryan knew everything he did by rote and he didn't make any mistakes.

Lily Baby was a mess. She served the wrong things to people who traded plates or glasses or cups. Everyone who came into the Pot almost immediately knew what was wrong with their hosts' attentions.

Some of the women tried flirting with Bryan in order to get his attention to themselves, but he didn't even notice their attempts.

Lily was not really paying any attention at all to anyone else.

One man got up and went around the counter and got his own meal. He also switched a couple of the drinks and poured the coffee.

Lily thought he was clever. She just watched and smiled. Actually, there should have been an aura around her. But she did appear to glow. She didn't notice.

It was a long, tiring day. The two floated on a hot sea of desire. They touched. Once the whole Pot was empty temporarily, and Bryan came quickly to Lily to hold her against his hungry body.

He trembled. He shivered. He groaned in severe pain and his hands were hard and rubbing on her in slow swirls. He kissed her absolutely witless. He was about as rigid as a human can be.

In contrast, Lily was just a malleable mass. Her eyelids were hopelessly heavy. Her eyes saw only him. Bryan. Her lips were swollen and red. She smiled a little and she was vague.

Now who in all this world would ever guess the two people were attracted?

Everybody.

The truck drivers leaving the Pot would compare as they'd ask each other, "What'd you order and then what'd you get?"

And another would sigh. "I remember when Betty and I were like that."

"Take her some flowers."

"I don't dare do something that stupid. She'd think I was sleeping with some other woman and had a very serious guilty conscience."

So the truckers offered, "We'll give you a note to show her you're pure."

He shook his head. "You don't know Betty good enough. You all do that, and she'd think I was guilty of even worse stuff."

And a guru suggested, "Take her out to a great view, park and discuss Life and Times with her and tell her how important she is to you."

"She'd listen," the guy admitted. "But then she'd ask, 'What'd you do to bring this on?' She has no soul." He shook his head in amazement. Then he told them, "She has a fantastic, hungry body, but no soul at all."

"Women are like that," another moony one contributed. "They just think we drive trucks and tell awful jokes."

"Yeah," another answered.

But then one asked, "Yeah, but did you hear the one about—"

And the soulfulness was pushed aside.

Out there.

However, alone at last and inside the Pot, the two lovers stood and just looked at each other and smiled. Then, not having done it in a long while, Bryan started obviously breathing. His breaths were quick and high in his chest. Anyone around could hear them.

Lily could hear. She thought something had upset him, so she went to him and said, "Can I help? Are you upset about anything? What's the matter?"

And he just smiled. But his breathing got worse. His lips parted to help with the breathing volume. His nose was no longer sufficient.

With a quick glance around and listening for any footsteps, Bryan took Lily against his needy body. He groaned in anguish.

Lily asked, "What's wrong?"

"It's daytime and the customers won't quit coming for hours and hours in one long, long day."

She agreed. "You're tired. You act exhausted. What all have you been doing?"

He replied quickly honest. "Watching you move around and smile."

She laughed and scoffed. "That wouldn't wear you out."

"It isn't being worn-out," he told his love. "It's being frustrated."

Lily *was* a neophyte. At the university, she'd been devoted to graduating and had a whole lot of female friends. She was a virgin, so she hadn't been fooling around with any men and listening to innuendos.

So she asked with interest, "Frustrated? Why? You want to change the menu? Quit making doughnuts? That would be a shame."

"No. I want to get you into bed."

She was a little shocked. "This soon?"

With some talent, he put the back of his hand to his forehead and mentioned, "I've been very patient."

But Lily was startled. "*This* soon? Don't you court me for a while—first?"

"Let's try it the other way around. I'll do the courting—later."

"Uh-uh. No. We can't be that rash. The courting comes first. *Then,* if you pass all the tests, you can…let's see…how do I say this? Uhhh. You're no help at all. If you behave well enough, you can kiss me and maybe I'll let you fool around just a little."

And Bryan lifted his hands and exclaimed, "Wow!" Then he steadied himself against the counter. "Was that an earthquake? Something sure rattled me."

She grinned. "No. I've given you permission to kiss me... again. You do remember that you've already kissed me out on the bench?"

There are just men who are smart enough to lead a woman along with her thinking she's in control. With his eye wrinkles white, he chided with a serious, sober face, "Who'd ever forget kissing you?"

Well, he *was* thirty. Men who are still single at that age are especially knowledgeable. And more outrageously, Bryan didn't move. He stood steady not reaching or grabbing. It was as if he acknowledged the strength of the moral ropes which held him from her.

It's a man like him who maneuvers a woman into seducing *him*. Men do that. A woman has to pay attention. In no time at all, a man like that will have the woman thinking she has to help him. She has to "save" him. Lead him along. He's so vulnerable and upset that she has to soothe him.

Guess how.

Yep.

So the neophyte stood close to the braced Bryan, whose full attention was riveted on her. She reached up to finger-comb his hair back from his suffering face. She asked with compassion, "Didn't you get any sleep at all last night?"

And he told her very seriously, "I dreamed about you."

"And that's what's made you so tired? Did I keep you awake? What did we discuss?"

Soberly serious, he told her, "You were all over me."

"I scolded you?" She scoffed. "Why?" And she almost smiled as she waited for his reply.

He told her, "You wanted me."

"To...do...what?" she questioned seriously.

He explained honestly, "To make love to you." His voice was roughened and a little raspy.

"Why...how shocking!" she exclaimed. "Did you?"

"I had you locked in my arms and I kissed you." His voice had thickened. Then he added, "You tasted pretty dry." Then he mentioned, "I was holding my pillow."

She thought that was hilarious. She laughed and her eyes danced with magic. She chided, "I'm not as soft as a pillow."

So he had to hold her against him. He nodded in agreement. He chided, "You're lumpy."

She was indignant, but he groaned and just held her closer.

Voices were heard outside the Pot. Some people were approaching.

The two in the Pot separated.

Lily adjusted her clothing and checked her headband. Her color was high. She was breathing rather quickly and looked very serious.

Bryan went behind the grill and tried to lift the counter.

Acting cool and assuming that she looked perfectly normal, Lily smiled and said to the new arrivals, "Welcome to the Coffeepot."

The truckers came to the counter and sat down. "Hi, honey." "Whatcha got for a hungry man?" "I don't think she's hungry—for you."

And she took them at face value and replied, "I've had one of Bryan's hot dogs."

With some surprise, she watched the hilarious re-action in the three with some blinking. Her comment wasn't that funny.

Bryan told the truckers, "Steady, there. Watch it."

And Lily gave him an indignant look, but she saw he was watching the men in a stern, male manner. Men are just so different. Their thinking, their conversations, their manner of communication, nothing is similar for women.

So she considered Bryan. He was a male. Actually, she probably wouldn't be so drawn to him if he wasn't that male. He was exciting for her. And she did understand that the excitement was probably mostly based in sex. He was of a different mold. He was a man.

Ah, yes. That he was. A man. And special. He was a darling. And he moved with such maleness. He'd calmed the men at the counter. While they smiled a lot and they coughed a little, they did behave.

Like not seeing mice, Lily didn't notice the men. She simply did as she was supposed to, and she didn't pay any attention to their chatter.

Bryan talked to them. He was easy, but he didn't allow any innuendos or jokes. The men enjoyed testing Bryan as much as they enjoyed the food. They were not offended by his chiding and control. They did push. But Bryan held the rigid limits.

How had he learned to do that? How had he learned what to say and how in such circumstances? And how did he know his own limits? How far he could go with them? It was fascinating and a little scary.

However it wasn't long before three older couples came into the Pot. They were traveling together.

Lily pushed together two of the tables and removed two of the chairs back to the wall so that the six could be together.

The newcomers were what then influenced the conduct of the truckers. And those counter men were well behaved. But they were mostly silent. They exchanged looks and smiled. They bit their lower lips on occasion. And their exchanges were brief and hardly heard. They still occasionally laughed, but they did behave quite well.

And the laughter was so genuinely amused that they cheered up everyone else.

When they left, the men at the table asked the truckers what route they were traveling and about roads. The younger men were courteous and the older ones smiled.

Other people came to the Coffeepot, and the two attendants were busy. They had no time to do other than to exchange a glance now and again.

And it was in that time, with the curiosity of the six travelers, that Bryan took them down to the basement to see the snake. They were delighted.

Lily didn't go with them.

When they returned to the ground floor without the snake, they bought doughnuts to take along. One of the women said, "Oh! I haven't seen doughnuts like this since I went to school in San Antonio! They had these for a nickel each at Woolworth's!"

And her husband commented, "These cost more."

Bryan said, "So do the ingredients."

Another of the older men nodded and shared, "So does the gas for the car...and so do the cars!"

The six went out exclaiming what things had cost before World War II and now. They shook their heads and shrugged and laughed about how things had changed.

The day went quickly.

It really did.

It just dragged for those two people who really wanted to be alone. Well, not entirely alone, just together, but not with anybody else around.

The day seemed to last forever. The clock was checked any number of times by one of the lovers or the other.

After lunch, Lily went for a nap. And it was a hurting Bryan who watched her walk across to her Cup. And he then could think of her lying on her bed.

In his thinking, she had no clothing nor any covering. While his eyes saw what he was doing in the Pot, his mind saw Lily sleeping restlessly, turning slowly on the bed, waiting for him.

At two-thirty, she came back to the Pot and her eyes were lazy. Her smile was soft. She drove him crazy inside his body.

It was about three when the Lamars' oldest boy came to spell Bryan so that he could nap. The days at the Pot were long days.

The Lamars' boy was Peter. Peter was a serious cook. He handled himself well. He did not chat. He was clean. He was tidy. He was getting good training.

At supper time, they all worked. Juan was there for the gas station, Teresa saw to the dishes and the Cups, and Bryan was back cooking. Peter helped Lily with the customers.

They did well. They were used to each other, and they melded well.

The doughnuts went out of the Pot like they weren't meant to stay any longer. Probably the most revealing thing was that no one who bought the doughnuts could resist taking out just one and nibbling on it as they drove away.

The watchers speculated how far the nibblers would drive before all those doughnuts in the bag or box were eaten. The hungry ones would be back. Doughnuts are addictive. Especially the squishy kind.

By ten that night, the lovers could close the Pot. Everyone had gone but just the two of them, Lily and Bryan. He looked at her seriously. His face was still.

She was smiling and surprisingly shy.

He was smart enough to take her against him in a warm, protecting embrace. His arms holding her were strong. And he kissed her. It wasn't a double-whammy, knock-down kiss, it was one that was sweet and very serious.

She looked up at him, and he was watching her intently. He said, "I love you, Lily."

She smiled and her sparkling eyes were like magic. She thrilled him and he groaned.

They went to lock the door of the Coffeepot before going up to Bryan's room. Lily asked, "Will the snake stay in the basement?"

And Bryan replied, "So far as I know."

She was still but her eyes moved around. "You *think* it does?"

He repeated quite honestly, "I've never seen it upstairs."

She considered that reply. Then she stated, "You don't look."

He smiled as he reminded her, "You don't 'see' mice."

"That's true. They don't bite."

"Neither does the snake." Bryan was soothing her. "He thinks he's human."

As they went up the stairs, the odd conversation kept Lily from acknowledging what she was actually doing there. "What snake ever thought it was human?"

Bryan considered, then asked, "The one in The Garden?"

She paused on the stairs, and Bryan thought he'd shot the whole endeavor. She would withdraw.

She said, "The Devil thought he was human inside the snake?"

So Bryan asked her, "Have you ever wanted to be a mermaid?"

She stopped on the curving stairs. "How did you know that?"

He watched her as he told her very seriously, "You'd lure any sailor."

She looked around. "There aren't any around here. They're over on the coast and they don't realize I'm here. I'm safe from them."

His voice was foggy as he told her, "You're safe from everybody but me."

"Uh-oh."

Bryan gently moved and lifted her in his strong arms. It was a dumb thing to do on those curving stairs, but he was apparently in control of himself and his feet and balance. A show-off. He carried her effortlessly as he went slowly up the stairs to his room.

His breaths were noticeable.

She asked, "Am I too heavy?"

"No."

"You're panting," she mentioned.

He told her, "I want you."

"You *pant* when you want a woman?"

"You get my lungs all excited and my body is anxious and tense."

She laughed softly and put her head back in a flirting manner. "Your lungs get excited?"

"And other parts."

So she inquired, "What...parts get excited? Your— feet? Or your shoulders?"

"I'll show you."

So she put her teeth into her lower lip and her own breathing was a little quick, high in her own chest, but she could control hers. After all, she wasn't carrying *him,* so she could breathe discreetly.

Then she noticed her heartbeat was a little wild. She took a breath and sighed as if relaxed.

But he kissed her, the double-whammy courting kiss. It was outrageously diverting. It spun the brain hopelessly confused inside of her skull. How could it possibly do that? She waited for her silly brain to settle down and supply an answer.

While she was reorientating herself...reorient? Was that a South Pacific maneuver? Why...reorient?

As she sorted that out, Bryan had reached the second floor and carefully set her on her wobbly feet, and she had to deal with rubbery legs that weren't at all reliable. They were no longer programmed to walk. She leaned against him, and he didn't mind at all.

He kissed her again.

As their lips parted in myriad soft little sounds that were excessively sexual, she told him, "Why would I be reoriented? I'm northwest European."

That stopped him and made him blink. But then he smiled. If she was reoriented, she had been disoriented—by him! So he helped in her stability by kissing her again. This time it was not only double-whammied but it was his Killer Kiss. No holds barred.

How sinful of him. No woman had ever— And he considered what hadn't a woman ever done? His brain declined to search that out. He was fuzzy headed. He picked Lily up again and took her into his bedroom. His brain didn't direct that. It was pure libido. How could a libido be pure?

He undressed her languid body. It was important for him to do that. For him, undressing her was like revealing a treasure so precious that he was stunned. He was breathing in sips and the squint-wrinkles at the corners of his eyes were white.

She smiled and pawed at him. She didn't have paws, she had hands. She pawed him.

She fumbled at his clothing.

She wanted *him* naked, too? That was probably logical. He tried to unbutton his shirt but his fingers couldn't handle that, so he took hold of the neck of the shirt and just ripped it down and buttons went everywhere in tiny pings.

She thought it was the ring of the bell clear downstairs. She said, "Someone wants in."

He grinned. "Yeah." He took off his trousers along with his underwear.

She watched him avidly with side glances and seemingly casual and a little bit bored. She noted that he had a tough time with the condom. Wasn't he practiced? Was this his first time . . . too?

Freed of all restraints, he eased her back on his tidy bed and got rid of the pillow under her head. It wasn't his muddled brain that did that. It was primal instinct.

And she lay under him. His body was in ecstasy. He rubbed his hairy chest against her softness, and they both moaned. She slithered under him.

How could she move? She moved in a fish wiggle and her soft chest shifted with the movements.

He found that mind-blowingly erotic. His breaths were hoarse and he shivered. He sweated. His hands were tensely gentle. His mouth was hot . . . scalding.

So was his body. His breaths. His hands. He was burning in fever. Not that kind. He wasn't sick except with love.

He made love to her.

The first time was so fast that she really hadn't adjusted to his invasion.

As he shivered, relaxed and lay gasping, she was filled with disappointment. She'd only just begun.

He was gasping and his body was heavy as he lay replete and breathing hoarsely.

She smoothed his hair back to soothe him. She was very alert, stilling her agitated, excited body. She said nothing. He was part rabbit. Rabbits are quick.

He was still gasping in a lung-searing way, but he finally said, "It'll be okay the next time. I'll be in control."

She wasn't sure what that meant.

He was still trying to control his breathing. Come to think of it, his breathing had been similar from the time she first met him. High. Fast. He could well *be* part rabbit.

At college, she'd heard women speak of this very thing. Long courting, fast completion. Zero. She felt like leaning an elbow on the windowsill and watching the cars on the highway. Boy, was that experience ever fast! And she wasn't thinking of the cars zipping by.

His breaths were slowing. There had been little conversation. He said, "It all began when you walked into the Pot. I've been in terrible shape since then."

"Oh." She didn't know what else to say. What was he talking about? He'd fumbled it. He'd lost the condom? Good grief. She could get pregnant on... that?

She became agitated.

He soothed her. "Next time, you'll get the glory ride."

She wasn't sure what that meant, either. And she was too green to ask.

When he separated from her, she moved and looked...and the condom was in place. She went limp with relief.

He asked, "First time you've seen a man?" His voice was husky and his smile was gentle.

She didn't know him well enough to tell him otherwise, so she said, "Ummm."

He moved his hand gently along her throat; his thumb touched her swollen lips. "I know you were innocent."

She looked at him.

Again he said, "It'll be better . . . next time."

Ten

When Bryan returned to the bedroom, he came to the narrow bed and settled down. He did that by adjusting Lily's still interested body to his lax one. And darned if he didn't go right to sleep! He was soothing his hands on her one minute and out cold the next.

And there Lily was, wide-awake and eager. She was *very* curious. Terribly frustrated. And he was *asleep!* But it was nice to be beside him, close to him. She loved his hairy body. Her hands were subtle as she petted him. He smelled nicely male. His breaths were slow and steady. He was alive . . . and asleep.

Not only was he asleep, he was down for the count, dead to the world. Out.

Lily's fires were stirred and eager. Her naked skin was exquisitely aware of his body. She ran her hand carefully through the crinkly hairs—on his chest.

She waited until his breathing was normal, then she boldly smoothed her hand gently down to his hair-covered tummy button. He made an odd breath. So she waited until he was again breathing normally, and she slid her—hand—down—farther.

He gasped. His breathing was odd. His muscles tightened.

She snatched her hand away as if she'd harmed him. And she watched his reaction with fascination. She held perfectly still.

He snorted and skipped a breath. He moved a little. But he went back into sleep in gradually snoggling snores.

She wasn't able to relax. She needed release. Some exercise would be a poor substitute. She would go outside and walk around the circle a dozen times to calm herself down. Then maybe she could sleep.

Very carefully, she tried to sit up on the bed.

The problem was that there was no room. That slender, single person bed allowed no subtle changes. And his sleeping body was possessive. When she moved, his hands and arms automatically shifted and pulled her back against him.

Only his breathing changed and that was briefly. Why could he do that? How come he could keep a woman in his bed that way? How many women had he slept with that his subconscious could react just so?

How would she find out?

She could hardly ask a man, "How many women have you slept with?"

Wait a minute. Why couldn't she ask?

It just seemed so...intimate. It was nosy.

Well, why not?

She had every reason for knowing what sort of man he was and how many women he'd slept with and whether he and they were healthy!

Her conscience mentioned that it was a little late to be concerned about such. However, although late, it was logical to find out. Who knew better than he as to how healthy his sex-teachers had been and how much risk she was taking being in his bed?

How strange it had taken her so long to find out such vital information. Why hadn't she asked to begin with?

It had seemed so...personal.

Sex wasn't?

Well, yes.

So she waggled his flaccid shoulder. His gentle snore snorkled a little, but he managed to settle down and snooze again.

He fascinated her. He was *out!* And he could be joggled or talked to or pushed with no real response back to her. He adjusted. He moved his hands and soothed her. He shifted. But he never really wakened.

Think how tired he'd been!

How stretched.

But his release had given him this hiatus of peace. Even her annoying intrusions didn't reach him. He countered with rearranging her, patting her and soothing her while he slept on.

She lifted the sheet and slid her feet out onto the floor. Then she cleverly slid the rest of her slowly out of his grasp. She was free, sitting on the hard floor.

He shifted and breathed. His hands moved in the vacated space. He was restless. But his eyes stayed closed and he settled down again, turning, taking up the whole of the skinny bed.

When his breathing was steady and deep, Lily carefully gathered her clothing and shoes. She crept quietly from the room and down the stairs. All the while, his breathing was steady.

Her steps down the stairs to the ground floor were a scary trip because she didn't know if the reportedly harmless snake was still in the basement. The lights and darks were filled with wavering shadows. That was done by the outside lights and the mesquite leaves.

She hoped.

Lily put her clothes on and unlocked the door. It was never locked. Anyone, who really wanted to be inside, could get in.

It is always strange to be outside alone in the night. No voices. No people calling to another. No bird songs. No chickens clucking. Off away, it was so still. A few trucks and an occasional car rushed by with brief sounds and were gone. It was so quiet.

She made the circle about five times and then unlocked the door to her Cup. She went inside rather moodily, somewhat thoughtful. Disappointed.

She showered and was aware she was washing not only herself, but she was washing away the essence of him which lingered on her body. That was a little sad.

As Lily put on her summer silk pajamas, which weren't a public garment, she considered it wasn't even eleven o'clock. She'd get in enough sleep.

She crawled into bed and lay alone. She considered the lacy leaves' shadows moving on the walls. Finally, she turned over, and she went dead asleep. Being a woman who had waited all day, and was only partially attended by a man in heat, was exhausting.

In the night, she was too warm. She wakened enough to remove one of the covers and found herself locked in a man's arms! She went, "Eeeek!" before she realized it was...he. There Bryan was, in her bed. How had he gotten inside?

The maid's keys which Teresa used.

How come Lily hadn't heard any of that? She was boggled by who all could have come into her Cup without her having one clue! She'd always been so secure there, and now she woke up with a man already in her bed!

His male voice growled, "You wiggle around thataway and you'll get me all stirred up."

"You *cannot* be in my Cup! What would Teresa think?"

"She'd think it took you a long old time to get me into your bed."

"Teresa? She would say that?"

"Yep. And she'd swish around and go looking for her husband."

Lily gasped dramatically, "How shocking."

"Why'd you sneak out of my bed thataway? I woke up and my arms were all useless and empty."

"Your bed is too little."

So he said, "This one's just about right. Let's see if it works."

"I'm so shocked you've gotten in here that I couldn't be interes— What are you doing?"

His muffled voice explained, "I'm looking for that little mole that's so sweet tasting."

"Stop that!"

"Okay. In a minute—"

But he didn't. He just went right on along doing what he wanted. And while she gasped and was shocked, she forgot all about protesting. She even helped. That was outrageous. Men can be so distracting. They bend women's morals. Their own are really quite scattered.

It was fascinating to be involved in the act again. It was…wonderful. How had she lasted all that time and never tried it? No other male had been Bryan.

His hands knew exactly what to do to thrill her. His mouth was practiced. How had he learned that? Was that legal? It was fabulous. She gasped and shivered and tugged at him. She moaned and sighed and helped.

He used her body by applying his so perfectly. And he drove her wild! He slid his sex where it should be and he took her to paradise.

No wonder there were too many people on this overburdened planet.

The lovers sighed as if they had been holding their breaths too long. They stretched and made sounds that were soft. They yawned and snuggled, and together they slept with smiling content.

The next day, Tim came by on one of his unnecessary visits. Yet again, he had no influence on their selling him the Coffeepot Inn.

Tim was logical and generous. He gave all the reasons they should be happy to get rid of the place and retire for life somewheres else.

The pair was sleepy-eyed and slow moving. They were tolerant. They went on about their work, and paid him enough attention, but they weren't interested. That was obvious, even to Tim.

Finally, as the time passed, Tim sat with a plate empty of those sinful doughnuts and with less coffee in his cup, and he really watched both Bryan and Lily.

They were lovers. It was so obvious. If they hadn't actually slept together yet, they would. Lily blushed almost continuously. Her eyes sparkled. Her lips smiled. She even hummed.

Tim wondered how come he hadn't been able to get her that way about him? He'd been so careful and so courteous and so available. Why the cook instead of the more solvent and known Timothy Morgan?

Women were such a puzzle. They were so hare-brained. They were so needed by a man. Just looking at a woman was entertainment to even a sated man. He knew there'd be another time. But it was Bryan who was the sloe-eyed, sated man and it was he who watched Lily with a lazy smile.

Hell.

So Tim lay back in his chair and watched the two with a sour face. It was like deliberately wearing a shirt made of coarse hair. He was punishing himself for thinking he could ever have had her. There'd never been one single chance, at all, for him, with Lily.

Actually, that was probably a good thing. If he'd snared her, he'd probably have spent too much time with her. Loving. Watching. Pleasing her.

He'd have missed opportunities to be the top seller in his group. He'd held that position in his business so long that no one felt they could beat him. But if he'd snared Lily, it could have happened. Love distracts a man.

So Tim considered the circumstances of this Lily Davie Trevor. She had her amorous cook.

Having to hoist himself from the chair, after too many of those wicked doughnuts, they waved aside Tim's effort to pay his bill. So Tim thoughtfully went out to his car, drove back to San Antonio and to his office there.

He sat and thought a while. Then he got up from his desk and went into his boss's office. It was, as usual, empty. Tim bravely picked up the picture of his boss's daughter for another careful look.

Jerry looked so sweet and pliant.

Then Tim's eyes closed a little as he considered. She hadn't sounded all that pliant and meek on the phone when he'd called her. Come to think of it, she'd been sassy.

So he called her again. It was only curiosity.

And she answered like she'd been wakened out of an erotic dream. The sound of her voice lifted the fine hairs along Tim's spine and on up into the hair on his head.

Lazily, she asked, "What are you doing?"

And Tim responded immediately, "I'm sitting in your daddy's office, waiting for him to show up. That sweet picture of you on his desk made me call you. You ought to get another picture made, wearing a coal miner's hat and clothes and smeared with coal dust."

In a smoky voice, she promised, "I'll do that."

Tim went on talking to her, saying, "All the guys around here would appreciate the change in your picture like that. It'd give us some peace."

And her slow, low voice asked softly, "A piece of—what." Not a question.

Tim looked again at the sweet, high school picture of this college woman. He took a steadying breath and asked, "You free for lunch?"

"Not today."

"When?"

He could hear pages being turned. A book? A diary? An appointment book? A racy magazine? What was she shuffling with thataway?

She said, "I can juggle appointments around and have tomorrow free."

"Name the time."

Jerry did that. And her soft laugh as she said goodbye was like ants in his blood. That soon?

Surely he had some brooding time to mourn losing Lily? Apparently not. Probably his subconscious knew all along that Lily wasn't seriously interested in Timothy Morgan.

Meanwhile, back at the Pot, the lovers were lost in a haze of passionate observation of each other. Their eyes were limpid. Their lips curved in almost smiles.

They were on hold. Their lives were being used, but they both just waited for ten o'clock that evening when they could turn off the lights in the Coffeepot and go on out to Lily's Cup.

When there was no one besides them in the Pot, Lily flung herself at Bryan, and he didn't object. He grabbed her and held her soft body close against his hard surface.

They kissed and panted, and his hands were careless.

She blushed and her eyelids were heavy. She told him, "Shame on you."

Bryan replied, "Yeah." But he wasn't influenced to change his hand around on her more discreetly.

Lily kissed back. She was a malleable mass. She made pleased sounds in her throat and she *rubbed* against him! She did. Her mother would have been so shocked.

Well, probably. Maybe. Supposedly.

And from Lily's memories came little bits of her mother's smothered laughter late at night. Hmmm. Her *parents?* Surely not.

As happens, the endless day ended, and Lily became just about breathless. She would draw in a breath because she needed the oxygen, but she felt a little dizzy. That was because she couldn't exhale. She didn't know why she couldn't.

But after Bryan got her to her Cup and undressed her, she found she was without any breath at all and she felt a little faint. Nervous. Shivering. Rubbing her knees together like a wicked witch rubs her hands.

Bryan smiled at her and said, "I've dreamed so long about having you in bed."

"How come you came and got into mine?"

Well, he *had* done that. He said, "I missed you. You left me."

She explained with earnest logic, "Your bed's too narrow for us to sleep together there."

In some shocked astonishment and disappointment he asked, "Aren't you going to let me stay with you tonight?"

"I suppose. But it would be scandalous if anyone found you there. What if some emergency came up, and they needed you? It would be outrageous to have you go out from my Cup."

"Yeah. I suppose. But what do I do when they come looking for me and find me in your Cup?"

Lily ventured thoughtfully, "Uhhh. We could say you're afraid of the dark? Or that you got away from the Pot because you don't want to listen to any more Pot stories repeated for the millionth time?"

"I think the count is more than that."

So she asked with real curiosity, "How can you be so patient when you hear those old, old jokes?"

"Some of them are new to just about everybody," he explained. "And they have such fun with it and laugh so, that they come back."

Lily thoughtfully suggested, "We could write a book about Coffeepot jokes."

But Bryan replied, "Then they'd know their jokes weren't original."

"What a tender heart you have." She lay there and put a hand up into his hair.

He told her, "I have other tender parts, too."

"Where?"

He showed her, and she was certainly surprised. She found petting didn't soothe him at all. She said, "This is what I do for a headache." And she rubbed him. He just got more excited. More active. More intense and urgent.

He suggested she kiss him and that just might help. But her kisses were stimulating to him. So he figured out something else entirely. She wasn't at all sure his suggestion could help. But it was remarkably unique, and she giggled in smothered laughter.

And at a time like *that,* Lily recalled her mother's smothered, nighttime laughter.

How strange to be in love with a man and only then understand parents.

It was a night of love. They found they could sleep on her bed, entwined and cuddling. Each was available to the other. He was greedy. She chided him and pretended to slap his hand, but he convinced her, every time.

In the morning, Bryan slid out of the bed and covered her with the sheet. He did that very slowly and was proud of himself for not getting back in bed with her.

As it was, he felt quite a bit lighter. After he dressed and stood watching her sleep, he disciplined himself and went out of her Cup and back to the Pot.

Then at a break, he went to her Cup and smiled at her sleeping so soundly. He sorted through to find her fresh clothing.

He gently smoothed his hand along her, and he held her discarded, scandalous silk pajamas to his face.

He almost forgot why he was actually there in her Cup. It was to get her up and dressed.

But she lay on her back. Her eyes were closed and her mouth was slightly open. Her arms were out and she was a dream of an angel.

His stern discipline had something to do with the previous night's loving. He was almost sated. But still he stood and looked at her.

His face was so vulnerable. He leaned and kissed her soft lips. She was so tired that she didn't even stir. He felt guilty for his greed. The guilt turned into satisfaction. It was *he* who'd taught her how to love.

Bryan put her clothes where she would see them, then he went back the Pot to the noisy group who wanted to eat... *now.*

Back in San Antonio, Tim went again into his boss's empty office. He called Jerry from there. That way the phone number came from her daddy's office and not from Tim's. Men do things that way. Men are crafty.

Tim had taken Jerry out to lunch the day before, and he'd taken her where she could show off. The place was of upgrade business people. She'd known most of those there. She'd had a great time.

So being connected by phone, they talked in a flirting manner. And she was a tease. Tim loved it. He said, "Lunch again? How about tomorrow?"

"No. I'm committed to taking some schoolkids to a free dentist tomorrow. The time is iffy. How about the next day?"

"I've got a client looking at some property for lunch. How about supper?"

"Day after tomorrow? Yep. I can do it. Supper..." she said aloud as she wrote. "... Tim."

He instructed her kindly, "My last name's Morgan. There *are* other Tims and I don't want you going out with somebody else who just happens to have the same first name."

In his ear he heard her saying slowly, "Morgan," as if she was writing it down.

Women do that sort of thing to fragile, eager, sweating men. They make a man think he has to work harder to get them. They do. Men are willing.

So when Jerry's daddy finally came into his office, he speared Tim with a hostile look. Tim was used to such a look, and it had no influence on him, at all. He said to his boss, "I have a brilliant idea for which you can admire, accept and take full credit."

They looked at each other with cold evaluation, then Tim smiled.

So on their next date, Tim decided to take Jerry to see the Coffeepot. It was unusual, and Jerry would immediately be charmed by the Cups. He told her about the Pot and its Cups.

She said, "I want to rent one Cup for a week...with you."

Tim was more than a little boggled. How strange. He'd wanted something like that from Lily, but from his boss's daughter?

So Tim released one hand from the wheel and looked down his nose at Jerry. He put the free hand on his chest before he said in a horribly stilted, fake voice, "You greedy beast! I'm not that kind of guy! I wouldn't do something like that 'til we're married."

Jerry laughed with such delight, while Tim was *shocked* by his own words.

But as he drove, he glanced at Jerry with sober eyes, and he found he could handle being married to such a woman. Maybe. Tim thought he ought to take another look at Lily. He could do it then with Jerry along and compare them. That's what he'd do.

The new couple drove to the Coffeepot Inn, and just seeing it made Jerry exclaim. She loved it. When Tim parked, Jerry got herself out of the car and looked around with a big grin. She said, "This is perfect."

It took a while for the pair to enter the Pot and meet the hosts. But they did go inside.

Then Jerry heard Lily's whole name and asked, "You kin to the San Antonio Davies?"

Lily agreed, "Yep," just like she'd been around there in TEXAS all her born days.

So Jerry said, "I know your cousin Patty."

Lily agreed, "Now there you have a jewel of a friend."

So Jerry said, "Yep," just like Lily had... and the two women were friends. Just like that.

When the Coffeepot traffic slowed, the four chatted and laughed and got acquainted. The ease of the two women rather boggled them, but the men were used to such happenings. And the four of them bonded in a rather remarkable way.

So with lunch past, and the Pot less busy, they called Peter and he came over to mind the Pot. And the four went across the field, over the fence and tramped along the hill in back of the Pot.

The day was perfect. Since it was so far out from San Antonio, the little animals were a surprise. It was the humans who intruded. The ranch dog came along after a time. He stayed away from them but he observed why they were there.

Tim whistled for the dog, who stood still but his tail wagged a couple of times to indicate that he'd acknowledged their friendliness. And having decided the humans were no threat, the dog disappeared.

The four explored the paths. Bryan knew them all. He led the way and found the spring. They all drank from it. They watched the birds and listened as the grasses rustled now and again.

It was a marvelous afternoon. Jerry especially loved it all. "I *never* get out of town. This is such a treat for me. You all are lucky you live out here."

It was Tim who said, "This land has been bought up. It's gonna be built up with houses."

Bryan said, "Ahhh. So that's how come you want the Pot."

Tim sighed with genuine seriousness. "They're going to be elegant places. The Pot will have to go."

Both Bryan and Lily said, "No."

But oddly, there was a little echo from Jerry who also said, "No."

Tim said, "What will be, will be. The clout the builders have is awesome."

This time all three of the others were in unison. They said, "No."

Tim just shook his head. His face was serious.

Bryan said, "I just thought somebody wanted the Pot. But I was right, you did mention the hill back here."

Tim nodded. "That was a slip of the lip. I've never done that before then. I guess my conscience wanted to warn you."

So the quartet was silent as they went back along the trails to the Pot. Lily was surprised that the other couple went back inside the Pot. She'd have thought they'd be embarrassed to stay there. They sat at a table, looking around, and had some iced tea.

Jerry didn't have much to say. She turned her head and watched. She listened to the people who came inside. She ignored Tim saying they ought to leave.

The odd couple stayed for over another hour. When they left, Jerry hugged Lily. She smiled at the sober owner of the Pot and asked, "May I come again?"

And quite seriously, Lily replied, "As long as we're here, you're welcome."

Also serious, Jerry replied, "Thank you."

So Lily had some time to chew on what might happen. She said to Bryan, "Tim said it would be an elegant place. The Pot would stand out like a sore thumb."

Bryan told Lily, "Nobody can move us or get us out of here."

Lily turned and looked at her love. How strange to be so involved with a man in such a different circumstance. Her great-granddaddy must have known Bryan was this kind of a man. Otherwise he never would have given her this Coffeepot Inn and allowed her to meet Bryan.

So Lily smiled at her love and said, "What will be, will be. But you're stuck with me."

Probably the most emotional thing that had ever happened to Lily—or Bryan—were the tears in Bryan's eyes as he reached for his love and held her. The applause from their luncheon guests wasn't even heard by the two, they were so emotional.

It was only a day or so later that Jerry took some of Bryan's doughnuts to her daddy at the office. So he wouldn't eat too many, Jerry passed the box around the offices. Then she went back to her daddy and sat across from him at his desk.

Jerry told him, "Save the Coffeepot Inn. Don't do anything about it. Leave it there."

Her father's face was sour as he took another bite of the squishy doughnut. "They don't budge."

"That's one of their doughnuts."

Her daddy took a quick, shocked breath, then he calmed. "They'll never know I ate one."

"I'll tell."

He looked at her like there was a grub on his doughnut. He said, "You take after your mother's side."

And Jerry replied smugly, "I know."

There was a peaceful quiet for some time. The only sound was her daddy chewing the rest of the doughnut. "Any more?" He lifted his eyebrows as he lifted the box.

Jerry told her daddy, "I like the Coffeepot right where it is. Build some Swiss châteaux on the hill."

Her daddy rose and became red in his face.

Did Jerry panic? No. She calmly made him sit back down and breathe. She told him. "The Swiss châteaux will sell like hot cakes . . . or Bryan's doughnuts at the Coffeepot Inn."

But it took a while longer than that before Jerry's idea was accomplished.

In the meantime, those around the Pot were contented and secure. Jerry had told them what would happen. The Swiss châteaux and the Coffeepot Inn would rub together—perfectly. Just like Jerry and Tim. And exactly like Bryan and Lily.

Then there were Teresa and Juan. And of course there were— Well, that's another story altogether.

**In February, Silhouette Books is proud
to present the sweeping, sensual new novel
by bestselling author**

CAIT LONDON

about her unforgettable family—*The Tallchiefs.*

Everyone in Amen Flats, Wyoming, was talking about
Elspeth Tallchief. How she wasn't a thirty-three-year-old
virgin, after all. How she'd been keeping herself warm at
night all these years with a couple of secrets. And now one
of those secrets had walked right into town, sending
everyone into a frenzy. But Elspeth knew he'd come for
the *other* secret....

"Cait London is an irresistible storyteller..."

—*Romantic Times*

Don't miss TALLCHIEF FOR KEEPS by Cait London, available
at your favorite retail outlet in February from

Silhouette®

TM

Look us up on-line at: http://www.romance.net

CLST

Take 4 bestselling love stories FREE

Plus get a FREE surprise gift!

Special Limited-time Offer

Mail to Silhouette Reader Service™

P.O. Box 609
Fort Erie, Ontario
L2A 5X3

YES! Please send me 4 free Silhouette Desire® novels and my free surprise gift. Then send me 6 brand-new novels every month, which I will receive months before they appear in bookstores. Bill me at the low price of $3.24 each plus 25¢ delivery and GST*. That's the complete price and a savings of over 10% off the cover prices—quite a bargain! I understand that accepting the books and gift places me under no obligation ever to buy any books. I can always return a shipment and cancel at any time. Even if I never buy another book from Silhouette, the 4 free books and the surprise gift are mine to keep forever.

326 BPA A3UY

Name	(PLEASE PRINT)
Address	Apt. No.
City	Province Postal Code

COMING NEXT MONTH

#1051 TEXAS MOON—Joan Elliott Pickart

Family Men

Private investigator Tux Bishop, February's *Man of the Month*, was determined to help feisty Nancy Shatner and keep her safe from the danger that threatened her. But who was going to protect her from him?

#1052 A BRIDE FOR ABEL GREENE—Cindy Gerard

Northern Lights Brides

In a moment of loneliness, recluse Abel Greene advertised for a mail-order bride. But when spunky wife-to-be Mackenzie Kincaid arrived, would the hesitant groom get over his prewedding jitters?

#1053 ROXY AND THE RICH MAN—Elizabeth Bevarly

The Family McCormick

Wealthy businessman Spencer Melbourne hired P.I. Roxy Matheny to find his long-lost twin. But the last thing he expected was to lose his heart to this spirited beauty!

#1054 LOVERS ONLY—Christine Pacheco

Clay Landon set about winning back his soon-to-be-ex-wife Catherine—no matter the cost. But would a seduction at a secluded hideaway lead to a passionate reconciliation?

#1055 LOVECHILD—Metsy Hingle

Jacques Gaston was a charming ladies' man who couldn't commit. But when he discovered beautiful Liza O'Malley had given birth to his secret baby, could Jacques find it in his heart to become a loving father and husband?

#1056 CITY GIRLS NEED NOT APPLY—Rita Rainville

25th book

Single father Mac Ryder didn't want delicate city-girl Kat Wainwright on his land. He knew that she wasn't prepared to deal with the dangers of Wyoming, but that wouldn't keep the rugged rancher from teaching greenhorn Kat about love.

You know where the MEN are....

SILHOUETTE®

Desire®

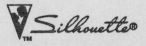